# THOSE WHO CURSE YOU

# THOSE WHO CURSE YOU

RAE RICHEN

**Those Who Curse You**
Rae Richen

Published in the United States of America by

Back Beat Publications
an imprint of Lloyd Court Press
3034 N.E. 32nd Avenue
Portland, Oregon, 97212
www.lloydcourtpress.org

Cover design by Diana Kolsky
Book Design by Amit Dey

Paper: 978-1-943640-20-1
E-book: 978-1-943640-19-5

Publisher's Cataloging-In-Publication Data
Prepared by Cassidy Cataloguing

Names            Richen, Rae, author.
Description:     Portland, Oregon : Back Beat Publications, an imprint of
                 Lloyd Court Press, [2024]
Identifiers:     ISBN: 978-1-943640-20-1 (paperback) |
                 978-1-943640-19-5 (ebook)
Subjects:        LCSH: Women architects--Fiction. |
                 Apprentices--Fiction.
                 | Disappeared persons--Fiction.
                 | Fire chaplains--Fiction.
                 | Fires--Fiction. | Rescues--Fiction. |
                 Family relationships-- Fiction. |
                 LCGFT: Mystery fiction. | Crime fiction. |
                 Thrillers (Fiction) | Action and adventure fiction. |
                 BISAC: FICTION / Mystery / General. |
                 FICTION / Crime / Amateur sleuths / Suspense. |
                 FICTION / Mystery / Action & Adventure.
Classification:  LCC: PS3618.I34 O54 2022 | DDC: 813/.6--dc23
                 978-1-943640-19-5

# WITH ADMIRATION

This story is dedicated to the late Dr. David Bell, friend and excellent pediatrician, and to the families and care providers at Albertina Kerr Centers in Portland whose work for children and adults with disabilities is amazing and encouraging to us all.

# PREFACE

December 1996
Clark Gulder, Archbishop
Methodist-Episcopal Church
Northwestern States

Dear Clark,

Abe Hallowell and I will be arriving at 10:15 a.m., on the day after Christmas, flight 2113, United Airlines. I look forward to greeting you in person at long last.

However, it is with great shame and intense grief that I bring the reverend Abraham Hallowell back to your country with such damage to his body and his soul. The recent bombing in his church here in Beirut seems to have shattered more than bone. It has crushed his will. He has lost the hearing in his right ear. His right hand has been amputated because of infection in the bone. As I explained over the phone, the doctors believe his right leg will heal with much therapy.

As I have written many times over the last years, our Christian and Muslim communities cannot thank you enough for sending us Abraham Hallowell. It is devastating to us that this should have happened just when our people are close to more peaceful times.

During these years of upheaval, Abe has served our congregants and the city of Beirut with courage and love.

I thank you for insisting he be given treatment at the hospital there in Portland, Oregon. If the Sisters of St. Joseph Mercy are as dedicated as Abe has been, they may be able to help him through this dark time in his life.

Sincerely,
Jean-Marie Biquet
Professor of Religious Studies,
American University, Beirut, Lebanon

P.S. Abe Hallowell here. I am learning to write with my left hand, so please pardon my scrawl. I read this letter before it went in the mail. I did some good here and made big mistakes. I need to warn you, I'm not the saint Monsieur Biquet has made me out to be.

# CHAPTER ONE

## SIX MONTHS LATER

Thirty-three-year-old Sarah Rohann jerked her battered green truck into a parking space on Altenbein Street, a neglected alley behind Saint Joseph's Mercy Hospital, Portland, Oregon.

She saw the call on her cell phone from Eleanor Whiting and figured she'd return that call this evening. Eleanor probably called about a detail in the Methodist parsonage she recently had redesigned to fit five families.

But now, it was too close to dark to stop what she needed to do here.

She glanced at the threatening sky and finally made herself look directly at her destination. Three deep breaths and the touch of soft wooden beads at her throat bolstered her courage. The beads lay hidden in the collar of her cotton knit dress. She'd worn them every day for five weeks.

Shoving open the door, she forced her shaking legs out of the truck cab. Her ancient leather purse bumped into her hip with unusual weight as she descended from the truck's high step. It reminded her of the danger she courted.

Every one of these searches took its toll on her nerves, but she couldn't give up. Kevin's life depended on her. She shut the door as quietly as possible and locked the truck cab. With a glance down the alley, she moved away from St. Joseph Mercy Hospital toward three derelicts – three slumped and beaten houses left stranded between new hospital construction and the wide swath of freeway behind and below them.

The Datsuns, Hyundais and Toyotas down on the freeway raced on top of what once had been a sparkling creek bed. The drivers knew nothing of the creek in the pipe below them. They were oblivious to the life up on this higher ground – life and death and tragedy in a cancerous sore on the north side of what appeared to be healthy urban tissue.

This small triangle of land on this bluff was slated to become an extension of the hospital parking garage. Awaiting the last phase of expansion, the old houses stood empty and inviting – too inviting.

Sarah forced herself to hold a steady pace toward the nearest house, a graying yellow monster with windows boarded over, and doors pad locked. She walked quietly, knowing very well that furtive hurry might alert potential squatters.

Six months ago, the second time her foster son, Kevin, had disappeared, Sarah and her eldest son Miguel had found Kevin in this house. He was upstairs, sprawled in an alcohol-induced stupor among the stinking bodies of five other boys. One of the boys still lay in a coma, in a nursing home out in southeast Portland. The others and Kevin had recovered.

Sarah caressed again the wooden bead necklace and its fat laughing Buddha which a healthy, drug-free Kevin had carved and presented to her five weeks ago. He'd waited until everyone else in the family had gone to bed.

"Mom," Kevin had whispered that rarely used word. "I carved these for your birthday."

He had peaked at her from under his blond bangs and had held out a box in which nestled the beads strung on silk thread. "See Mom, these are all the woods I've used in the houses and altars and stuff I've built since I came to live with you. That Buddha in the center is gum wood. He was a bitch to carve, I'm telling you, but I hope he makes you feel good when things aren't so cool."

A week later, Kevin received a letter from his biological father, from the Sheridan Federal Correction Center. Sarah had no idea what was in the letter, but Kevin disappeared that night. She'd been searching for him ever since.

These houses were among her daily round – before work, the flop houses and transient hotels, after work, the gang hangouts like these.

Sarah walked as unobtrusively as possible to the back of the first house. The door still hung open, tethered by only one broken hinge as it had been the last time she'd come in here. She pushed the door out of her way and ducked into what had been a kitchen. The linoleum had worn away and the sub flooring showed through rotten boards, brittle and thin. She kept to the edges of the room, sure that the floor would give way if any weight were put on it.

Sarah tiptoed through the main-floor rooms.

*Nothing here but my own footsteps in the dust.*

She combed the house from attic to cellar as quickly as she could, not wanting to meet unexpectedly with any of Kev's friends. After checking the last closet, she hurried out, disappointed not to find Kevin, but relieved to be outside for a minute.

Between houses, she felt a chill wind rise as the sun lowered behind oppressive piles of dark cloud. This night was going to see a heavy storm.

Sarah crept quickly into the second house. The first sign that something was different stood like a beacon on the kitchen counter.

A beer bottle. Five more bottles were strewn on the table in the next room. And the house smelled like garlic – recently cooked garlic. Sarah's nose twitched at the unexpected odor. Mold, she expected, but garlic . . .?

Sarah hurried toward the nearest door – the basement entry. Reaching toward the door handle, she hesitated.

*I'll go there last. Up first this time,* she thought.

She climbed the back stairs out of the dining room to the first landing where she wrenched open a door she remembered leaving open two days ago.

*They were here ... someone was here.*

The light from the dusty windows on the landing was barely enough to show her the missing second step on the next flight. She knew the step was gone. She'd memorized the dangers. If the sun were shining, she could have seen clear through the step to the basement.

Up here, the odor of garlic grew stronger. Her hand slipped up to her beads as a shiver threaded down her spine. Someone had been here. If it was Kevin, pray God he was still here, but alone.

Sarah's nerves tightened with each creak of the stair steps. As she rose toward the second floor, she tried to remember the layout above her. Each of these three abandoned houses was a permutation of the same floor plan. Each house had a basement, with an old sawdust burning furnace. The other two sawdust bins were empty. In this house, the bin was strangely full. The sawdust had packed itself down over years of humid winters until it was a wet and evil-smelling mass. During each visit, Sarah searched this basement, but she didn't like it. The windows had been nailed shut at some time in the past. This basement felt like a trap. That was why she often put off searching down there until last.

On the main floor, each house had a large living area to one side of the front entry hall – in this house, the left side. The stairs took off from the side of the hall opposite the living room. At the first landing, the front stairs met the servant's stairs which rose from the back part of the house where Sarah had entered. Above, on the second floor, were four bedrooms, a bathroom, a linen closet and a set of steps leading to the attic. In this house, the attic steps were hidden in what appeared to be a closet of the northeast bedroom. The northwest bedroom had a door out to a balcony and beside that door, a very small window, high in the wall.

As she neared the top of the stairs to the second floor, Sarah heard a rumble far below her. She stopped, holding her breath. A moment later she decided it was merely the sound of a truck on the freeway in the gulch behind the houses. She'd never heard such a deep truck motor before.

She held herself stiffly still, listening for the rumble to subside. When it did, she breathed deeply and forced herself to take the last step onto the second floor. She began her usual systematic search of the four bedrooms and their closets. The odor of garlic was strong up here, but no sign of the feast, no pizza boxes or food crumbs marred the dusty floors.

She opened each closet door with apprehension, standing back in case one of Kevin's old gangs, Coxwell 13 or Die Ratten, were still hanging around the house.

She'd met some of the gang members around her home – young boys who shaved the blond and brown hair from their heads and glared at her with innocent but angry blue and green eyes, daring her to comment on their style. A couple of the boys were into lifting weights to achieve thick necks and big arms. Tattoos of swastikas and roses adorned their newly developed muscles.

They'd begun coming by the house in ones and twos during those last months Kevin was with her. Sarah sensed a desperate urge from a few of them, a need to see that families really existed, that life could be different.

Others were clearly hanging around, trying to lure Kevin back into the streets and away from his new family. Miguel had warned off two of the boys who had made threatening remarks towards Akesha, Sarah's foster daughter. Sarah only found out about those remarks during this last week because Miguel used them as examples of why Sarah should stop looking for Kevin. Miguel wanted her to let him and the police handle the search.

Sarah knew Miguel worried about her, but she also knew that she could handle the gun that was in her purse. And she couldn't stop looking. Kevin on alcohol or drugs was a danger to himself. Every day that they failed to find him, he was more likely to make a wrong decision and get himself killed. She couldn't merely wait for others to find the time to hunt for her son.

Searching the closets had left Sarah sneezing, unable any longer to smell the garlic. Mold in the old wood raised her allergens to a high level.

At last, she arrived at the door to the attic. With her hand on the pistol in her purse, she stepped to one side, opening it softly, slowly. No one was in the shadowed stair well. She touched her beads and began to climb again.

As soon as she topped the attic stairs, she heard sounds. Downstairs, on the main floor, something heavy and metal fell to the floorboards, the front door squealed open, then latched closed. Quick footsteps crossed the sagging boards of the front porch. Sarah raced for the attic dormer window which looked over the alley in front of the house.

Far below, on the weed-cracked sidewalk, a man stopped running and looked back at the house. He wore an old Filson jacket, its black and red squares covered with the dirt of years. On his head was a knit night-watch cap, pulled down beyond his eyebrows. He yanked up his collar as he glanced around the lower portions of the building.

Furtively, the man glanced up toward the second floor. Above that, her form at the attic window caught his eye. He jerked back as if she'd hit him from that distance. Whipping around, he ran across the street and yanked open the back door to the eye clinic portion of the hospital. As he slid through the door, he chanced one last glance toward the house.

Something he saw made him straighten up suddenly, slither into the building and pull the door shut behind him.

Sarah frowned. She couldn't place the man, certainly not the little bit of his face that she had seen, but something about the way he moved reminded her of someone . . . someone not so thick set, but someone who would have run the same way.

He must have been in the basement, she thought. Thank God he chose to escape! He wouldn't take kindly to being trapped with me between him and the door.

Suddenly, an explosion of glass drew her attention back to the house. The sound, directly below her, was echoed by another spray of glass at the back of the house.

*He set off something downstairs!*

She twisted away from the window and nearly fell over a heap of wool. From the wool two bare feet stuck out. She stared, frozen at first by fear of the bundle, then by fear of what she would find. Trembling, she reached out, tentatively pulling back the collar of the woolen overcoat.

The young face which stared up at her was not Kevin's pale face, but she knew the face well, knew it shy and knew it sullen, knew it vulnerable and behind a mask of hardness. Kevin's best friend, blue eyes opened yet blank, face gray, a stubble of red hair grown over his head.

As she touched his cold skin, Sarah whimpered, "Bruce." Incongruous thoughts assailed her. *Thank God it's not Kevin. Selfish thought. Poor Bruce. You'd hate the hair . . . Always so clean shaven . . . Bald even.*

And as a third window exploded below, she thought, *I can't carry him.*

Nevertheless, Sarah grabbed for Bruce's arm, pulled his body to an upright position and tried to hoist him over her shoulder. She couldn't just leave him here given what she suspected was happening in the basement.

Under his clammy weight, she staggered toward the top of the attic stairs. Once there, she was forced to drop him. Grasping both his wrists, she backed down. "I won't let your head bump," she whispered as if Bruce cared. "There now, only two more. We'll make it."

As soon as she reached the closet below, she could smell the smoke of fire on the first floor. She lowered Bruce to the closet floor.

"I have to leave you here. I'll be back. Got to figure it out."

# CHAPTER TWO

In the basement of his Portland, Oregon hospital, Abraham Hallowell took a breather from physical therapy. He watched the older gentleman and the lady who worked at the other end of the physical therapy room. He knew from talk around the hospital that she had lost her legs to bone cancer and was working to learn how to transfer from wheelchair to bed or toilet or whatever and back again.

And he thought he had seen the two of them in his new congregation here in Portland. Possibly her cancer treatments had kept them away most Sundays since he had become the minister at Wesley Methodist.

Abe liked the way her husband cheered for her successes and urged rest between failures.

He had learned their names: Arthur and Amanda Charles. Somehow, despite the cancer, they laughed with each other, and they touched each other with affection. They had what he always wanted – a solid life together.

He went back to his own therapy, but his therapist was, for the moment, off getting a ball of some kind. So, Abe got into his exercises.

He practiced locating sound in the room. Losing the hearing of one ear had left him out of touch with where sound originated.

After a few moments he began his stretches. He reached for the ceiling with his left hand, but his right remained in its pocket—his missing right hand. He didn't like to bother people with the empty space where the hand once had been.

He leaned over, trying to touch his toes. In a blink, his world went black, and his back screamed at him. The last thought he had was *Somebody, please call my children.*

*    *

When he came back to the present world, Abe lay on a gurney. He felt the movement of the wheels over the floor tiles, the turn of the gurney into another room. The pain in his back grabbed his attention and dragged him down into the past.

In an aura of red and green haze, he stood once more before his congregation. Out the nearest window, he could still see the ancient cedar that shaded this church. He glanced to his right and saw once again the children and their mothers. He began reading in Lebanese French a passage from the Last Supper. He raised the wine, just as he had done on that fateful night.

Something heavy flew toward him. Years of baseball games came to his defense. He moved his left hand as if to open a glove and catch the object. With his right, he raised the chalice of wine.

And then he woke up, sweating.

"Mr. Hallowell," the nurse said. He couldn't find her at first, then realized the sound came from his right, near his bad ear.

She said, "Doctor Dennis is coming in a few minutes to tell you what he has found."

"Has someone called my children?" he asked.

She smiled. "Yes, Arthur Charles insisted. He heard you say something about children as you blacked out, so he got us to call."

Abe relaxed a little. He thought, *Arthur Charles? Oh, and his wife, in the therapy room.*

His nurse said, "I thought you would want to be awake enough to talk to Dr. Dennis. Here is some orange juice to help you hold out for dinner."

She rolled up the knee part of his bed and then his head.

He felt groggy but noted how important she thought the coming of Doctor Dennis must be. He tried humor to sound her out. "Do I need a tux and a tie for this meeting?"

She laughed and said, "Just a tie. Doctor Dennis is very informal."

As she set the glass on the tray table, she added, "Extremely informal."

"Good. Can't tie my tie anyway."

She glanced at his arm, where even in his sleep he hid the wrist end under the covers. As she exited his room, she turned and smiled, saying, "Bow ties. Great problem solver."

He snorted, and then lay back trying to shake the ominous memory of his dream. He couldn't change any moment of that event, no matter how often he dreamed it. Fear, guilt, grief – his legacy and his inheritance from that one instant.

After minutes with his eyes closed, he realized the doctors must have used something to cut his pain. An odd lack of sensation, or more, the sensation of not having a back made him more aware of the previous pain.

He took his orange juice, drained it, and set the glass back on the tray table next to his bed.

*Here I am again, back in a hospital and out of control.*

As he closed his eyes, he remembered the couple from the therapy room. He remembered the small woman, Amanda, her white hair, her smile at her husband, her silent work to move from the wheelchair to the ordinary chair and back again. And her husband, Arthur, an old-world type – a gentle man, clearly in love with her and supportive of her every effort.

Abe thought, "May you succeed, Mrs. Charles. He needs you to succeed."

His friend Dick Street brought his children to the hospital. He saw the fear on their faces, especially on Andy's face – Andy who never admitted to feelings.

Abe assured them he would get better. "This is a temporary thing," he said. He hoped that was true.

They talked and planned how to keep things together. As little Peter left, he turned back and said, "I love you, Dad. Work at well."

Abe waved and gave him a thumbs up. Dick took them home with a plan to stay with them and enlist help.

*    *

And then Abe slept through another fitful effort to stop the object that was thrown at him. He saw his hand once more, and then he saw the object fly down and right.

Doctor Dennis woke him. "Abraham?"

"Ahhh. Oh. Doc." Abe looked at a man whose hair stood on end, a tired man with his white jacket pulled on so quickly that the collar still lay inside the neck of his shirt.

"She said informal," Abe said, and then realized he'd said it aloud.

He tried to sit up but failed.

Doctor Dennis pushed his shoulders. "Don't just yet. Are you awake enough to understand me?"

Abe thought a moment and then said, "So far I understand you."

"Good. We X-rayed that back of yours. There is still shrapnel in there."

"Shrapnel," Abe said. "Yes, that would be just."

"Just? Just what?" Doctor Dennis looked puzzled.

"Just what I would expect," Abe said. *He didn't say the rest of what he meant. Justice for Abe Hallowell. Justice between him and the dead – the many dead.*

"Well," Doctor Dennis said, "we are trying to figure out how to get it out. Not easy. Not at all, because it is right next to your spine, the nerves. The damned thing is curved as if it wants to hug the spinal cord. It's too near, only millimeters. We've called in a specialist. He's coming over from Pill Hill, you know, the University hospital. Be here this afternoon."

"My physical therapy . . ."

"Oh, that's on hold, man. We've got to get this thing out. Why didn't they find it when you were in New York?"

"I . . . I guess they were more concerned about the infection in my . . . my hand."

"That thing must have ricocheted in there. Didn't you feel it hit you?"

Abe thought back to that moment. The moment he realized the missile was a bomb, the moment he knew he should have let it hit him instead of trying to catch it with a second baseman's glove that didn't exist. The moment he doomed all those women and children.

"Abe?" Doctor Dennis looked worried.

"I didn't feel anything," he said. *Nothing but horror.*

"Well, I don't know how it got there, and I don't know why it hasn't pained you before this, but it's in there and it's going to be a buzzard to get out."

*   *

The specialist was special enough to figure out that they should "leave it lay". In fact, he said they had to leave it lay and just hope it didn't move.

The therapist told Abe not to try that bending over stretch again. And then he gave him other exercises he should do to regain his balance and keep his legs and arms strong.

On the second day of his tests for other possible shrapnel, Doctor Dennis and the specialist found nothing else. Both doctors were clearly worried about the location of that piece of metal, but they could not get at it safely.

Abe asked to be drummed out of the hospital so he could be with his kids.

A few hours before he was scheduled to go home and resume his life with the children and his congregation, he had some welcome visitors.

"Hello," the gentleman said as he wheeled his wife through the door. "We were worried about you. We are Arthur and Amanda Charles. We were working in the therapy room when you had that problem."

Abe put down his exercise list and took a deep breath. *What luck. They are here.*

"I remember you," he said. "Mrs. Charles, you work very hard. I hope that transferring stuff is going well."

Her husband wheeled her to Abe's left. Somebody must have told them about his deaf ear.

She smiled, "I've decided it is a dance. Transfer in, transfer out. Do the Hokey-pokey and turn the chair about."

Abe laughed. "I hope to keep up with you. You must be tired after all that dancing."

She smiled. "I am, but what is going on with you?"

"I seem to have a piece of metal in my back, and they are having the dickens of a time figuring out what to do about it."

Over the next half hour, Abe, Arthur and Amanda talked enough to become friends. When Arthur wheeled Amanda out of the room, Abe knew he needed the two of them. He determined to meet Amanda at the school where she volunteered with children, if only to absorb her strength and ability to face down fears.

But as his door closed, he struggled to stay awake, avoiding the dreams that always came – the dream of an explosion, of holding Elani in his arms as she died, of Elani whispering in Arabic and in French, "I'm so sorry. So sorry."

# CHAPTER THREE

Sarah Rohann dashed from the bedroom into the hall where smoke roiled up the stairwell. The house was so old, its wood so dry from years of neglect, that the fire had taken hold very fast.

The pile of fuel in the basement bin would have been filled with rotting sawdust, moisture – a deadly combination.

The man in the Filson jacket . . . How did he delay the explosion until he got away from the sawdust bin?

She saw that the fire had spread to the first floor. The man must have left the basement door open, drawing a draft.

It didn't matter how. What mattered now was getting out. She stared at the thickening smoke and tried to remember the outside of the house.

He may be watching the front. Go out the back door.

Sarah ran into the bathroom to run water on her clothes before dashing down the stairs. Turning the tap in the sink brought her only sputters of air.

Damn. Of course, there's no water. The house is abandoned.

As she headed for the stairway, Sarah pulled the turtleneck collar of her dress up over her nose. The smoke rolled toward the landing at the bottom of the stairs. She couldn't see as far as the windows on the landing. Remembering the missing step, she also knew that the fire would come up from the basement through that path.

*Trapped up here.*

Backing into the northeast bedroom, she took up her burden once more. "I can get you onto the balcony . . . Police . . . forensics . . . They'll find out how you died . . ."

Sarah tugged Bruce's inert body out into the hallway toward the next bedroom, repeating a litany to give herself strength.

Between the two rooms stood the chimney flue, plastered over, except for a small door. She heard the loud rush of air behind that little door.

The old laundry chute and dumb-waiter shaft. Another way for the fire to climb.

Even as she and her awkward burden passed the chute door, the paint on it began to blister and peal. She didn't have long. But she couldn't leave Bruce's body to be consumed.

*That's what the man wanted. No evidence. No murder to investigate.*

The paint on the wall next to the chimney peeled back. Sarah pulled the boy's heavy body into the southeast bedroom because across the room was the door to the small deck.

She stumbled and dragged her human cargo. She tried the brass deck door handle. Yanking on it, she felt bile rise in her throat. For the first time, she realized she might not get out.

The door to the outside deck was locked and it had no window.

Frantically, she glanced back out into the hallway. Smoke had begun to rise up the stairwell, cutting her off from the western bedrooms.

"Oh Bruce," she whispered.

She slammed the door to the bedroom to slow the progress of the smoke from the first floor. The chimney wall next to the door was already painfully hot. Casting about in panic, Sarah saw the small window at shoulder height. It provided light on the space and sat to the right of the deck door. Maybe she could get to the deck that way.

The only window in the room. Its size and height indicated that it had once been enclosed in a closet that no longer existed.

Sarah's fingers scrabbled at the window's swing-opening armature, loosening its thumb screw, then pushing on the window frame. No motion. She pushed again with all her might. Still nothing.

It was painted shut.

She struck at the window with her bare fists, pounding in an effort to break it. The thick glass distorted the Maple tree outside.

Smoke filtered under the door from the hallway. She glanced at Bruce's body and realized he could be more than a responsibility. He could be a source of tools.

She rolled his body over and unbuttoned his jacket. "Thank you," she whispered, thinking nothing odd in the care she took for his feelings. "It's just a jacket, Bruce. We have to get out of here."

Rolling him again, she pulled off the garment, then ran to stuff it under the door. Smoke seeped into the room, but the garment slowed its rate. Her eyes stung and the back of her throat felt dry. She pulled her turtleneck collar up again over her mouth and nose.

The clack of the metal buckle, made when she rolled Bruce's coat off, had given her an idea. Back at his body, Sarah unbuckled Bruce's thick leather belt. Watching her hands through a fog of smoke-induced tears, she ripped the belt from its loops and stood about two arm's lengths from the small window, her feet braced apart. Rearing her arms back as if a batter at home plate, she brought the full force of the buckle against the window.

She swung back again. This time her efforts produced a long diagonal crack in the thick glass.

Sarah swung the buckle once more against the glass. The entire window seemed to shiver a moment. Then, through the watery veil over her eyes, she watched it fall in shimmering droplets, leaving only one sharp shard stuck in the bottom of the frame.

She gulped in the blessed fresh air as it rushed past her face. Almost immediately, however, she noticed that hot air rushed out. She had created an exit. She had also created a draw for the fire.

She swung the buckle once more, dislodging the last shard slightly from its place in the caulking. She reached to grab the shard but stopped short at the sight of blood running from the palm of her hand up her forearm. She had cut herself on the buckle.

She pulled her knit sleeve down over her hand and grabbed at the shard, pulling it out of its place and dropping it on the floor of the room.

Smoke now seeped into the room from cracks in the overheated plaster around the chimney as well as from under the door. Pulling up her collar again, she coughed and gasped for air inside her turtleneck as she bent to hoist Bruce's body. Heavy, too heavy for her.

"I can't leave you. I can't let him get away with killing you."

She had used up strength and oxygen just punching out the thick glass.

*How can I save Bruce?*

Somehow, her oxygen starved mind now thought of it as saving Bruce. Her knee scraped against the belt buckle. She regarded it almost stupidly, then looked up at the window.

High, but wide. The metal swing armature, bolted to the sill and the frame, had done no work for years. Why not make it do one last job?

Sarah slipped the belt through the three loops in the back of Bruce's levis. Erratic thoughts invaded her mind. Thoughts like composing an apology to Miguel for dying and leaving him alone in the world to care for Jeff and Akesha. She couldn't seem to cope with planning how to deliver the apology.

She dragged Bruce as close to the window as possible, then lifted his body until she could rest his stomach on her knee. With slowed movements and great effort, she threaded the belt over the metal window armature. Then, lifting her knee she pulleyed Bruce's body up toward the window.

Behind her, she could hear the flames eating at the stairwell walls. Their crackle had been in the back of her consciousness for so long that, mentally, she had turned the sound off. Now that she couldn't look in that direction, she became aware that the whoosh of flames grew louder.

Still, she concentrated on lifting Bruce. She had learned from Jeff and Akesha's track coach not to look over your shoulder at the opponent – the surest way to lose a race.

The leather of the belt bit into her already cut palm, but Sarah pulled grimly. With the leverage of her knee, she was able to raise Bruce closer to the window. Then, she had to wedge her shoulder under his chest and keep pulling and pushing until she had him at the windowsill.

As she turned sideways to the wall, she saw more smoke reaching tentatively through the plaster at the chimney and clothes chute wall. She closed her eyes and gritted her teeth, pushing up with her shoulder and pulling down with her hands until the buckle reached the armature at the sill.

She gripped the belt with all the strength in her hands – hands that had wielded a saw and hammer all their life. She was glad now for the power in them, prayed it would be enough. She rose slowly, Bruce's body on her shoulder rising into the light from the wide window. At last, she was able to stand straight, one shoulder against the wall. Bruce's center of gravity lay above the sill. She stood on tiptoe, pushing his body into the opening.

"It won't hurt long," she whispered. "Better than burning."

She twisted his body carefully, not wanting to drop him inside to start all over again. She pushed his head and shoulders out the window, then started to lift his legs.

His body fell out so swiftly that the belt's metal end whipped her jaw as it unleashed from around the armature. One moment he was in the window, the next he was gone.

Behind her, Sarah heard the crash of wood – some part of the house caving in. She whirled. The stairwell!

Trembling from exertion and lack of air, Sarah watched in horror as the smoke spread toward her. Above and behind her, the window offered no easy exit. There was no one but herself to hoist her body to that sill.

Her nylons stung her legs as the heat became intense. The pain was so great that without thinking, Sarah flicked off her shoes and grabbed at the waist of her pantyhose. She ripped them off and felt blessed relief from the heat, but immediately realized the relief was temporary. Her feet burned from the heat of the flooring. She would die in flames if she didn't get out that high window.

Outside, she heard the scream of a fire engine. The back of the house – up against the freeway walls.

*They'll never come back here in time to find me.*

She reached toward the armature on the window and tried to pull herself up. The nylons in her hand seemed a nuisance until she took another look at them. Quickly, without clear thought, she wrapped them around the armature, tied the feet together and placed one bare foot against the wall.

Pulling herself up with the nylon rope and climbing with her feet flat against the hot wall, Sarah rose toward the sill. She put one foot out the window, pulling herself up until she sat on the sill. Raising her hands to the upper window frame, she steadied herself to look at her options outside.

One leg was in the heat of the room, the other out in the fresh air. She gulped oxygen into her lungs and glanced about her.

She sat sideways in the window. The small balcony hung behind her, about three feet away. Too far. A young Bigleaf Maple tree hovered about two feet off to her left. It must have been in its sixth or seventh year, left alone to grow up quickly in this neglected yard. Its youthful bark appeared almost as much green as it was brown. It would be as flexible as a whip.

Sarah wriggled a little further out of the sill, reaching for the sapling with her toes. Her arms overhead kept a firm grip on the window frame as she stretched toward the tree. Her toes touched and then grabbed at the upper branches. She drew her foot toward her, using all its flexibility as if it were hand.

Below her on the freeway, two fire engines passed from east to west heading for the hospital off ramp. In five minutes, they would arrive.

In five minutes, I'll burn if I stay here.

Inside the bedroom, her leg curled up closer to her body, her foot pushing against the inner wall to help maintain her balance. Her skin tightened in response to the growing heat in the room. Sarah knew without looking that her opponent was gaining on her in this race.

More fire engines flashed past down in the freeway gulch just as she reached with her left hand, slowly, slowly drawing the leaves and then the small branches toward herself. At last, the main stem came into her hand, whip thin and frighteningly tall.

She glanced out, gauging the probable angle of her fall. Naturally, the sapling leaned toward the sun and the freeway wall which stood only thirty feet behind the house. It would probably whip that direction at first. Then it would break. She knew it would break at some point in its descent. Maple wasn't as supple as a birch sapling. There would be no gentle dropping her on the ground and then whipping back up to its original height.

The question was how to control when and where it would break and therefore where she would fall. She didn't want to be smashed against the concrete wall which separated this yard from the freeway.

But inside the house, she could feel, the intense heat at her toes and knew her opponent ran in her lane, preparing to pass.

So, she pulled up her inside leg. Holding the sapling with her left hand and the window frame with her right, she maneuvered her leg onto the sill, foot flat against the sloped outer piece of wood.

She lunged. Pushing off with her foot, she swung her other arm out and caught the Maple stem three feet below where her left hand gripped it.

For a moment she flew. Her feet scraped on the rail of the little balcony behind her, and then she had the sensation of being poised in air, of stretching her slender body out into a perfect dive, toes pointed, arms straight above her head.

The Maple whipped toward the concrete wall, then slowly bent toward the earth.

Control lasted only seconds. The snap of the stem wood sent her dive into a crash.

The jagged edges of the stem scratched her right wrist as the green inner bark ripped away from the break and tore down the stem for two feet. Her hands still gripped the now useless upper stem of the tree as she fell the last fifteen feet.

She tried to tuck and roll as she landed, but the muddy weed bed made the roll impossible. She tucked and caved in upon herself, expelling the last of the air from her lungs and jarring her head against her shoulders. Sarah felt herself roll to one side, a jolt of pain running up her right leg just before the world blackened. In her darkened mind, she became aware that the fire engines had screeched to a halt on the front street.

Above her body, the rose of sunset reached to meet the orange and yellow flames of the burning house. Then, black clouds and smoke covered the sun.

# CHAPTER FOUR

In an upper office of his church, Abraham Hallowell dragged a pencil through his unruly hair. The gesture didn't help him concentrate. He needed to write, yet this afternoon he was too empty even to think clearly.

After finding great friends in his own congregation, after working on therapy with cheering from Arthur and Amanda Charles, Amanda's cancer had returned. Abe's children had enveloped her with love during her last days. His friend, Amanda, had died. His children grieved. Arthur, struggled with his grief. Abe deeply felt the need to be with them.

Part of his need to help must be to continue the work that Arthur and Amanda had started here at the church.

If he finished this grant proposal, he might be able to keep the old parsonage in operation as a half-way house. Five homeless families would get back on their feet during the next year.

Amanda and her ally, Eleanor Whiting, had renovated the house, taking care of it almost entirely without him with the help of an architect he had never met, but who, it appeared, had mostly donated her time.

However, the cost of food and electricity was more than he had hoped.

Abe had to write this grant proposal soon. The time was coming when he could only care for his youngest son, Peter.

Unable to think clearly, Abraham slapped down his pencil and stood to stretch his body. He leaned his left hand against the office door jamb, stretching his body away from the wall. At thirty-eight, he felt old. The sharp pain in his leg stabbed, but he tried to stretch beyond it.

Closing his eyes, he controlled the urge to cry out as the ache suddenly knifed him. He refused to give in, either to the torture in his body or the torment in his soul.

For his children and his parishioners, he tried to take care of what was left of himself. But today, his strong legs needed their run, his shoulders missed the weightlifting he'd neglected for three weeks. The time he ordinarily used caring for his health had been spent helping his old friend Amanda Charles die in a family of love.

He knew he should exercise in the hall since his office was too small to contain six feet two inches of man. He started for the door. The door tilted crazily.

Abraham made a quick grab for the side of his desk and tightened his grip to keep from falling over. The walls and floor spun around him.

I will not be dizzy, he thought desperately. I will **not** be a soggy vegetable.

With his eyes closed, he suddenly heard the wail of fire sirens nearby, maybe down in the gulch where the freeway ran next to the hospital area.

He won a minor victory by opening his eyes and concentrating on something – anything. The fog of white before him coalesced into paper. As he focused, the individual sheets slowed their apparent motion and became separate items on his desk. A familiar bit of formal note paper and fine Spencerian script arrested his attention. He leaned over the already memorized words. Picking up the paper, Abraham read again the short note. He felt again the old man's sadness.

"Reverend Hallowell,

I am enclosing a check as recompense for your services at Amanda's funeral. It was a good memorial. The things you said about Amanda were fine and I thank you for them.

Please use this to get something for your children. They are truly "special" children in ways that the medical community cannot define. Amanda loved being their grandmother.

Sincerely,
Arthur Charles"

Abraham sat down heavily and rested his head on the high back of the old leather chair.

He noticed that the sirens had halted. He hoped that fire was not in the hospital. Or in the neighborhood near it.

His gaze glanced over a wall of worn books. Had the ministers who sat in this chair before him known this sense of inadequacy after funerals?

He could hear Amanda Charles clear, soft voice. "Abe-boy, you were left alive. Get on with the work."

Ministers were supposed to have figured these things out. If he couldn't accept the death of a twisted, pained and wonderful old lady, how dare he offer solace to others? How offer hope to little Peter?

Abraham closed his eyes, grimacing at the ache in his heart. He knew he had to keep going, but some nights 'getting on with the work' was gut wrenching.

He glanced at another wall, the photos of the ministers of this church from 1920 to today. All venerable men, some with beards, some clean shaven, and the last one, the one with green eyes and copper hair, the one who supported the people of today, a man he hardly ever recognized as worthy of the space on the wall.

He glanced at the watch on his right arm and then pushed his arm back into his jacket pocket. Six-thirty. Time to get down to the police station for his stint as Police and Fire Chaplain. His second job helped make ends meet – and he was needed. There were times when he was all there was between some officer and his unspeakable terror.

But today it was so hard to get out of the chair . . .

The phone on his desk jangled Abe's taut nerves.

He fumbled it up to his good ear. "John Wesley Methodist Church."

"Hallowell, that you?"

"Yeah, Bob. What is it?" He recognized the gravelly tones of the fire chief and in the background the noise of fire pumps.

"Bad fire. Old house in your neck of the woods. Two victims – well one victim, the other, God knows what to make of her."

"Where is it?" Abe hoped God did know about the Her – Bob didn't ask for outside help very often.

"We're behind St. Joseph's Mercy. Altenbein Street – it's an alley really. The one that's still alive, she's incoherent."

"I'll be right there." He hoped Bob didn't think Protestants gave absolution. He hoped absolution wasn't needed.

"Better beat the police over here," Bob said. "She needs someone to talk for her."

Okay, she wasn't dying. Abe knew the area. Half a mile south of his church. He'd do it on foot. No use wasting time parking a car.

* *

Within four minutes, Abe skirted fat hoses to get to the back of the emergency vehicle where he spotted a woman wrapped in a blanket. At first sight, he noticed how pale she seemed. Her hair had been wrenched out of what appeared to be a neat knot at the back of her head. Brown and gold wisps waved about her face, whipped by the growing wind. The woman stared up at the rising flames, her dark eyebrows raised in fear or worry.

Bob Chappell stood next to her, a hammy hand on her shoulder. "You're out now, Missy. You're safe. It's all right."

"Everything is rotten" she whispered, still staring at the flames. "— rotten to the joists. They'll fall through."

Bob stared up at the flame as well. "I'm not sending any men in there, Missy. You don't need to worry about that."

Bob's men trained hoses on the roofs of the neighboring houses, but this house was gone, and Bob knew it. "What the devil were you doing in there anyway?" he asked her.

"He might have been in the basement. I never thought of that. He might have been down there with that man."

"What man . . . oh Abe. Thanks for coming." Bob quickly stepped between Abe and the woman. "Weird." he whispered. "Maybe drugs. Every minute a new revelation. Found her lying in the back yard. Back there with a dead boy and no idea how she got there."

"What did you need me to . . ."

"Couldn't get a lawyer for her myself, but I figured she was going to need someone to stand up for her when the police come. Called you first. They'll be here in a minute. Better talk to her."

Abe ducked around the burly fire chief and knelt in front of the woman. As he looked up, he was startled to see clear brown eyes and a smooth complexion under smudges of cinder and mud. He had expected mottled skin and the opaque glaze of a drug ridden mind.

"Miss," he said, capturing her attention for the first time. She glanced at him; the flames she'd been watching reflected in the dark color of her irises. "Miss, I'm Abraham Hallowell, pastor. The chief thinks I should talk to you before the police come. What happened here?"

She blinked and glanced back up at the fire. "I was trapped in there. I pushed Bruce out the window . . ."

*The dead boy*, thought Abe. "Did this Bruce attack you?" he asked her.

"No, he was dead," she whispered, still not looking at Abe. "Pulled him from the attic. Pushed him out the back window. Want to know what killed him."

Bob's voice answered that one. "It was a broken neck."

Bob's words cut through her dreamlike trance, "No," she said gazing at Abe. "It wasn't broken before I pushed him."

Abe felt cold spread across his shoulder blades. She stated so calmly that she'd pushed Bruce out the window. It was as if she'd spent all her emotions on doing it and had nothing left for remorse.

"Miss, what is your name?" he asked gently.

"My name," she said, stalling for memory of it, "My name is Sarah . . . Sarah Rohann."

"Are you hurt?"

Her smile was brief. "My leg hurts right up to my teeth. The sapling broke. I knew it would . . ."

As her voice trailed off, Abe saw the sheen of sweat on her lip. Her color had gone white beneath olive tan.

"Bob, this lady is in shock."

Bob took a quick glance at her, "I agree. Seemed right enough when I found her, though. And the police are going to be interested in what she was doing with a dead boy."

The woman's whisper nearly escaped Abe. "Forensics."

At that moment she crumpled over onto his shoulder.

As Abe stood up, holding the woman in his good arm, he heard the police sirens.

"She needs an ambulance," Abe said, laying her down on the grass.

"You tell Officer Reese."

"I'll do that."

# CHAPTER FIVE

After the ambulance left, Abe ran to the backyard. Police Captain Reese followed him as fast as a big man could, but by the time he caught up, Abe stood in the back yard near the burning house.

"Thing's gonna collapse," Reese said, pulling Abe's arm.

"She said 'the sapling broke. I knew it would.'."

"What the hell are you doing back here?" Reese said, heading both of them back to the driveway.

Abe said, "I'm trying to get the picture of what happened before it's all gone."

"Let Chappell figure that out," Reese said, "We've gotta get outa here."

"There it is," Abe said, pointing at a broken tree between the balcony and the empty window. "God, did she try to climb down that spindly ..."

Reese yanked on him. "The roof ..."

Abe saw the roof moving under its own weight as flames leapt out of it. He grabbed Reese's arm and pulled the big man around the corner into the driveway just as the first timbers flew past them. Even Abe heard the whack of wood on concrete as the roof threatened to plow into the concrete wall and spill the fire onto the freeway below.

"Bob . . ." Abe shouted.

"Got the freeway blocked off in that lane," Bob Chappell hollered back. "Get out front now!"

When Abe and Reese arrived at the alley, a stiff spray of hose water nearly knocked them over. Abe had a momentary memory of black and white film, of children, of dogs and fire hoses, and then Police Captain Reese brought him back to the present.

"What was all that about that broken tree?" Reese asked.

"She said something like 'I knew the sapling would break.' I think that's how she got out the window – grabbed the maple sapling and rode it down as far as she could until it broke."

"You're nuts," Reese said. "How could she?"

"I think there wasn't much choice," Abe said.

"Well, forensics and Bob's expertise are going to tell us a lot. Meanwhile, she's under guard at the hospital because I think she killed that boy."

Abe said, "Let's wait to judge until she's coherent enough to tell us what happened."

"She told Bob she pushed the kid out the window."

"Reese . . ."

"All right. I'll wait."

*   *

Late at night, Abe pushed through the swinging doors to the west wing of St. Joseph's Mercy. He'd been here often enough during the last two days to see that Sarah Rohann had friends. But after the first time, he'd made a point to come very early or very late and miss the crowd that hung about her door waiting to visit.

Among them, Abe had recognized Muhammed, the Halal grocer from the neighborhood open-air market. And yesterday in the waiting area, he'd met the old plumber who helped him with the ancient water system at John Wesley church.

Several shapes, sizes and languages of teenage kid, and a passel of construction workers waited to see her, too. The construction workers finally made sense when Jack Darnley, the plumber, told him Sarah was an architect and builder. But the kids?

He was afraid she was about to be accused of murder and the kids hanging around added fuel to police suspicions. Captain Reese had been great about getting her into the ambulance, but he also was anxious to understand more than Sarah Rohann seemed able to tell him.

Today the police got a statement from the dead boy's mother that Sarah Rohann enticed her boy, Bruce, away from the bosom of his God-fearing family. The woman described the bedlam of the Rohann household – several foster children living with Sarah and a whole gang of who-knew-what kind of boys hung out around her house and shop.

"And no father," the woman had thrown out. "No man at all since her grandfather died, unless you count that old drunk who came with the building."

There was no gang of boys waiting as Abe strode up to her door. A sudden feeling of being an intruder made him stop. The nurse had said to go right in, but Sarah Rohann had no reason to welcome him. He knocked gently.

"Come in."

He pushed the door open and beheld her, pale and sad, and amazingly fragile for one so determined. She lay against the pile of pillows. One bedside lamp softly lit her face. The dramatic contrast of her dark brows and hazel brown eyes to the sunny warmth of her wheat-colored hair surprised him just as it did each time he visited.

Her dark eyebrows rose in surprise.

"Reverend Hallowell," she said.

"Abe," he corrected. "How's the leg?"

"Much better. The cast itches, but it's the burns on my hands they're worried about. I think I'll be out of here tomorrow though."

A chuckle slipped out of Abe. He already knew how difficult inactivity must be for this woman. He'd watched as Bob's fire investigation had traced her harrowing escape out the back window of the burning house. This afternoon, he and the fire chief had climbed a ladder to the small balcony at the back of the house. Through the hatcheted door, they'd studied the charred room from which she'd leapt.

Bob's low whistle expressed their awe. "She wanted that boy's body out of there awful bad. She risked her own life to make sure we had a chance to find his killer. And swinging down on the Maple sapling – little gal's got more chutzpa than I have."

But here in the hospital, Abe, approaching Sarah's bed, noted dark shadows beneath her eyes. He was glad she was confined a little longer. It would keep her out of danger.

Still, he could sympathize.

"It's hard to rest, isn't it?" he said. "Especially when your mind says `It's only my hands'."

She nodded. "You sound like you've spent plenty of time in a hospital." Then her gaze swept over the arm tucked into his suit coat pocket. Her face flushed.

Abe worked to ignore that glance. He smiled at her and plunked himself down in a chair next to her bed. "Don't worry." He shrugged his right shoulder, but his arm remained in the pocket. "This was several months ago. I miss it, but I don't mind much anymore."

The truth was his arm had been giving him trouble – acting up ever since he caught and carried her to the grass two days ago. The pain he often felt in his missing hand had been a dull ache all day. But he sure wasn't going to say so to this woman.

To put her at ease, he quickly changed topics. "You've had quite a tribe of visitors."

The flush rose again, and her dark lashes lowered to hide her embarrassment. "Foster children, friends."

He tried to keep his gaze from the lace at the neck edge of her night gown, but the way it touched the smooth skin over her collar bone drew his attention.

"How many kids out there were yours?" he blurted.

She gazed straight at him again, a hint of defiance in the tilt of her head. "One adopted son and three foster children. They've been with me for several years now."

He smiled to himself over the thought that `several' couldn't be very long in the life of one so young. She was probably no more than twenty-eight or nine – fresh smooth skin, natural laugh lines around her eyes – Abe found himself fumbling to keep the conversation going without asking about yesterday's mob of visiting construction workers.

"And the other kids?" He could have kicked himself for that nosey question. He blamed his stupidity on his infernal throbbing hand.

"The others are friends of my children – the high school track team, Kevin's buddies . . . They like my cookies and the space to kick back in." Sarah sat up, abruptly. "Have the police been through the burnt house?"

Abe could hear her voice tremble, afraid of the news he might bring. Ignoring the cold sweat caused by his insistent pain, Abe spoke softly, protective of her feelings.

"Bob Chappell – the fire chief – went through the house this afternoon. It's still got hot spots, but he was able to get down into the cellar. No sign of your son. Kevin didn't die in there, Sarah."

"The gases from the stored woodchips . . ." she began.

"You were right. They did explode. It was a mess down there, but Bob's thorough. He'd have found something."

She fell back against the pillows, relief filling her eyes with unshed tears.

"It's time you went to sleep, young lady," Abe said gently. "Please, let the police look for Kevin. You gave them his photo. Even with his blond bangs over his eyes, they will be able to recognize him. And I know the neighborhood hangouts, too. Sarah, you rest."

"The autopsy?"

He was afraid she'd ask that. "No word."

"How long?"

"Depends on the caseload. A week maybe."

She shuddered, covering her mouth with a bandaged hand. "Caseload . . ."

Abe hated his ineptness. "That was kind of a crass way of putting it," he said. "I'm sorry . . ."

Behind him a new voice interrupted Abe. "Well, the priest. Haven't you religious types anything better to do at ten-thirty at night?"

"Miguel!" Sarah frowned.

Abe turned. A youngster – barely out of his teens and into the self-importance of young manhood – a boy of olive complexion and flashing dark eyes slipped into the room. His alert gaze went to Sarah's tears after barely a flicker over Abe.

"I don't want him upsetting you, Mom."

"It's not Mr. Hallowell who is upsetting me," Sarah said quietly to her son. The gentle reminder that his cold manners might upset her, hung in the air between the three of them.

After a defiant moment, Miguel softened, but almost imperceptibly. "You should be sleeping, Mom," he said, sidling past Abe to the far side of Sarah's bed. Miguel put the back of his hand to her forehead in the time-honored way of fretting mothers.

Sarah smiled up at him indulgently. "No fever. I've been sleeping all day. This is Abraham Hallowell – my son Miguel Salvador who takes a dislike to anyone who might harm me."

Abe stood and reached his left hand across the bed. "I'm glad to meet a man who protects his family."

The young man eyed him carefully, then slowly extended his own left hand, giving Abe's a firm short shake. Abe recognized that Miguel gave in to this outward form of politeness only for the sake of his mother. Afterwards, Miguel's gaze followed Abe's movements with the careful wariness of the wild animal newly trapped in human surroundings.

Perhaps hoping to turn the men's watchful stand-off into a normal conversation, Sarah prodded, "Mr. Hallowell saved me from wondering what the police were up to."

Miguel did not pick up on the offer of a topic.

Abe didn't want to force the issue. He'd heard the epithet 'priest' spat out by Miguel when he first entered. Perhaps someday he would know what caused Miguel's anger against men of the cloth. For now, Abe wanted to allay the boy's fears and leave him in peace with his mother. Besides, he needed to get home and take something against this pain.

He glanced down at Sarah who watched him, silently.

Does she share her son's disdain for my calling?

It shocked him to find he cared so much what Sarah Rohann thought. But there it was. He faced it squarely as he'd taught himself to face all of life's rip-snorters.

I'm infatuated with a woman with the courage of a mother bear, a woman suspected of murder.

Hesitantly, he touched her bandaged hand where it lay on the crisp hospital sheet. "You do need sleep, Sarah. I'll keep you posted."

Apparently unaware of the daggers her son was glaring at Abe, Sarah turned her hand over, enclosing Abe's fingers briefly in hers. Aware that her hands had been injured, he didn't grip, but realized her fingers were warm. He reacted and then stopped his thumb from caressing the inside of her wrist.

"Thank you for coming," she said. "It's hell being cooped up in here when I know Kevin's in danger."

"You're the one in danger, Sarah," Abe said harshly. "Stop going to these places by yourself."

"She will," Miguel said abruptly. "Good night, Mr. Hallowell."

Abe kept his tone calm in spite of Miguel's pushy attitude. "Good night, Mr. Salvador." He nodded at Sarah's bodyguard-son, then, while his gaze lingered on her dark eyes, he allowed his thumb to brush her wrist after all.

"Sarah," he bowed very slightly before walking out of the room.

Out in the deserted hall, Abe passed the posted guard. Down the hall a way, he let out a frustrated breath. The boy was a dragon, his fiery mouth set to torch ministers and priests. Abe had seen it before. Miguel's distrust was probably the result of venomous treatment at the hands of some self-righteous crusader. Abe knew some who called themselves 'God-fearing' but wielded 'god' like a vengeful weapon.

Unbidden, a particularly vivid memory of vengeance came to mind. Raw agony shot through Abe's missing right hand. He gasped, grabbing his arm with his left hand. His body twisted to one side in a spasm that sent him against the wall. Resting there, he forced himself to breathe deeply, to will away the phantom pain. With great effort, he fought off the dizziness that always followed these episodes. His body knew righteous vengeance too well.

\* \*

Thirty feet behind him, Miguel watched Abe from the doorway of his mother's room. His young eyes narrowed at the disgusting sight. Miguel marched back into his mother's room. Making no effort to hide his anger, Miguel noisily straightened the books on Sarah's nightstand.

"All right, Miguel. Out with it."

Miguel slammed down the hospital water pitcher, slopping water on the tray. He grabbed a handful of tissue and began mopping. Sarah reached over and stopped his hand.

"Miguel, say it."

He let out a long breath, finally looking at her. "You know he's on drugs, Mom."

"Oh Miguel! Just because he's a preacher . . ."

"Not that. It's not prejudice. You could have seen it too if you were looking. He had beads of sweat on his forehead. And his jaw muscles were working sixty miles an hour."

"That could be anything – tired, maybe overworked . . ."

"There's always some better explanation for you, isn't there?" Miguel said angrily. "You believe what you want. 'Kevin's been hurt,' you say. You risk your life looking for him instead of facing the truth. He's chosen to go back on cocaine or alcohol. And now this guy – Overworked! My God, Mom – out in the hall that priest was doubled over by withdrawal symptoms, leaning against the wall and moaning. It's drugs. Plain as day."

Sarah's eyes widened. She stared at her grown son and then turned her face to the window. Blinking out at the glowering night clouds, she fought to bring up a clear picture of the man who'd come to her rescue after the fire. His red-brown curls danced in the wind as he gazed up at her, questioned her and then folded her in his arms as the world began to spin.

"No," she whispered. "No. It can't be."

Miguel snorted. "It is."

# CHAPTER SIX

Two days out of the hospital, Sarah saw her small family of two teenagers off to school and then she promised Miguel she would only work on the house they were renovating for the Jackson family.

"Mom, the police are looking for Kevin. That priest says he's looking for Kevin. You keep our work schedule moving forward or we won't be able to take care of Jeff and Akesha."

She saluted him, with her bandaged hands. "Sir, yes, sir."

"Not taking any funny business from you," Miguel said, quoting Sarah's own grandfather who had used that line on Miguel when he was a wild teenager.

Sarah laughed. "You don't quite have Grandfather's gruff voice."

Miguel eyed her over his safety goggles.

She promised. "I'll be at Jacksons, ordering the plumber around, or at the hardware store getting what he needs."

"And nowhere else," Miguel said.

"Jack-in the Box for lunch."

\* \*

Once he'd wrung that promise from her, Miguel was free to leave for the southwest hills of Portland where he worked to finish the kitchen at the home of the Walter and Joan Schreibens. Finishing the Schreibens' kitchen was going to keep their company afloat.

On the other hand, finishing the Jackson home was a long project, a little at a time as the Jackson's could afford each step. The Jackson's were both employed but underpaid and so had been living in a trailer when Sarah met them.

The African-American Cooperative Bank had underwritten their loan to purchase the property and would help the Jackson family get the permits as each part of the renovation came up. As they saved, Sarah was able to buy lumber and other necessities to turn a derelict house into a home.

That same bank had another non-profit arm that provided apprenticeship opportunities first for Miguel and now for Jeff and Akesha, the foster children in Sarah's home.

As soon as he had become a Journeyman Carpenter, the non-profit part of the co-op Bank hired Miguel to help teach younger apprentices. When he became a Master Carpenter, Miguel still taught for the school. He loved kids.

His students and his family all worked once a month on homes for Habitat for Humanity. The donation of hours was a requirement for earning their apprentice recognition. But the kids and Sarah enjoyed these opportunities to create a better community.

So, Sarah hopped in the old Chevy truck and drove off to meet Jack Darnley, the plumber who was set to install a kitchen sink at the Jacksons. She knew Miguel was correct about not hunting for Kevin. She'd nearly died and that would have put her kids out on the street with nothing.

Kevin now had to be the responsibility of the police.

As for Pastor Hallowell, Sarah hadn't seen him since the night Miguel said he was exhibiting withdrawal symptoms. She hadn't wanted to believe it, but if she never saw him, she couldn't make a judgement.

Pulling up to the Jackson home, Sarah first noticed the orange paint on the front porch. She'd seen that graffiti sign before. The gang for which Kevin once sold drugs.

She slumped over the steering wheel for a moment, and then swung out of the truck in anger. She whipped back into the truck bed and found the only paint she knew that might cover the huge C of the orange spray paint.

She found the white can, but as she pulled it out, she remembered the great pain in her hands. The cast on her left leg slowed her pivot, nearly sending her to the ground. As she recovered, she heard a car pull in behind her.

She whirled, spray can pointed to paint any gang member who threatened.

Out of a beaten Subaru, stepped Abe Hallowell.

He stopped halfway out of his car. "I'm that scary?"

She lowered the can. "Thought you were someone else," she said.

He smiled. "I'm not here with the police, and Officer Reese has more than you in mind as a suspect. He's thinking Bruce's murder was a gang killing."

"But that man was older."

Abe closed his door and walked toward her. "We've got older gang members. Sometimes it's them running the younger ones."

She nodded. "But what gang, and why."

"Was Bruce part of a gang?"

She nodded. "Bruce was part of the Coxwell 13. That's what they called themselves because they all live around Coxwell and 13th."

Abe stared at the house. "And that's why there's an X, a 3 and a C painted on this house?"

"Yes."

"Do you have a camera phone?"

"Yes."

"Please photo that before you paint over it."

Sarah pulled out her phone and handed it to him. "Could you? My pointer finger isn't working yet."

He chuckled and took her phone. He fumbled a bit, but had taught himself how to do this with one hand.

While he pointed the camera he asked, "You were going to paint white, let it bleed through and paint white again? Spraying with no pointer finger?"

"I don't have a crew to scrape and repaint today and I don't want the Jacksons to see this on their house."

"Don't you think the Jacksons ought to know what they are moving into?"

"Oh, they know. They are moving here from their trailer park because here there is more community that will stand up for them when the racists get on a rant."

"Racists? Who knows you're working on this house?"

"The whole neighborhood."

"Including the Coxwell Thirteen?"

She stared at the orange paint, answering slowly, "Yes, but Kevin wouldn't do this."

"Who in the gang might want you to stop looking for Kevin? Who might be warning you, and not the Jacksons?"

"I don't know. How did you know I was here?"

"I drive the streets visiting people who cannot go out, people who are sick, or tired, or angry or afraid. I know your truck because Officer Reese had to arrange for it to come back to your house."

She said, "Reese says you are a chaplain with the police and the fire department and that's why he called you."

"Yes, Bob Chappell called actually. He thought you were going to be accused of murdering Bruce and he knew you weren't making any sense, so he called to have an advocate."

"Thank you for coming. I was pretty out of it that day."

"Have you really given up looking?" he asked.

"No. I keep my ears open and my eyes on the community, but I don't go into scary places alone."

"Except this graffitied house, which now qualifies as scary. Let's go in together."

Sarah took a deep breath and decided to face her own concerns. "Miguel thinks you're on drugs."

He handed her the phone and looked her in the eye. "I'm a priest or a pastor, therefore I must be into the wine?"

"No, at the hospital he saw you doubled over in what he believes were withdrawal pains."

Abe leaned back onto the hood of her truck and faced the house. "Before I forget, could you send that photo to Officer Reese? I think he gave you his phone number. Then, I'll explain."

Sarah watched his face. He didn't seem to be anything sinister. He was the man who had come to her side when she couldn't talk for herself. But she did see his shoulders slump a little as if he had hoped never to have to 'explain' again.

She turned to her phone and with some effort, forwarded the graffiti photo to Officer Reese with the house number and the information about her renovations for the Jackson family. Texting wasn't easy, since her thumbs were also somewhat tied up in her bandages.

When she finished, she also leaned against the hood and said, "Okay. I'm listening."

"Someone threw a bomb into my church in Lebanon."

She raised an eyebrow at him.

"Not Lebanon, Oregon. This was in Beirut."

"Ah," she said. "Middle East, Lebanon. Mediterranean Sea, Lebanon."

"Yes," he crossed his long legs and leaned toward her. "I was holding the communion chalice. Part of the chalice sliced through my hand and part of it is still in my back."

Sarah sensed there was more, a lot more, but he didn't say, so she waited.

"Miguel is correct," he said. "I was suffering from withdrawal. I had been trying not to take my pain medicine. It turns out I still need some when the pain hits."

"Opioids?" she asked.

He nodded. "During the first week in the hospital, after they… after they removed my hand and found it too dangerous to try to remove the shrapnel, they gave me oxycodone. In the second week, they stopped that and put me on an anti-depressant that seems to reduce chronic pain. What I take now is called Cymbalta. I hadn't taken any of it for several days, but that night my hand was something fierce."

She waited.

He said, "I can text that name to you if you want to look it up. It's not an opioid. Miguel . . . well, I feel Miguel deserves to know. He's afraid for you."

"He is. And he has reason to hate priests, but I'll let him tell you about that when he knows you better."

Abe glanced at her. "So, there is a chance Miguel will know me better?"

She shrugged. "Let's see what comes up."

# CHAPTER SEVEN

"**O**kay," Abe said. "But for now, we should make sure this house is safe for you."

"Thank you."

"Should you be on that leg this long?" he asked.

"I get the cast off next week. This is just a walking cast, and it doesn't hurt."

"But it gets exhausted, I bet."

"Yes, it does." She smiled.

Sarah rifled her keys out of her purse and led the way in.

Inside, they found no one, and nothing was disturbed, though Sarah knew the place must look like it had been hit by a tornado because of all the lumber and hardware lying about.

Abe said, "Nice kitchen. When's the move in date?"

She glanced at him and realized he was teasing. The kitchen was ready for the plumber, but all he could see was the framing for cabinets and counters.

She decided to riff with him. "Move in is set for next week."

He went along with her. "I can see it all. Breakfast table with bench seating here. Doggy door there. Cat litter over here."

Sarah smiled. "You have a dog and a cat?"

"The kids wish. Cat, but no dog."

This was the first she knew about kids. Somehow the idea that he had a family shocked her. Why had she even imagined a grown man might not have a loving wife and three kids?

She tried a comeback. "Cats are easy care," she said.

"And boy do we need easy care," he said as he wandered over to the window above the future sink. He opened and closed it. "Nice slider," he said.

"And beyond it, a backyard in great need," she added.

"All in good time. Sarah what were you hoping to accomplish today, with bandaged hands and a cast on one leg?"

"I'm waiting for Jack."

"Plumber Jack?"

"Yes, today the kitchen and bathroom, next month the basement for laundry."

"Next month?" he asked.

She nodded, "Necessary monthly budget for the Jacksons."

"Got it," he said. "Can I wait for Jack with you?"

"You afraid the Coxwells are coming?"

"Frankly, yes. Got a paint scraper?"

\*    \*

Half an hour later, over Sarah's objections and finally her thanks, Abe had scraped the orange paint off the siding of the front porch. Jack Darnley arrived.

"Hallowell," Jack said in his usual taciturn greeting.

"Jack. Kitchen and bathroom today?"

"Yup. Didn't know you were part of the crew."

"Just the graffiti crew."

"Good. Hate the stuff," Jack said, and walked in to greet Sarah and start into the kitchen and bathroom piping.

Abe swept paint chips off the porch, then he set the scraping tools back in the future living room and went on his route, visiting shut-ins and then to the police station, checking with Officer Reese about the search for Kevin and the Coxwell 13 gang graffiti.

Officer Reese said, "That kid, that blond kid, Kevin, he was part of a gang that sold drugs. We've got his dad in Sheridan, but the older members of the gang probably are still at it."

"You think maybe they've got Kevin back into sales?" Abe asked.

"Would not be surprised. We couldn't prove the kid was selling before, but he sure had an alcohol problem. He went to Adolf and Sarah Rohann's after a thirty-day rehab program and has been back into the program twice while his dad was incarcerated."

"Adolf?" Abe asked, more than a little afraid of the answer. Why the devil hadn't he thought there might be a husband?

"Grandfather," Reese said.

"Ah!" Abe couldn't believe how that buoyed him. There was no chance his relationship with Sarah could be anything more than friendship, so where could he go with this false optimism?

"Yeah. That kid, Miguel? Originally her grandfather's project, now he's grown, he's her son and business partner, carpenter."

Abe remembered being impressed with the framing in of the kitchen cabinets. "She do carpentry, as well?"

"Sure, couldn't take care of all those kids if she just sat around drawing designs."

"All those kids?"

"Well, Miguel and the other two. You must have met them at the hospital."

"Yes. Just never figured out who was friends and who was family."

"Well, I can tell you every bachelor carpenter and electrician I know wants to be more than friends," Reese said.

Reese seemed to watch Abe's reaction to that statement, so Abe tried to move the topic without showing his pang of jealousy. "The graffiti has meaning, but what meaning?" Abe asked.

"That graffiti makes me think Kevin's gang is warning her to keep away from Kevin," Reese said.

"Or is it Kevin, warning her?" Abe asked.

# CHAPTER EIGHT

Three miles away, on the east side of Eighteenth Avenue near Atfalati Street in North Portland, three turn-of-the-century wooden buildings bared their peeling paint to the afternoon sun. A darkly handsome man walked purposefully past the old relics, heading for the northern end of the block. His age was difficult to pinpoint – young body, graceful and sturdy, supporting a head with glossy black hair. His soft mouth was partially hidden by a trim mustache. Brilliant black eyes gazed with benevolence on his present world. But the lines in his forehead and at the corners of his eyes disclosed past grief that even the sun of springtime could not erase.

As he strode, Miguel Salvador thought about the buildings and their owners. Each in its dilapidated way revealed an attitude toward the community.

On the most southern structure, the lower story sported a garish yellow coat of matt paint. The chalky color, slapped on three years ago, had run down to contaminate the sidewalk. Letters, three-feet high, in graying blue, announced the Adult Movie store. Smaller print refined the impression for passersby. Marital aides were included in the offerings. Miguel always snorted at the hypocrisy of that ugly sign.

Any pedestrian could see that the upper two floors of this and the next building were inhabited by mysterious shipping boxes, by crooked piles of chairs and by few people. Even those who lived there had privacy guarded only by crooked shades and faded bedspreads. The bedspreads refused to remain hung on their nails at the window frames. They defied their owners right to privacy, drooping to reveal the tired faces and care-worn hands of the lonely.

The building next to the porn shop was a used bookstore. Georg B. Kerns sat in the sun in a chair reading a book. Ever since Miguel could remember, Mr. Kern's used bookstore had barely made enough each year to pay the rent and feed Mr. Kerns.

"'Lo, Miguel. Read gut books, yah?"

"Those back copies of Woodworking Magazine that I bought from you. They helped solve a coving problem I had."

"I vill more dat type hunt for you," Kerns said.

"Thanks, Mr. Kerns."

"Booky to you, knabe. You become man now, so call me Booky."

"That a nickname or a description?" Miguel joked.

"Name is Georg Buchstein Kerns. Meine mutter, she read a lot. I become Booky long ago, because . . ." he waved at the store front where several layers of books lay piled on the window shelf in helter-skelter fashion.

Miguel laughed. "Not much of a stretch from one to the other. Have a great day."

"Vill do," Booky said, as he returned to his reading.

The central building on the block remained unpainted since the owner had moved out twenty years before. Muhammed, the grocer who rented the street floor invested in window bars, but not in paint. Inside, his broom and his whitewash bucket conveyed grey cleanliness.

Muhammed Dinawari came out of his store, broom in hand.

"Miguel," he said. "I like your new garage door."

"Thank you, Mr. Dinawari. Color makes everything better."

"If you own the building."

"Even if you don't."

"Hmmmph!" Muhammed Dinawari grunted and continued sweeping small leaves from one place to another.

The lack of investment in paint revealed what Muhammed believed was the transitional character of his neighborhood. All who could, were only passing through. All others, including Muhammed's Halal grocery, were stuck here by unhappy circumstance.

But Miguel was not just passing through. And he was no longer stuck here. When he and his mother had been tenants, this neighborhood had seemed like a prison. At thirteen, Miguel had quit school to take care of his dying mother and the future had held no hope for either of them.

Then Adolf Rohann had bought the third, most northern building at the corner, and had made the tenants, including Miguel, shareholders in their home. Adolf had insisted Miguel return to school and had hired nurses for his mother. He also had taught Miguel to make a future with his hands. Adolf's granddaughter, Sarah Rohann, had become his mother's last and best friend.

When he was seventeen, Miguel's mother had died here in a beautifully decorated room, surrounded by loving people. Just before his mother's death, at his mother's request, Sarah had adopted Miguel. There had been loud objections from the social worker and the priest. After all, Sarah was not of the faith and she had been only twenty-eight and not quite finished with her architectural degree.

But because of the written testimony of Miguel's mother, the judge had given Miguel a new parent barely ten years older than himself. In truth Sarah had mothered him since he was fourteen and only occasionally did it occur to him that she had been little more than a girl herself when it all began.

The stern and loving Adolf had become his great grandfather. Miguel had learned the family trade quickly. And now, at twenty-three, this neighborhood was not a prison to him. It was his chosen home.

Each building revealed the worldview of its occupant. Even the home of Miguel Salvador revealed his frame of mind. This northern-most building was separated from its brothers by a narrow delivery drive. The building had recently been painted a soft beaver-fur tan. The windows were framed in blue. The street floor windows had been replaced by an enormous garage door, painted to match the wooden siding, and framed carefully to look as if it had always been part of this building. A smaller door with a glass window gave entry to a well swept office. Elegant black calligraphy on the window announced proudly that "Rohann and Salvador" were Architect and Master Carpenter/Cabinet Makers. The lettering was Sarah's favorite font and her careful work.

Muhammed Dinawari suddenly waved his broom at Miguel and shouted, "Hey. Those boys!"

"What?"

"I forgot," Muhammed said, "Those boys used to come by all the time?"

Miguel couldn't understand the question, so walked back toward the grocer. "Yes. Boys used to come. Have they been here?"

"Today. They come by looking for Sarah."

Suddenly Miguel felt fear. "Which boys?"

"White boys. You know. His friends. They hang around when Kevin was here."

"Did they go in?"

"No. Ernst, you know he never answers doors. They knock and yell a little, then walk around back."

"Thanks. I'll check," Miguel said.

He took off for the back of the building searching for anything – any sign they might have jimmied a window or gone up the fire escape stairs. Sarah's truck wasn't back there. The windows were intact, and the doors and windows at the top of the fire escape didn't seem to have been touched.

Muhammed had followed him. He searched the rhododendrons and azaleas at the back and the side. Miguel joined him.

Miguel said, "It doesn't look like they did anything or left anything."

"They were not back here very long. Just seemed to be looking for Sarah."

Miguel looked at him. "Looking out of anger?"

"No. More like what used to be – looking because they enjoy … maybe enjoy home and …"

Miguel snorted. "And her cookies."

"Her cookies are care, you know. Some of them don't get much of that."

Miguel nodded. "Don't I know. They didn't ask for Kevin?"

Muhammed shook his head.

"Then they know Kevin isn't here."

"Yes. They must know."

"Thank you, Mr. Dinawari."

"Miguel. You are a man now. I am Muhammed to you."

"Thank you, Muhammed. I wish I always felt like a grown up. But this thing with Kevin – it's really blowing my mind."

"Any grown up would be as worried and as protective as you are. I hope we find him."

Miguel nodded. "Thank you."

They walked back toward the front.

Muhammed said, "We watch. All of us watch for Kevin, even the porn shop fellow."

"Thank you all. The porn shop fellow?"

"Not a bad man, just has to make a living and hasn't got, you know, groceries or books."

Miguel shook his head. "If he had better merchandise, he might be able to make a better living."

"Yes, and he has discussed this with me. Looking to get out of this business but can't see a way."

Miguel, "Well, maybe someday, we can figure that one out."

Muhammed smiled. "Someday, when your family is together again."

Miguel nodded, but he thought, Sarah worries about Kevin. I think he just went back to his previous comfort zone and doesn't need us at all.

The lyre chimes over his front door set in motion as Miguel stepped into the office. Sarah's truck was gone. He'd heard her say that she would work at the Jacksons today.

Miguel laughed at how she'd managed to be absent just at this time of the week. He knew that the bookkeeping needed to be caught up so that the billings could be done for the month's work. No wonder she'd insisted that he take bookkeeping along with the carpentering classes at the community college. This way they could share the onerous job of staying indoors and wielding a pencil instead of a hammer.

Miguel looked into the woodworking room behind the office and waved at the older man who built a cast for a plaster cornice. Leathery old Ernst Schumacher gave Miguel a sardonic smile and returned to his task. Miguel headed for the desk and took out a ledger, sat down in the swivel chair and made entries in the computer account books. He resigned himself to the task and worked steadily for two hours, checking figures, collating receipts, making sure he'd documented everything. By mid-afternoon, the silence of the office began to bother him. His concentration wavered toward the window. Unconsciously, he watched for an old and battered truck.

# CHAPTER NINE

A little after two thirty, on the third floor of the tan and blue building, Sarah Rohann closed the door from the fire escape. This was her quick access to the drafting room on days when a fragile idea struck her. Some ideas wouldn't survive the greetings required by a front door entry.

She entered and took up the ringing telephone. "Rohann and Salvador," she said.

"May I speak to Sarah Rohann?" asked a woman's voice.

"I am the Rohann," Sarah said.

"Ah good," the woman said. "I am Eleanor Whiting."

"Of course, I remember you, Mrs. Whiting."

"I'm calling again to represent the Building Committee of John Wesley Methodist Church. We are interviewing contractors for a renovation of a portion of our church building, so we'd like to talk to you. We enjoyed your design for the parsonage renovation."

"I saw it once after your committee finished doing the work. That was a nice job of room dividing."

Mrs. Whiting said, "Your ideas made the work very much easier for us old committee folks. So, that confirmed that we'd want to call you again. Plus, you were recommended to us by Amanda and Arthur Charles. May I talk to you about this bigger project?"

"Oh, yes Arthur and Amanda. I renovated their home for Mrs. Charles's wheelchair access."

"Yes, that's what they told me. Amanda died six weeks ago."

Suddenly, Sarah felt the world whirling. She put her head down on her sketch board. "Oh!" She said, "I didn't know! I'm sorry. She was such a wonderful person."

"Yes, we will all miss her very much," Mrs. Whiting said.

Over the next minutes, Sarah wrote down the time and place of a meeting with Mrs. Whiting and Arthur Charles for their church building.

After hanging up, she stared at her drafting table, seeing the face of Amanda and the caring and worried face of Arthur Charles. A loss of a sweet and lovely person. A loss of a great friend.

Then, she straightened, as Amanda would have her do. She began working on a design for better storage space in the Jackson's garage and their basement.

As she sketched, Amanda Charles' face kept appearing in her sketches, instead of a floor plan of Mr. and Mrs. Jackson's basement storage space.

And then, she realized that Abraham's dark and penetrating gaze also appeared before her on the page. The man's body hurt him; she was sure of it. Twice this morning she had seen the color drain from his tan face and beads of sweat form suddenly on his forehead. Something still was very wrong, but he ignored it. Why?

She wanted to make things better for him, not ask him to scrape the paint where Coxwell 13 had marred the front porch.

Did his pain have anything to do with his conflict towards her? Men had been attracted to her often. She thought she recognized that pull in all its forms. With most men, she had a ready technique – a clear brush off.

Yet Abraham's attraction, if that's what it was, seemed to be paired with an equal repulsion. Whenever closeness had begun to build between them this morning, he had worked very hard to resist it. His reaction to her was far from smooth, certainly not suave.

Was that why, for the first time, she had wanted to encourage instead of discourage?

* *

Down on the main floor of the brown and blue building, Miguel worried. By five o'clock, high school athletes began passing on their way home from school. Sarah always arrived by the time Akesha and Jeff came from track practice. Slamming the finance ledger closed, he returned it to the desk drawer, and turned off the computer. In the woodworking room, he waved at Ernst who turned off the saw to hear him.

"Where is she?"

"I ain't seen her, Miguel. I thought she was still out at the old Victorian she's finishing up. Thought I heard the truck around two, but she never came through this way."

The old man pulled his safety goggles back over his eyes and fingered his work, anxious to return to it.

Miguel went back through the office and out onto the street to look for the truck or any other sign of his adoptive mother.

Out front, he met Muhammed who swept the sidewalk in front of his Halal Grocers.

"Seen Mom?" Miguel asked him.

"She not off looking for him again, is she?" Muhammed asked.

"Geez, I hope not," Miguel said.

Mr. Kern came out of his used bookstore. "You look for Sarah?"

Miguel nodded.

"She in your driveway drove, about two something."

"Thanks, Booky," Miguel said and trotted around his building. Sure enough, the truck sat at the back of the driveway near the fire-escape. Miguel shook his head and enjoyed the joke on himself. He'd spent an afternoon on those lousy books when a pleading look in her direction would have had her taking over from him. He supposed he should be proud of all the work he'd just done, but he would much rather have been building something. He shook his head and climbed the fire escape to take her by surprise.

* *

Sarah drew at her drafting table. Occasionally she glanced up at the long cross-cut saw that hung above her desk. Its teeth were worn, and its wooden handles rubbed a dark almost black with the sweat of the hands that had once used it – Grandfather's hands and his brother. The saw reminded her of the wonderful and patient old man. She had never met his older brother, Elijah, but she imagined him, a mentor and a solid friend for Grandfather when they came together from Finland, looking for a new life.

When late afternoon sunlight warmed the paper on her drafting table, Sarah leaned her forehead onto the white heat of it and thought about how she would miss knowing that Amanda Charles graced the earth. She closed her eyes to savor the memory of her morning talk with Abraham.

She wanted this memory to take her mind off of the sadness she had visited after he had left. In the early afternoons, she now made it a habit to spend an hour sharing water bottles and letting the street people know she was looking for sixteen-year-old Kevin.

Her foster son didn't want to be found, but she wanted him to know she hadn't given up caring. After so many weeks, she grew fearful of the condition he would be in if he ever did come home.

Before he had lived with her, illegal drugs had been Kevin's father's major source of income. Alcohol had also been Kevin's major food.

* *

"Mom," Miguel's voice woke her. "You haven't really recovered, have you? Let me see those hands."

Sarah smiled. Teresa's son had become such a nurse when his mother was sick, that he couldn't seem to give up nursing. She held her hands out to him. He began to unwrap the right bandage.

"Can't have an infection go undiscovered here," he said. "How is Jackson's house coming?"

"Plumbing's in," she said. Sarah knew she wasn't going to tell him about the graffiti, and now she was thankful the front porch had been scraped so that even the shape of the missing paint wasn't a hint as to the letter that had been there. Abe knew what he was doing.

"Boy," Miguel said. "That must really hurt."

"Yes, but it's getting better. Not so red, see?" Sarah said.

"Humph," he grunted. "Let's have the other one."

She held it out. As he unwrapped the bandages, she said, "Mr. Darnley got the bathrooms and the kitchen piped in and he set the toilets in on both floors. If we finish the counters and put in the sink, the Jacksons could start moving in soon."

He studied her hand. "Flex your fingers. Don't want 'em to get too tight."

"Should we do the kitchen cupboards next week?"

"Mom, I'm promised to the Schreibens until their kitchen is done. How about if Jeff and Akesha start learning to do finish work at the Jacksons after school."

"That's a good idea, except they have track until 5 p.m." she said.

"What good is track doing us when we need all hands to keep this company going?"

"Track is keeping them in school. You know that, Miguel."

He glowered toward her basement design, flicked his eyes to her drawing board, over her clever use of hash marks that created a sweet lady's face as well as the dark-eyed grieving half-expression sketched next to it, and said, "Okay, Five to nine at Jacksons."

She countered. "Six to nine. They need to eat. So do you."

"Okay, Mom. And I'll come to Jackson's as well. Those two can learn some new skills besides yammering and running."

"Hey, Mr. Salvador. Don't you forget that you love those two kids. They are not dragging us down. They are keeping us alert."

Miguel looked at her. "I think I'd like a little less action in this house."

"Well, remember that fact the next time you meet someone stealing bikes in our alley. Parenting is not a quiet and calm way to live life."

"Yes, ma'am. And I'm sorry I was such a brat."

She laughed.

Miguel said, "Now let's go down and replace those bandages before the two dervishes get home from track practice."

As Sarah rose, Miguel glanced back at the drawings. He recognized Amanda. And he feared that he recognized the guy, with the grieving eyes, too.

"Mom," he said. "You can't do anything with those fingers but straight lines and hash marks. Let's get more of your fingers free so you can really draw."

*    *

Half an hour later, Sarah was rebandaged with a little more of her fingers out so she could at least text and draw curves.

She and Miguel were in the kitchen when the back door banged open. In rushed Akesha and Jeff.

"I'm in," Akesha announced.

"She's on the hurdles team," Jeff said proudly. "She can stretch and count strides and stretch and not look back and she's great."

Akesha jumped up and down, dragging her foster brother, Jeff into a hopping dance.

Miguel noticed this was the same way she had jumped up and down in excited fear the night two years ago when he'd cornered these two kids in the delivery drive.

He'd caught them in the act of making off with Sarah's bicycle. At fourteen years old, Akesha was so afraid of going to jail that she'd held tight to the bike and to Jeff and done this dance of fear with tears streaming down her shiny face. Little Jeff had been paralyzed with fright.

"I don't want to go to no jail with them pimps," Akesha had cried. "I don't want to be with them women. I don't want them get they hands on me. No, please no!"

Miguel pried the bike from her hands and lay it on the ground, all the time talking to them as evenly as he could make himself. "If you don't want to go to jail, how come you to steal?"

"Me and Jeff here, we taken care of each other, but they ain't no food."

"You look for jobs?"

"Nobody gonna hire no fourteen-year-old 'cept newspapers and with no bike we can't do 'nough to eat. Them fancy guys wants us to work, but, oh please, we don't want that! It kill my mamma. Oh, please, no!"

"You. Kid," he zeroed in on Jeff. "You want a job?"

The scrawny freckle faced kid had to work to push the words past his teeth. "A r...r...real jo...job."

"Where's your folks?"

Jeff's head ducked. He couldn't even begin to say it.

So, Akesha had filled in the blanks. "His mamma drinks. Jeff don't drink though. He with me. We our own selves, with nobody else. Ain't nobody gonna make us drink and sleep around."

At the time, Sarah had been up in Seattle to bid on a church renovation. So, at twenty-one, Miguel had made his first executive decision for Rohann and Salvador. "You kids want to learn to build houses?"

"Build houses? Like hammer and saw and climb on the roof?" Akesha stopped, mouth open.

"Ya gotta work hard, sun and rain. You'd learn lots of things, but they're not easy."

"Cl...cl...climb on r...rooves?" Jeff looked even more afraid.

"Not everybody gets on the roof. Some do plumbing, some hammer – lots of different jobs."

"Kin we work for you?" Jeff seemed a little less shrunken.

"If you can work your tails off," Remembering what Sarah had always said to him, he added quickly, "and if you go to school every day. That's your first job."

Akesha grew two inches taller. "Go to school? You gotta be cracked man. Ain't no school wants me back. I seen 'em all."

"If you work for us and live here, that's rule number one. You go to school every day and get at least C's on your grade card."

"L..live here?" Jeff looked back up at the beautifully cared for building. It was clear he had never lived anywhere as nice. He grabbed Akesha's arm. "We...We can try school, huh?"

Akesha's protests died on her lips. She saw how much Jeff wanted to live here. She shrugged her thin little shoulders and bit her lip. "Well, I don't know. I like to climb. Maybe there's one school might of forgot me."

\* \*

And now Akesha, a straight B and A student jumped for joy instead of fright. Miguel smiled. He put an arm around Jeff.

"How's the shot-put going, Buddy?"

"I'm g...getting it out f...farther. And the J...Javelin, too. Did you know the Ro...Romans used th...them?"

"Really," Miguel like to hear Jeff talk. He stuttered less and less as he survived more and more challenges. Miguel knew Sarah was right to want them to continue with track. Looking forward to teamwork at the end of the day kept them studying.

But that first year of catch-up had been a doozy. It had really refreshed Miguel's grasp of English, Math and history and had given him a big appreciation of what teachers work hard to accomplish.

Still Miguel never regretted that decision.

And on this day, he enjoyed the noise and the excitement that were part of parenting.

"Okay," Miguel said. "Sarah can't cook so I brought home take out from Pastinis, and then we're off to learn how to finish cupboards at Mr. and Mrs. Jackson's home."

"What about homework?" Akesha asked.

"Whatcha got?" Miguel asked.

"Ge . . .Gee…ometry," Jeff said. "And essssay for hi..history."

"And you?" Miguel asked Akesha.

"Biology and the same Geometry."

"Okay," Sarah said, "Bring them. We'll take some time to get them done. We can talk about your essay as we work. During dinner you can give us the low-down on what the topic is and Akesha's biology, too."

"I gu…guess, we have to fin…finish the ta. . .table first then the cupboards, so  . . .so we have a place to do . . .do  homework," Jeff joked.

Miguel and Sarah laughed.

"That is one good idea," Sarah said.

Akesha said, "Can I use the planer?"

Miguel knew she was avoiding the sandpaper duty, saving her newly long and polished fingernails.

"Okay, gang," he said. "I'll do the sanding."

# CHAPTER TEN

Abraham rolled over and slammed the knob on the alarm. Six o'clock. He burrowed into the covers and let the pictures reconstruct themselves in his mind. He could almost get the warmth and the smile, but the color wasn't right. She was there, but not as she had been, so vividly alive in his dream. The twist of her braid was good, but her hair was so much softer, so many more indefinable shades of cream and brown.

Something more than the color of her hair eluded him. That moment or two when her confidence had wavered. They were significant somehow. But those moments didn't tally with the rest of her cool sophistication. A beautiful, highly educated woman – a woman who could handle all those teenagers and taciturn Jack Darnley with equal grace – how could that woman suffer doubts?

He'd almost worked that enigma out in the dream, but the alarm had shattered the dream. Now reality intruded again.

Sounds of his children filtered into his lair, forcing his body back into action for another day. He smiled at the two boys' laughter that wafted up the stairs. They had to eat soon, and he was the chef.

He stretched and stood. Eyes still heavily in debt to sleep, he went through his morning exercise therapy, dutifully at first, and then with a little more enthusiasm as he felt the breathing and stretching begin to enliven his body. There were moments when the power of his body was a pleasure to Abe. When no one was around, and he temporarily forgot his hand, he felt good, even young and vigorous.

Dreaming of Sarah Rohann had made him aware of his body and its needs in a way he had not allowed for a long time. For a moment, he permitted neither the hand nor the image of her watchful son, Miguel Salvador, to intrude on his fantasy. He could almost feel the vibrations of her laughter as he held her against him. So close . . .

So unlikely!

Abe made a quick grab for the front of his dresser to keep himself upright.

He recognized the narrowing of his peripheral vision which heralded another bout with his equilibrium. He held tight to the dresser front and waited it out. As the buzzing subsided and the walls spun more slowly, he caught sight of himself in the mirror.

He mocked himself with a dry imitation of Amanda at her most realistic. "Abe-boy, if she's Beauty, then you're Beast for sure. Leave her be. Get on with the work."

He focused his attention on the surgical dressing that surrounded his rib cage. No blood, and no seepage this time. That was a good sign. He pulled off the bandage and reached back to test the skin around the old wound. Was it his imagination or was it finally beginning to close? How could any wound continue neither infected nor healing for years? Shrapnel hovered in there somewhere, but all of Dr. Dennis's x-rays and the combined head shaking of St. Joseph Mercy physicians had not found a safe way to get it out. Too close to his spinal column.

Abe felt its presence daily but ignored it. It would go or it would stay. He had work to do. Its stab made him break out in a cold sweat occasionally. It pinched a nerve that controlled his leg when he was tired, but he rode over it with the steamroller of his obligations to others. He paid it no more heed than this daily change of dressing.

* *

Scrubbed and dressed, wet hair curling about his neck and face, he walked down from his attic room and strode down the hall toward the boys' room. On the way, he knocked on Deborah's door. His seventeen-year-old foster daughter was usually awake before him.

"I'm up, Dad. Finishing my calculus. Can I use the iron after breakfast?"

"Sure, Honey. Hope it's not a big project. Ironing that billowy skirt of yours made us all late the other day."

"Sorry. Just a short-sleeved blouse this time. Ten minutes tops if you fill the iron with water for me."

"Deal. Breakfast in fifteen. Could you help get Peter to the table?"

"Sure. Only two more ridiculous problems to go on this assignment."

"Thanks, Deb."

In the boys' room, dark haired, handsome Andy giggled and waved his right hand uncontrollably. "That Pete ... Peter ... funny."

Little Peter went into his gorilla-eating-a-banana routine. It was funny. And it was just like the gorilla, Sampson, they had all seen in the Portland Zoo last summer – right down to the glowering eyebrows, and the big hand scratching a distended belly – finding a flea and eating it. Peter was very observant. And he was delighted with his audience.

Abe and Andy clapped for the performer and then Abe untangled his ten-year-old gorilla from the covers. Lifting him, he carried the slight boy across the hall to the bathroom. "Time for intermission, Sampson. Got to use the facilities before the Zookeeper has to clean the cage."

"Yeah, Zookeeper, New Keeper. I was about to laugh too hard. What took you so long? You do your exercises twice this morning?"

"Nope. Just did them verrrrrrry carefully."

"Dizzy, huh?"

"Once, a little."

Peter looked up at his dad, unembarrassed by his position on the toilet or his dependence on others. Fourteen-year-old Andy always made Abe wait outside the bathroom and was angry for a long time afterward. Peter just took what had to be and kept up his end of the conversation.

Andy's attitude was understandable. He was an adolescent, and he had more contact with healthy children than Peter. He knew that regular guys would have locked the door and had the bathroom to themselves. Those guys would be able to comb their own hair and stand around afterward, ogling the girls, looking cool. Andy never felt cool. His wheelchair and his uncontrollable limbs saw to that.

Because of his constant embarrassment, Andy's anger was volcanic. Peter seemed to have no anger.

Andy had already transferred himself from bed to wheelchair – a laborious process – and waited in the hall when Abe carried Peter out. Abe pushed the door as wide open as it would go.

"Call me when you're ready, son," he said over his shoulder as he returned to the boys' room. He heard the wheelchair catch on the door jamb two or three times, but he did not go back to help. Helping only added insult to injury. It was not appreciated.

Abe propped his weak boy among pillows on the bed and began getting together the clothes Peter would wear to his school. Facing the mess of drawers, he wished he had time to sort the socks. Matches were hard to come up with, but it was usually as much as he and his foster daughter Deborah could manage to get the right clothes in nearly the right drawer on laundry day. Andy helped as much as he could, but the process was slow. For Peter, the process was exhausting, but he tried.

"Dad?" It was Deborah, sounding desperate. "Dad, I can't figure out how to vandalize this last problem."

"Okay, Deb. I'll be down in a few minutes. Maybe I can remember how." Had she really said 'vandalize'? He'd have to be dredging to get any statistics out of his brain at this stage of life. Only vaguely did he recall that there were such processes as integrating problems and ... whatever she had said. "Vandalize" was what he might do if he tried to help her.

Maybe he needed a refresher course in math. Deborah had come to his home because her parents had asked that he take her. Their rural hospital could not keep up with her health needs. Deborah's parents knew about Abe from Amanda Charles and had asked that he take over her foster care when the previous foster family had needed to move to another state.

Since her arrival, Deborah had become ever more able to get where she wanted and do what she needed. Now Abe was the one who had to keep up with her.

*Irony*, he thought.

Peter was nearly dressed when Andy called angrily, "Dad, I stuck."

"Coming. Excuse me, Pete."

"You comin' right back?" Peter, helpless on the bed, sometimes felt a fear related to falling. He hated to be left this way for any time.

"I'll get Deb to bring you to the kitchen. Okay?"

"Okay."

"Deborah," Abe called, "could you help Peter get to breakfast while Andy and I finish up in the bathroom?"

"Be right there, Dad."

Halfway across the hall, he remembered his daughter's problem. "I'll help with the math while you iron."

Andy's frustration spilled out vehemently in barely understandable words. "Damn! Corner too small ... Door too small ... nothing work 'ight. Shit! Go back hospidal. Hate here!"

Abe grimly gripped the handles on the wheelchair and shifted it to the correct angle. "Let's use the bed pan, son. You're too tired to make the transfer."

"No! Get out! I do myself!"

His dad winced at the shame Andy felt. He hurriedly set up the transfer board and removed the side arm on the wheelchair before he left. Outside the bathroom, he listened as Andy, crying bitterly to himself, worked every muscle available to him, shifting his body from the chair to the toilet, missing and then grabbing the steel bar nearby for support, cussing and muttering until Abe could hardly stand not to just pick him up and do it for him.

Deborah's bright face saved him. She wheeled cheerfully out of the boy's room with Peter on her lap. One arm worked the controls while the other kept a firm grip on her little foster brother.

"Hi, Dad," she said, "We're on our way to see what is inside the Crunchies. Peter says it's air. I say it's little balloons. That's why you hear the pop when you chew."

Rolling down the hall, Peter began singing.

"Pop when you chew.

Pop when you chew.

Goin' to find out

Just why they do . . ."

Peter giggled and Deb joined him to sing it again.

Abe laughed at their silliness and relaxed a little against the wall. Andy was right. The corners were too tight, and the doors were too small. If Andy was to have anything but frustration, Abe had to make some major changes in this house. They couldn't afford it. But for Andy's sake, they would just have to go into debt. It was hard enough for Deborah to get around even though her arms did what she told them to. Andy's arms only minded him sometimes, after great mental effort. It wasn't fair to make him cope with so many obstacles.

If the African American Cooperative Bank also turned him down on the loan he'd requested last month, Abe didn't know of another bank that might help him out. The first banks had simply told him that he couldn't have the money and that he ought to think about taking on a less challenging child.

Get rid of Andy! That's what they meant, as if that would not hurt anyone. Andy was hurting all the time. This was his fifth foster home since his father had left and his mother had given him up. He was fourteen and he'd been rejected over and over again, all his life. He had been with Abe less than a year – didn't trust Abe's love, wouldn't admit his love for Peter and resented Deborah's greater mobility and good humor.

Abe pushed away from the wall and hurried into the kitchen to fill the iron and help put breakfast on the table. On the way by, he dodged into Deborah's room for her hairbrush.

In the breakfast room, Peter was already strapped into his chair at the table. The straps kept him from falling over. He looked like a frail six-year-old, but he gamely tried to help Deborah from his confined position. She wheeled in carrying the silverware. Peter distributed it as close as possible to its destination on the breakfast table.

"Hey, Dad." Deborah said. "I checked the Crowd Funding and we've enough for three months at the motel for the Richardsons.

That astounded Abe. "Already? You just started that site three weeks ago."

"I know. But a picture of twins learning to walk is pretty powerful – almost as good as kittens playing."

"I hope those were photos from the back. Don't want them to have to live with that face recognition stuff when they are teens."

"From the back and wobbling. Very cute and very generic. Can they move soon?"

"I'll call Don at the motel and see what he's got. Three weeks ago he had a two bedroom for that price."

Deb's smile grew. "Let's have them over for dinner after they move. Those kids are the cutest."

Abe nodded. "Mom and Dad Richardson are pretty cute, too."

"Yeah. That Mary is a little doll, but Art is so tall. How'd they ever find each other? Were they sitting down?"

Abe stared at her.

"Just a joke, Dad."

"Not a joke I'd trot out when they are here."

"Not till we know them better, eh?"

"Right."

The fund-raising for the Richardsons was amazing, but he needed to keep his family moving toward their school morning. "I'll see the Richardsons as soon as possible. I know they are worn out by being separated in the shelter."

"Now all we have to do is find an apartment."

Abe decided to change the subject.

"Deb," Abe said, "I grabbed your brush and some pins from the dresser. I saw a style yesterday I thought would be good on you. Want to try?"

"What's it like, Dad?"

Abe tried to find word for the way Sarah's hair had looked. "Long, sort of twisted and then pinned at the back – just one pin holds it somehow – that's the part I'm not sure of."

Deb wheeled closer. "Twisted?" She looked skeptical.

"Yes, but not real tight." Abe was hard pressed to give his description anything like Sarah's chic-natural quality. "Twisted, but very soft around her face."

# CHAPTER ELEVEN

Deborah looked slowly at her dad, a light of understanding made her alert. He was not looking at her but off into space with a vague, not-quite-with-us expression. Deborah tried to keep the fun out of her voice when she led him on. "What color was it, Dad?"

He tried to recapture that elusive hue in words. "All cream and brown. The twist showed off the different colors."

Deb could hardly keep her voice straight. "Really? That good, huh, Dad?"

He heard the fun in her bubble of laughter. "Deb! Really, it would look great on you. I thought so at the time."

"And what color was her dress?"

"Deborah! Do you want sophistication or a good laugh on Dad?"

"Ooh! Sophisticated Lady!" She dodged the hand towel Abe tossed at her head. "Truce! King's Ex. You win, Dad. Let's try it."

"I don't know." He stepped around her studying how to tackle the project – whether to tackle it. "Might be too old for you. Probably make you look too grown up for the high school guys. Nah . . ."

"Dad . . ."

"I'll try and see." He pulled out the cereal boxes and some fruit and milk from the fridge. Breakfast set, he took hold of Deborah's heavy brown tresses and tried to get the brush through without tangling. He'd never known what a trick it was just to get through this curly length every morning.

No wonder Deborah had such remarkable arm strength. It was not to be blamed on the wheelchair races after all. He twisted to form a ply of hair, straight out from the center back. When his wrist was completely upside down, he saw the need for another hand to make the next twist.

"You better do this, Hon. It's a two-fisted job."

Reaching back, she took over. "Thanks Dad. Do I just keep twisting?"

"I think. Until it's one rope." Abe went to the hall and listened to Andy splashing in the sink. Andy must have made it back to the wheelchair. The sink was three feet from the toilet.

"What about those hairs that are falling out?" Deb brought his attention back to the kitchen.

He strode back in, still listening for Andy. "I don't know. Let's see if I can tuck them in. Oh. I'm sorry. I got that finger caught while I was using this one to tuck. Oops. I guess I better back out while I can get away. This is like trying to untangle a fishing net."

"Is this as close as you've ever gotten to long hair? Come on, Dad."

"Well, my wife had very long hair, but she always had it tied up."

"Really? How long?"

"Oh, I was never real sure – maybe three, three and a half feet."

"How far down her back did it go?"

"I don't know, Deb. Let's see if we can get this taken care of and get breakfast on."

"Ellen . . . isn't that it?"

"What?"

"Her name . . . your wife, I mean."

"Oh. It was Elani."

"Was she beautiful?"

Abe stopped trying to move away from his daughter's questions. He turned to be sure he had her attention. "She was beautiful on the outside. It wasn't enough to make her happy."

Deborah stared at him. He so rarely talked about his life before coming to Portland. Now she had a clue about why. His wife had died. Did she kill herself? Deb knew that was too much to ask her dad now. She began twisting her hair again. "It probably takes practice is all. Can you ask the lady how she does it?"

Abe hesitated. "I'm sure you have the right technique. You wrap the rope of hair in circles at the back of your head and then push the end of the rope through the circles. I'm not sure where to put the pin. There was just the one."

"I can't seem to get it. Is she a parishioner? When will you see her again?"

"I don't know. She's an architect. I might see her, but ..."

Deborah was aware he was trying not to talk about the woman anymore. She decided to give him permission not to take the subject seriously. "It's nothing. Just if you see her."

"I'll try. I better get this iron ready as promised. Can you finish the table?"

"Sure, Dad."

Peter, quiet as a peeping cat, obviously had been listening to the exchange. He sat up and began chanting.

"Deborah with hair to there.

Gets all tangled, everywhere.

Bubble gum makes hair smell yum.

Twisted and tied sounds kind of dumb."

"Peter," Abe said. "Chant the silverware into its proper places."

Peter obliged, impromptu as always.

"Places, places!

Put them through their paces.

Left fork, right spoon,

Dirty knife lays down at noon. . ."

As Abe pulled down the ironing board from its cupboard near the kitchen, he glanced at his son and daughter with pride. She and Peter had arrived under his wing at the same time two and a half years ago. Peter had been able to walk with the aid of braces then, but his Duchenne Muscular Dystrophy had begun its rapid advance.

It was his alarming rate of decline that had forced his move from his parents' home. His mother, Laura, had wept as she hugged him goodbye. His father, Grant, had been the stoic, damning himself for not being able to provide, even though it was the health care system that really failed Peter. Peter, by then, required constant attention and frequent trips to the only hospitals that could provide his care – here in Portland.

Grant and Laura had been able to visit Peter about every six months since. Abe had been able to drive him to their dryland farm in southeastern Oregon once, for his grandma's funeral. It had been a very long drive and the hours of sitting had left Abe limping for two weeks. Abe still marveled at Peter's understanding of his parents.

"They love me, but they don't have a lot of money and I'm a lot of work," Peter often said.

Abe added another fact. "They don't have a lot of money, but also, your local hospital couldn't help them help you," Abe said.

"The people were great at the hospital," Peter said, "but the system stinks," Peter said. "Country hospitals don't get enough money from their city hospitals."

Abe agreed with Peter, but he wondered how much hurt was being concealed by the statement of fact.

Peter's empathy for other people showed how much emotional stress he suffered himself. Only a boy who had experienced rage himself would have been able to stand by Andy as many times as Peter had done. He waited out the screaming and the violent language. He endured Andy's vain and further enraging attempts to throw something at any one in range.

Peter always waited until the cursing subsided into sobbing and then put his arms around Andy and held him as tight as his weak limbs could hold. He alone really knew Andy's grief and rage. And Peter alone was allowed to comfort it.

Deborah was altogether different. Her spinal column had been damaged at birth. As Peter knew, Deborah's ranching community had not been able to provide for her early medical and therapy needs, so she had been brought to the children's hospital here in Portland. Her young parents had been forced to relinquish her to the care of the state during her first year. They visited her whenever they could, but financially could not even do that very often. They were like a loving aunt and uncle to her now. Although she cherished their letters and visits, they were not the primary source of love her new foster father had become. The foster families before Abe had been exhausted by the hospital visits and worry. But they too, still communicated their love to her.

Spina bifida may have left her legs useless, but it had not damaged her mind. She may have been too much for her remote community's medical system, but she was not too much for herself. She was her own best cheer leader.

"Can't walk?" she seemed to say to herself, "well then I'll have to roll fast." and she took up racing in the hospital halls.

"Can't dance? Then play ping pong." And she became state champion under eighteen, girls and boys. She made more trips to ping pong tournaments than she had ever made to hospitals.

It was for her that there was a ping pong table under their dining cloth. A few trips around the table each night, and she could have the net set up and a tournament going. She beat her two-footed school friends (as she called them). She beat Abe regularly and gave his friend Dick Street a run for his money, stringing them along just to keep them playing before she dropped the winning point in the near corner.

Without Deborah's brilliant smile and youthful exuberance, Abe felt he would have been a very old and morose man indeed.

He allowed himself to watch Deborah tease Peter about his "artistic placement of silver artifacts" before he made himself go back down the hall to deal with Andy's clothes.

Getting Andy dressed was no fun for either of them. Nothing Andy wore was able to conceal the fact that his legs were too thin and his back crooked from the neglect he had suffered in the early years of his life.

Even Andy was aware that if his timid mother had been braver or his violent father had cared enough, his body need not have deteriorated this much. He would always have the effects of cerebral palsy, but they could have been minimized with proper therapy when he was very little.

Now, his therapy consisted for the most part of a holding action, trying to keep his spine from becoming even more S shaped. Abe hoped that if Andy ever gave up his anger at the world, he might be able to concentrate some of that energy on improving his physical health.

"Picked out what you want to wear, son?"

"Peter your son. Andy wear desig. . .ner jean."

Abe ignored the bait. "Here's a pair designed by Levi Strauss – French I think."

"zhunk!"

Abe, unsure of the word, took a guess. "You going punk today?"

"Gar...bage."

"It may be garbage, but it fits. Want it?"

"Why not?"

Abe took this as the best he would get and began helping Andy dress.

\*    \*

After breakfast, the boys and Abe were brushing their teeth when Dick Street arrived with the van to take the older kids to high school. Dick wheeled himself up the not so well-built ramp to the front door and was roped into helping Deb with her math. Dick was a senior student of physics at nearby Reed College and much more qualified to vandalize a math problem than Abe.

Problem solved, Abe and Dick helped Deborah and Andy onto the lift that deposited them in the van. He and Dick had worked out this arrangement early in their friendship. Abe and a good friend bought the van, Dick bought the gas and did the driving. After Dick dropped the kids at the high school, he went on to the Reed Commons for his tutorials. Sharing the van made independent living possible for Dick and took a load of responsibility off Abe's shoulders.

As the van pulled out, Peter waved and shouted, "Safe journey, Dick."

# CHAPTER TWELVE

A be looked down at Peter. "Well, little Pete. It's down to you and me, old buddy. Think we ought to get rolling?"

"Roll 'em out, Dad."

After scooping Peter into the car, Abe put the little wheelchair in the trunk, tossed his briefcase and old jacket in the back seat and headed out to the school. As they drove along, the silence seemed to deepen. Abe took a sidelong glance at Peter in the review mirror. His expression was thoughtful. Abe sensed a whamo of a question coming and braced himself.

"Dad? How come Andy gets so mad?"

Abe thought a moment, decided what answer was fair to Andy and finally said, "Andy can't do the things he wants to be able to do. He's very frustrated."

"But Deborah wants to run, and she doesn't throw things." Abe heard the almost whispered admission that followed. "I want to run, but I just get more sick."

Abe slowed down to concentrate on his answer. "Peter, I'm going to tell you something you must always remember, but never talk to Andy about. I talk to Andy about it at the right times, but you just need to keep it in mind when you let your brother know you care about him. Can you do that?"

"You mean know it and not let Andy see that I know it?"

"Andy or anyone else."

"I can do that, Dad."

From experience, Abe had no doubt that Peter could keep secrets when they might hurt someone. "I think, Pete, that the big difference between you and Andy is the love you have known. Your parents and your grandmother loved you very much and did for you as long as they could. Even after you came to me, they call and visit when they can.

"Andy didn't get any of that. From the time he was born, Andy was not loved. His Dad wouldn't let his mother take him to doctors, tried to hide him away. His mother wasn't brave enough to do it in spite of the dad. To Andy, it looks like she didn't love him."

Peter nodded. "So, it's no loving that makes him angry. He just pretends he's mad about not running."

Abe was always non-plussed by Peter's perception. "It's something like that. Not having love makes not having muscle control hurt more."

"But you love him."

"He doesn't trust me yet to keep on loving him."

Peter looked straight at his dad. "Maybe some of his tantrums are for finding out if you will love him. He doesn't do them as much when Dick is taking care of us, you know."

Abe was hit in the stomach by that revelation. "No," he said softly. "I didn't know."

"I think he's afraid Dick will just tell him off. Dick has been real sick, too – that polio stuff, he had. He wouldn't put up with Andy throwing things."

Abe was going to have to mull that one over and see how it should change his method of dealing with his older son. "The wisdom of children," he thought.

"Peter, see where we are?"

"Muldowney School! Let's hurry. Maybe I can paint with the computer today, if I get in early."

Abe was always relieved that Muldowney School held Peter's affection. Without it, Peter's life would be much more constricted. This public school served several counties and was part of the state's effort to provide as good an education as possible for its medically fragile students. Peter had been in a regular school and class for as long as that was possible, but he needed constant medical attention.

In this school, Peter had therapy, daily exercise, time to make friends, as much education as he could stay awake for, and he had loving attention.

Abe pulled in the circular drive. A waiting staff member took Peter from the car to his wheelchair and whisked him through the big electronic doors.

# CHAPTER THIRTEEN

On Tuesday evening, Abe met with the board of his church. The biggest topic came as a recommendation from the program committee and the building committee. Together, they recommended building a chapel on the second floor out of what had once been a storage room and a classroom with a sink.

Abe had met with these committees as they discussed this prospect, but he believed the chapel a distraction from other things the church could be doing for the community. He felt especially grated by the pushiness of the Building Committee chair, Eleanor Whiting.

"You know, Abraham," Eleanor had said at one meeting, "Not all of life is a social justice problem. Sometimes people need a place to meditate."

For Abe, most of life was indeed a social justice problem that should have been solved yesterday. "Wasn't that what Jesus was doing for most of his teaching? – creating community, saving the sick, overturning the tables of the money changers?"

Arthur Charles said, "Jesus, Buddha, Mohammed, each took himself off to the wilderness on occasion – an opportunity to think about what he should do, how he should be ready for tough times."

Abe nodded. "Yes, they did. But we already have a sanctuary."

Eleanor said, "Now there's a wilderness if I ever saw one."

Abe frowned. He felt certain that once they knew the cost, that would be the end of it. Still, he tried to keep an open mind because Amanda had asked him to do that.

"For small celebrations of any kind," she had said. She had added softly, "Pray about it, Abe."

He prayed. Mostly, he admitted to himself, he prayed the board would get over the idea.

The room was out of the way for most people, and totally inaccessible for his own children who had a difficult time getting into the sanctuary of the church.

At the end of the board meeting, Abe packed his briefcase when Arthur Charles stopped to say something to him.

"Abe, thank you for not speaking against the chapel. I know you don't see it. But wait. It will be an opening to other things."

Abe smiled at his friend, "Art, so far, I can't even find a door into this idea."

Art nodded. "Well, isn't that a good description of life? Blank walls everywhere until we step back and see that some walls have windows and doors in them?"

Arthur smiled and put his hand on Abe's shoulder. "It will come into view one day soon. Come to our first meeting with the contractor next Tuesday."

Abe thought fast for a reason not to be there. "Deb has a tournament that night."

"Give her a high five from us," Art said.

"Will do," Abe said, knowing that for a moment Art had forgotten Amanda could no longer send high fives to the kids. He walked out into the dark of nine o'clock at night.

After the meeting, Abe felt soul stricken. He missed his old friend, Amanda. His children missed her. She'd been like a grandmother to them. Her death was hard on many people, especially on her husband of fifty years.

His children were with Dick, probably studying or helping Debbie practice her ping-pong serves, so Abe sat in his car, remembering Amanda's sweet ways and her admonitions.

After a few moments, he started the car and just began driving aimlessly. It didn't take long for him to realize his driving wasn't so aimless. He was at the Jackson house and saw lights on inside.

He thought Sarah might be working late and dangerously alone, so he stopped.

As he approached the front porch, he saw that the scrapings had been painted over in a way that pretended to be testing paint colors. He smiled anticipating teasing her about that.

He reached to knock, but the door opened.

Miguel stood there, just looking at him.

Abe said, "I was afraid Sarah was here working by herself."

"Afraid or hopeful?" Miguel said.

"Would you want her working here at night alone?"

Miguel leaned on the jamb. "No. She might have unwanted visitors."

"Might have unwanted ogres guarding the castle as well."

Miguel actually laughed at that. "What's up, Pastor?" he asked.

"What's up is that I just left a contentious meeting and drove past not looking for another one."

"Just drove past?"

"I knew she was working on this house. So, lights on? I decided to check her safety. Bet you would have done that yourself."

"Yes, and I'm not an ogre, just careful."

"I appreciate that," Abe said.

"The cops have been to question her. Did you send them?"

"The circumstances of Bruce's death sent them. I don't send the police anywhere. I'm a chaplain there, and at the fire bureau, which is why the fire chief called me. He realized she was in no condition to speak for herself, and she was found next to a dead body."

"The fire chief called you? Why?"

"He hoped I could make some sense of the situation, but she was going into shock, so I sent her off in an ambulance as the police arrived."

Miguel stood up a little straighter. "Do you now understand what happened?"

"Yes. After she was better, she was able to tell me and the police why she dropped Bruce's body out the window. Took some determination, and courage to get him and herself out of there."

"Stupidity, more like, but she's allowed stupid once in a while in a crisis situation."

"Maybe stupid," Abe said, "but she desperately wanted the police to know how he died and find who did it."

"Yep." Miguel glanced around outside. Finally, he said, "Want to see the progress?"

This took Abe by surprise. "Uh … sure." He checked his watch. "Got some time before the kid sitter has to get home."

He could tell the mention of kids took Miguel by surprise, but Miguel stood back and waved an inviting hand.

Abe said, "I noticed the really careful framing of cabinets the other day."

"You build, too?"

"Not as well as your group. Used to do a lot before I moved to Portland." He didn't say before I lost my hand, but that was what he meant. Lost his hand and with it, his urge to create.

"Well, our little company has apprentices and they have done quite a bit since you saw framing."

Abe stepped into a transformed kitchen that had a new smooth pine table, a pine bench that wrapped around two sides, new cupboard doors, and new countertops with a tile backsplash.

"My goodness!" he said. "Quite a change!"

Miguel smiled.

"I see," Abe said, "that Jack got the sink in, so are the bathrooms next?"

"You know Jack Darnley?" Miguel asked.

Abe nodded, "Helped with plumbing at our house, too." He didn't add that Jack was a member of his church. He didn't think Miguel wanted to hear about church.

Abe looked at Miguel. "This is beautiful, Miguel."

Miguel glanced at the floor and then up again at Abe. "Thanks. I'll tell the crew."

Abe smiled. "Well, can't keep Dick waiting. He has physics in the morning, so I'd better get home and take over kid care."

Miguel said, "Abraham, right?"

"Yes."

"Thank you for checking on Mom. She does take risks."

Abe couldn't stop a laugh. "That's an understatement if I ever heard one."

"Yeah, well Kevin knew we worked here, so I told her not to come here alone anymore. That gang was dangerous."

Miguel walked with him toward the door. "You said kids. How many kids?" he asked as if casually curious, but Abe knew this was no offhand friendliness.

"Three," he said. "The kids are great." He crossed the threshold and turned to wave at Miguel. "Thanks for the tour."

Miguel raised his chin in acknowledgement. "See you around."

Back in the car, Abe took a deep breath, turned on the motor and drove around the block where he could sit a minute and digest the previous prickly conversation.

First, the police. Were they still thinking Sarah killed Bruce? And second, did the tour of the kitchen represent a truce between himself and Miguel? Or was it a gauntlet thrown down? A statement like, 'I can produce real things, priest, while you deal in things that evaporate in the sunshine.'

Abe shook his head. No telling what the tour meant, and he probably wouldn't know for a long time. But Miguel had said, "Thank you for checking on Mom." So maybe he did understand that Abe was just checking.

Or was that what Abraham Hallowell really had been doing?

"Damned if I know," Abe said to himself as he started toward home again.

# CHAPTER FOURTEEN

Officer Reese stopped at Abe's desk in the Northeast police precinct. "Gotta problem," he said.

"Yeah? And it is …"

"Your fire death. It was drugs in the beer or pizza. Neck broke after. When she tossed him."

"That's a problem? She told you that's probably what happened."

"She did. And I didn't believe her at the time."

"So, we're days late on ident of the man who set the fire."

"That's it, basically. I could have a line-up of the gang that's been graffitiing her place or get her down here to look at photos."

"Wait a minute. Graffiti on the Jackson home or her home?"

"Both, actually. She's now sent me photos of stuff at her home."

"She live near Coxwell and 13th?"

"Mere blocks. Atfalati and 18th," Reese said. "I thought she was doing it to divert attention, but now I'm taking it seriously."

Abe stood up. "Reese, I think we've had this conversation before."

Reese nodded his head. "Yes, and I fell into the trap again. It's just that it was unbelievable that she would rescue a body and risk her own life."

"Easy …"

"I know," Reese said "Easy answer is often too easy. Can you be there when she comes to ident these guys?"

"You know, Reese, she probably knows the kids. Kids around that area are part of her life with teenagers. But it was an adult who ran away after the explosion in the basement."

"So, photos?"

"You can sure try it, but the guy was wearing a hat pulled down and he was running away."

"Well, there's a couple of guys in that neighborhood that run kids for a living. In and out of jail, never off to prison. I've got a line-up of photos that can help us narrow it down if she saw his face at all."

"Okay. I'll be there. But I have a motel to visit first." Abe grabbed his coat and took off for the Triangle Motel to secure a room for the Richardson family.

As Abe left, he noticed a blue Chevrolet parked across the street and he grew certain that the driver, a fellow with pale stringy hair and a dirty blond beard, had just photographed him coming out of the police station.

When he got a block away, he told his Bluetooth phone to call Reese.

"Whatcha got?" Reese said.

"Blue Chevy parked in front of the station. The driver photographed me, and maybe others exiting the station."

"I'm on it. Thanks."

*   *

Having put three months down on a two bedroom with a kitchen for the family at Triangle Motel, Abe returned in time to meet Sarah.

Miguel came to the police station with Sarah to look at photos. Abe greeted them and showed them the photo ID room. Reese took over helping them get started.

As Abe came to the entry of the police building again, he saw two young white men, about Miguel's age across the street, lounging on the wall of the library annex. He was pretty certain one was slovenly the driver who had photographed him earlier.

Abe thought the two were more interested in the goings on in this building than in visiting each other or the library, so he stepped where he could take a photo through the window without them being aware.

In the photo room, Officer Reese had set out a book of local suspected drug dealers. They were all about the age that Sarah had described. Miguel kept insisting that she was looking at the wrong age group, so finally Officer Reese said, "Mr. Salvador, could you help us out? I'd like you to look at some photos that might be the graffiti artists in your neighborhood."

That move let Sarah concentrate, but she wasn't sure of any she looked at. She did identify a couple of possible men, mainly by the way they scrunched their heads down into their collars and by the wide size of their shoulders. but she had only seen the man's face briefly and from the second-floor window.

"A very dirty window," she added.

Miguel, on the other hand was able to identify several folks he'd seen tagging buildings in the area – not their buildings, but derelict houses and empty businesses.

Abe tried to stay out of the identification area while they worked. He didn't want to influence Sarah or distract Miguel, so he just went about his work, talking quietly to a fellow who came in off the streets asking if he could be arrested so he could stop drinking.

Abe talked to the man about his goals and the steps he could take to reach them. Then he set the man up with an AA meeting and a counselor at a nearby shelter.

Later, he sat down with Officer Sidney Seneca to discuss a recent shooting that the police had interrupted.

"I should have gotten there sooner," Sidney said. "The victim is in the hospital and the shooter saw me and then killed himself."

"What's the prognosis for the victim?" Abe asked.

"Bum leg for a while, but he'll be all right."

"Can we get him any help? like extricate him from the gang? Any leverage?"

Sidney nodded. "Mom."

"Only Mom?"

"Dad came out of the woodwork and back into his life, so that's good."

"Good. Big responsibility for both of them. Good folks?"

"Ebenezer Baptist minister vouches for both, they just got separated along the way, but they both want this kid to be back in school and safe."

"Sid, what about school counselors? Teachers? Principal?"

"I could talk to Mom and Dad about getting him with a favorite teacher and into the night high school until he catches up again."

"I think anything you can do to salvage the survivor, that's a big plus. Are you a praying man?"

"Not much. Never learned how or why."

"How do you feel about the kid who shot himself? What was his name?"

"Frank Jameson. He was real shaken. I tried to talk him out of it, but he didn't know me, wasn't listening, something."

"Can we sit here a minute and imagine we can talk to Frank now? What would you like to tell him?"

Sidney leaned his head on his hands. Abe did nothing, just waited for Sid to think and feel.

Finally, Sid said, "God, Frank, I wanted you to live, to serve your time and have a life. I wanted you to get beyond this. I wish you had heard me or believed me."

Now Sidney was crying softly and whispering, "I wanted you to have a life, Frank. I want you to live, but that's gone."

Abe put his hand on Sidney's arm. "Yes, we want him to know he was loved, even for that few moments in the street, and now, while you're talking to him. I believe he hears you. He hears you now, Sid."

Sid glanced up. "They haven't found a family. How's a kid get to be eighteen with no one?"

Abe said, "It's way too easy to imagine the ways that can happen. Here's something I hope you will do. Write a short note to his family, whoever they are. Tell them what you hoped for him in that few minutes. He was shaken, maybe because he suddenly realized the enormity of what he'd done. He wanted that moment back, too. Tell them why you wished you could have saved him."

"Write it?"

"Write it. Put it in a drawer and think about what you will do for the next kid like Frank that you meet. You can't save Frank, but you can be aware of the Franks that need help before something like this happens to them."

"Okay, Abe. I'll do it for Sammy, the kid in the hospital. Boys and Girls Club, something, something has got to help Sam."

"Good idea, Sid. Now go home. Sleep."

As Sid gathered his gear to go out to the car, Sarah came to the door.

"Find anybody likely?" Abe asked.

"A couple of maybes, but I just can't be sure. I didn't see enough of him."

"And Miguel?"

"Known graffiti artists." She smiled at the term. "Some need more practice. Maybe a class in calligraphy at the community college."

Abe said, "Won't surprise me. Right next door to the class on 'What Not to Call Others."

"How about, 'How to Succeed Without Harming Your Neighbor?'"

"Way too thoughtful. It'd be labeled a Lefty College."

"Our present leader would call it a Wimp Socialist College."

"Doesn't serve enough Orange Sherbet in the Hair Design classes either."

Abe followed her out as they joked around about the state of the nation. He felt almost at ease until he realized there were only two of them.

"Where's Miguel?" he asked.

"He's going through the same group I went through, trying to see if he's seen any of those folks hanging around the office or any of the houses we've been renovating. He'll be along in a minute or two."

The two of them stepped out onto the front porch of the precinct. And there sat the same two young men across the street.

Abe pulled out his phone, opened his photo of the men and made it bigger.

"You know these two fellows?" He asked, without pointing out who they were.

She looked at the photo and said, "These are the two white guys across the street, aren't they?" She didn't look at them, only at the photo, so Abe was thankful for her quick mind.

"Yes. Been there about an hour and a half, just lounging away the afternoon."

"Miguel might know them," she said. "Let's go back inside and ask him."

# CHAPTER FIFTEEN

Miguel took one look at the photo and said, "This is not good. They were fired from the apprenticeship program. Tried to sell me heroin. I turned them in."

Abe said, "Have they made attempts to get back at you since then?"

"Well," Miguel said, "they did once end up in a dumpster in an alley." He started toward the front door.

Sarah said, "Stop."

Miguel stopped and looked at her, a question in his raised eyebrows.

Sarah said, "You can beat up on them, or you can plan a long-term strategy that puts them where they belong."

"Okay, Mom. What strategy?"

Abe said, "They know who is important to you, right?"

Miguel glanced at Sarah. "They do. I think they may also know about Akesha and Jeff."

Abe asked. "Could they be the graffiti on your building?"

"Don't think they know their letters, yet."

"I'm serious," Abe said.

"No, it's all Coxwell 13 marks."

"Might they be selling?" Abe asked, "Either to the Coxwells or with the Coxwells?"

Miguel thought a moment, "I suppose any of those ideas may be possible."

Sarah said, "Or trying to throw suspicion on Coxwell."

"Also a possibility," Miguel said.

"So." Sarah said, "Strategy one is to exit from the back of this building, a direction I bet Abe knows."

Abe nodded.

"And then," Miguel said, "We check on Akesha and Jeff and warn them always to travel together."

Abe said, "How about if we ask Officer Reese to learn more about those two before we exit out the back way?"

"Sure," Miguel said. "They've got a record."

"And Reese and Sid Seneca can keep an eye on their affiliates and customers," Abe added.

Miguel faced Abe and asked. "What was going on with that Officer Seneca. How did you get him crying?"

*Ah*, thought Abe, *back to the religion thing already.*

"He was feeling bad about something that happened on the street. You can ask him, someday, but he's gone home to sleep right now."

"Gone home to feel guilty?"

Sarah stepped back, startled at Miguel's vehemence.

Before she could step in again, Abe said, "I hope he got rid of the guilt here and can really sleep tonight."

"Hmmmph."

Abe shrugged and walked off toward Reese's office to get his take on the two fellows pictured in his camera. He heard Sarah talking behind him.

Sarah said, "Miguel. You teach Jeff and Akesha not to make snap judgements. Going to start practicing that good habit yourself?"

"Mom . . ."

"Might try it now," she said.

And then Abe turned the corner and didn't hear any more. He took a deep breath and decided not to ask about Miguel's obvious dislike. He'd just wait and see what happened.

* *

Reese knew those two in the photo immediately. Matt Langren and Dorsey Templeton seemed to be high on his list of people to watch because he believed they were responsible for several drug killings.

"They like to send messages about paying your bills," he said.

"So, do you already have a watch on them?"

"Yep. They followed you here and are lounging across the street like fools."

"Maybe not fools," Abe said, "but threatening. Do you think they know you have your eyes on them?"

"Do you mean are they across the street because of you, or police in general?'

"Yes, are they here because you follow them or because they have a thing against Miguel Salvador? They tried to sell him heroin and he got them kicked out of an apprenticeship program."

"Ah!" Reese said, "So, he was the one."

"Yes, and they have attacked him in an alley at least once," Abe said.

"Well, that's a combination of influences that muddies the waters."

"How so?"

"We thought Salvador might be selling."

"On what grounds?"

"Location, location, location. He's living in the middle of a rough neighborhood. He has a foster brother that's in and out of rehab. He has money."

"Wait a minute, Reese. He has a foster brother because his mom has foster children. She's out searching for that kid and Miguel is scared because she takes these awful risks. He has money because he's a master- carpenter and does excellent carpentry. Take another look at this situation."

"You see the way he looks at you?"

"Reese, he's not required to like me. Not liking me means he's human. I don't like myself quite frequently."

"Why is that?"

"Long story. The point is, Miguel is not your man, but these two are very likely."

"Geez, Hallowell, when did you become a policeman?"

"Never. Hard enough to be an ear for the force when bad things go down. But I can offer perspective. Isn't that what you hire me for?"

"Yeah, yeah. I'll keep after these two."

"And Kevin? Rescue, not capture."

"I know that's what she hopes for, but the kid has gone south several times."

"He goes south with alcohol, not viciousness," Abe said as he walked out into the hall.

Miguel walked in front of him toward Sarah. Abe wondered where Miguel had been while he talked to Reese. When he caught up to him, Miguel was already talking to Sarah.

"Mom, the back door is down this hall. Let's get over to the school and talk to Jeff and Akesha." He glanced at Abe. "Oh, thought you left."

"Nope," Abe said. "Reese is looking at those two pretty carefully already, so let's get out of here and you make sure Akesha and Jeff keep safe."

"You coming out, too?" Sarah asked.

"I have another job. But I like your idea about strategic planning. Let me know what I can do to make that work."

Sarah smiled. "We will, thanks."

As Abe got into his car, he saw Miguel in his rearview mirror gesturing to Sarah and pointing toward Abe's car. Sarah leaned on the hood of her car and nodded at Miguel.

Abe thought, I wonder what dirt on me he's selling her.

# CHAPTER SIXTEEN

A be took himself off to John Wesley Methodist Church to get news about parishioners who might need him. He called the shelter to let the Richardsons get ready to move on Friday to the motel.

Then he went into the church office to pick up his list of people to visit in the hospital. Mrs. Stevens handed him the list and then looked at him, one eyebrow raised.

"Mrs. Whiting wants to know your schedule so she can set up a meeting with the buildings committee."

Abe reluctantly pulled out his phone calendar.

Mrs. Stevens went on, "Mrs. Whiting is worried because this is the third meeting since the board voted, and next they are meeting with the most likely contractor."

Abe knew Mrs. Whiting probably hadn't used the word 'worried'. She was given to more colorful language combined with little patience. He guessed he'd better find a date.

"How's tomorrow? Tuesday afternoon?" He suggested.

"Needs to be night because the contractor works days."

"Tuesday evening then? I'll have to check with my kid care person." He hoped Dick could come over for the kids.

"Perfect," Mrs. Stevens said. "Got that in your gadget there?"

Abe nodded as he typed it in. He should have known that Mrs. Whiting would make Mrs. Stevens her ally in forestalling any procrastination on his part. Mrs. Whiting was a force.

"Seven o'clock," Abe said. "I'm off to Emmanuel Hospital first for Elmer Quigly and Fran Wilson."

Mrs. Stevens smiled. "Safe travels."

Abe smiled. He knew she was quoting Peter. Everybody in church loved Peter and his fun habits. Someday, he hoped, they would love Andy. Of course, that wouldn't be until Andy trusted that they really cared about him.

*   *

At Emmanuel Hospital, Abe helped Mr. Quigly get in touch with his daughter who lived across the country. She promised to get on the next plane back to Portland. She also promised to make sure her dad had good care and all the information he needed to make a decision about his cancer.

Then Abe visited Fran Wilson, who wanted to get out of her hospital bed yesterday, but still had to find out why she got dizzy whenever she stood up. Fran had a tough time with inaction. It felt to her like laziness, and in her book there should be no laziness. The small, fun book he brought her would be devoured a few minutes after he left, and then she would be back to fretting.

He bet, given half a chance, that Fran would be up and cleaning dust bunnies out of corners in every room on her hospital floor. Cleanliness was not *next* to Godliness in Fran's book. No sir, Cleanliness *was* Godliness.

*   *

Tuesday evening at the church, Abraham glanced at the watch on his right arm and then pushed his arm back into his jacket pocket.

Sixthirty. Nearly dark. Half an hour until the Building Committee meeting with the contractor.

Irritated at the thought of the meeting tonight, he tried to relax, eyes closed. But rest eluded him. As he saw it, his congregation was about to make a mistake.

Eleanor Whiting, determined and efficient chairwoman of the Building Committee, usually seemed more in tune with what money ought to be used for.

Amanda had said, "We need a place where God is more accessible than the dizzy rafters of that behemoth sanctuary the last century bequeathed us."

There were so many people in need of food and shelter – what good would a remote chapel do them?

He dragged out his watch again. Twentyfive minutes until he had to deal with chapels. He had enough time either to check on his children or do a little work on the sink in the kindergarten room. He reached for the phone and began to punch in his home number.

No.

Tonight, he needed to be alone for a while. After all that happened to Miguel and Sarah in the last weeks, he couldn't be upbeat and cheerful. The kids would hear his sadness, and they'd worry about him. He'd better leave them in the capable hands of his friend, Dick Street and kiss them goodnight when he arrived home later. Hanging up, he turned instead to gathering tools for plumbing repair.

The claxon sound of the side doorbell twisted his already tired nerves even tighter. He sighed heavily but stood.

Leaving the quiet of his office to help yet another needy person took great energy tonight.

At the church door, Abraham's left hand grabbed the handle and swung the door awkwardly to his right. He looked out and then down. What he saw solidly thunked him in the chest.

The lights of the street reflected in the dark brown eyes that gazed up at him. The porch light touched hair that shone all shades of brown and gold. It touched angles and curves in a face held picturestill. He believed he could see laughter barely contained. Her mouth did not smile; but it had to be controlling the mirth she must have felt when looking up at so dumbfounded a man.

He knew the streetlamp revealed his worn hardness. His fear for her must have been evident.

Sarah Rohann backed away from him toward the steps of the porch.

"Sarah what's happened. Has something . . .?" he finally managed.

After a moment's hesitation, she stood her straightest and asked. "You were expecting a taller architect, perhaps?"

Her humor helped him regain himself.

"Oh! I thought contractor . . . you're this evening's architect?"

"Yes, and I get to do these presentations because I'm the one with the suit."

Abraham laughed and took in more than her face for the first time this evening. To excuse his wandering gaze, he reached down with his left hand and took charge of the computer bag sitting at her feet. "Let me help you with this. We'll be meeting in the room right off this hall."

"Could we please meet in the room that's to become the chapel?" she asked. "It's much easier for committee members to imagine changes when they are actually in the space."

"Certainly. I'll leave a sign at this entrance to send the committee on up. Is this everything or is there more in the car?"

"This is it. There's already a screen in the chapel space."

"Been here before, Sarah?" he asked over his shoulder as he hefted the computer up the stairs.

Stupid question, he thought. She's knocked sense out of my head.

"I've been here several times," she was saying, "but somehow, I always missed you, Reverend Hallowell. Why isn't your name on the reader board out front?"

"Reverend Baily retired. I haven't gotten around to changing that yet." He said, knowing he hadn't even thought about getting around to it.

"I thought you were the police and fire chaplain, not the pastor of John Wesley."

"A pastor puts together whatever God presents as opportunity to serve."

She laughed. "They under-pay you, but want to build a chapel, no wonder you weren't at the meetings."

Now he laughed. "Chapel in an unreachable location, yet."

"Well, the committee has had very good discussions."

"Oh? Who did you meet?" He turned sideways on the stairwell to look down at her. The grim lighting of this hall did not diminish the shine of her very dark eyes.

Why is small talk so hard?

"I met your secretary, Mrs. Stevens. The first time, she said you were at a nursing home. The second, you were at the hospital with a family. During the last Chapel Committee meeting, you were home with a sick child. This afternoon, you were at another meeting somewhere outside of the building, so I got the measurements I needed and left."

Abe hadn't realized how much he'd been away from the building these last two weeks.

"I did intend to be here for the Chapel Committee last Thursday. Sorry I missed you." He turned back toward their destination.

She said, "I could use your perspective no doubt, but Mrs. Whiting, the committee chair, has explicit ideas about what is needed. So, I had guidance aplenty."

Abraham turned quickly. The gleam of humor in her eye was not imagined. He chuckled and headed on down the hall.

In the room, he busied himself with finding a table for the computer projector while he watched her pull down the screen from the overhead carrier.

He suddenly realized that such a simple act could appear to be a slow dance. Every move she made reminded him of the mental picture he had conjured – a picture of her flying down from a burning window.

"Miss Rohann?"

"Hmm?"

She didn't contradicted him about calling her Miss, but that wasn't conclusive. What he knew of her so far indicated she had never married. Adopted Miguel … what? When she was twelve?

He tried to remember what he meant to ask. "Uh … Is there anything else I can get for you?"

"Hmm? Oh, no thanks. Excuse me, I was thinking about the windows."

"Windows?" The room had none – a major drawback he thought.

"Three windows. They'll be right there in that wall. Outside of that wall is a lightwell between the church and the parsonage."

"Windows are a great idea. But won't they look into the upstairs bedrooms?"

"They'll be stained glass – translucent. Your family won't be giving up any privacy."

"My family doesn't live there, Miss Rohann. It's not a parsonage any longer. I own a house in another part of the city."

She hesitated fractionally before going on.

*Is this insecurity?* he wondered.

She was thinking aloud, "Not a parsonage . . .? Does that house still belong to the church?"

"Yes. It's temporary housing for homeless families."

She looked surprised. "Oh, I nearly forgot. I gave Mrs. Whiting ideas about how to divide a large house to make five suites and a shared kitchen. I never saw the house, only the floor plan. I wanted to give her ideas and not charge her a design rate. I didn't know it was the parsonage she asked about. Do you have a large enough congregation to afford gestures like that?"

"Not yet, we don't. The house is a joint effort with other churches in the neighborhood."

"Did you talk the other congregations into that, Reverend?" Her look of contained humor was on again.

"We all agreed there was a need." He'd nearly forgotten the long meetings, the cajoling and arm twisting which that feat had cost him.

But she seemed to understand right away. "You are persuasive," she said and quickly turned back to her rolls of drawings of the church. She dropped one and seemed inexplicably flustered as she retrieved it and rearranged them.

She pivoted suddenly. The pleats at the bottom of her skirt flared out in the movement.

He blinked.

She spoke hastily. "There's one measurement I still need. The city's drawings have this wing about two feet closer to the street than reality. I'll go down and check."

He stopped his business with the projector. "If I'm not here, Miss Rohann, I'll be in the kindergarten room on this floor, two doors down."

"Great." She took a tape measure from her purse and whisked out of the room.

Abraham Hallowell gripped the table to keep himself from watching her walk away.

*What kind of fool are you?* he thought.

The tension in every part of his body told him what the foolishness was. She was young, fresh, beautiful, and as happened whenever in her presence, his hormones raced.

It didn't seem to matter that he was old before his time – that any such longings were useless for him. His mind and body paid no attention to facts. The past three years of building immunity to this urge had come undone the moment he first saw her, dazed and fearful at the burning house.

Abe, he explained to himself, you've a sink to fix and would be a lot better off doing that.

But his heedless hormones remembered each moment when she smiled at him over the last weeks. And tonight, three times she'd answered to "Miss".

# CHAPTER SEVENTEEN

S arah propped the door open with the metal measuring tape. She didn't need this measurement; she knew how far the building was set back. She needed to get outside – away from the unexpected Reverend Hallowell. The moment he'd opened the door, she'd sensed tension in him, just as she had sensed it each time they met over the six weeks since Bruce's death.

But why? Did her face betray the sudden jolt of awakening his appearance had given her? She'd seen him at work, helping Officer Sidney Seneca through a difficult time. That he was a compassionate man, a dynamic speaker and a man of strong convictions, she already knew.

But tonight, looking up into his angry amber eyes, she'd become aware of a desire to make his life – what? Happier? Safer? She had no idea.

What a joke on her. Would she never be able to control the impulses bequeathed her? Grandfather had gone through hell, sure that her nature was as promiscuous as that of his wife and daughter. With love and apprehension, he had watched for Sarah's fall. No man had worked harder to teach a beloved child how to walk the narrow path.

And yet, this new and forbidding man with the unruly copper hair and broad shoulders had, over the last weeks, forced other needs to the surface.

He had a family.

Back when her grandfather was alive, unwilling to disappoint him, she would not have let this happen. It had burst forth suddenly – attacking her at the very door of the church.

"Keep busy. Learn to work with your hands. Do something and do it well." She could hear grandfather's voice, see his gnarled, busy hands whittling, carving, hammering, sanding. His antidote to isolation was to teach her to do well what he did.

Build.

That's what she was here for. To Reverend Hallowell she was a builder. Perhaps, he also thought she might be a murderer.

She had to go back inside and become a builder for this church. Without this job, she stood a good chance of not being able to hold together the company and the family she had built. Sarah stood tall, tugged at her skirt zipper, and straightened her jacket. She reentered the sanctuary determined to do and do well.

\* \*

Under the kindergarten sink, the Right Reverend Abraham Hallowell bit back a familiar Arabic curse and tried again, muttering to himself in the LebaneseFrench that had always served his mother in times of stress. Normally, he got leverage on these pipes by holding the wrench with his left hand. Then he'd add pressure with the leather-covered end of his right arm. But this pipe just twisted along with him and wouldn't let go of its grip on the nut.

With two good hands, he could have held the pipe still with one while he twisted the nut loose with the other.

Abraham sweated it out, determined to get this thing. His frustration mounted. It had to do with a lot more than this plumbing, but plumbing was going to bear the brunt of it.

He stopped suddenly. The soft sound of her shoes came into the room. He thrust his right arm up in the space behind the sink and closed his eyes, hoping he'd been fast enough.

"Reverend Hallowell?"

"Under here."

"The sign outside doesn't list plumber as a pastor's occupation."

" 'Reverend' covers all kinds of fixit." His voice sounded almost normal to him. "Did you get the measurements?"

From inside the sink cabinet, he couldn't see her. Still his memory told him more than he wanted to know. Unbidden, the clear image of her reminded him that she was out of bounds.

Suddenly, she knelt on the floor next to him, her head and shoulders above his inside the wide cabinet. The wrench she had found, she fitted to the pipe – a useful and efficient offer of help, but considering his present state of mind, not wise for her.

"Okay, Reverend, on the count of three we pull simultaneously."

He felt the sting behind his eyes and the flush of color to his face. He could hear his own breath turn ragged. He pushed his right arm farther up into the space behind the sink-well while he gripped the wrench more firmly with his left.

On three they both pulled. Nothing happened. Miss Rohann said, "Huh!" and brought both hands to bear on her wrench. On three again, nothing budged.

"You know Reverend, you might as well get that right arm into this. Even without a grip, it can provide enough push to get the job done."

Abraham swallowed hard. He looked at her directly for the first time since she'd knelt next to him. Her gaze rested on him, dark gentleness. He forgot the image of sleek sophistication he had carried with him for six weeks. The light from the room shadowed her cheek. There was enough light for him to see the raise of one eyebrow and the almost imperceptible smile. Slowly he lowered the arm, watching her face. Her smile became encouraging.

He put the leather-protected end of the arm on the wrench and knew she had to see it, but she merely began the countdown once more. On three, they both twisted in opposite directions and pulled until the nut gave way.

"Look out!" She shielded his face with one palm. "You don't want that grit in your eyes. Come on out. The rest can be done from out here." She backed away from him, shaking the grit that had landed on her hand.

When he pulled himself out and sat up, she knelt on the children's "sharing carpet", directly in front of him, twisting the wrench mechanism.

After a moment, she looked up and smiled. He dropped his gaze to his right stump and back up at her. Her gaze had followed his down but held there where his hand had once been.

The arm throbbed. His throat constricted. The stump grew and became an ugly thing between them.

"Tell me why you hide your arm, Mr. Hallowell?"

He studied her serene face. Didn't she see how ugly it was? Looking away, he tried his voice. "No one knows who threw the bomb into the church. My hand was . . . it was. . . they had to take it off. But others died – children died while I held them. Their mothers . . . their mothers were already . . . They trusted me."

He glanced back to see the salt tears brimming in her compassionate eyes.

"And that day is always inside of you," she said. Her gaze held his captive. Under her deep scrutiny, he felt himself letting go, allowing her into his soul. Her soul met his and beheld his pain and struggle.

"Why hide your wrist tonight?" she asked. Her gentle voice disarmed him.

"Ugly . . .!" He'd blurted before he thought.

Appalled, he swallowed the thought that followed hard on the heels of this first. He knew she heard the unspoken. How could she not? Since he'd met her, and tonight, since he'd opened the church door, he had felt desire even in his missing hand.

The silence between them lengthened. He dared to look at her. Her head bowed over her hands in her lap. The thick knot of her hair shown all its shades of cream. Lashes of the same subtle colors framed her fragile lids. Her face spoke only of a tranquil innocence.

Only the tightening of her lips gave a sign of agitation. Without raising her eyes, she whispered, "We're all flawed. In some, the flaws are so deeply hidden you cannot see them with your eyes."

He sat in silent wonder. After a moment, she looked up and he knew she had spoken of flaws in herself.

"But…"

The front doorbell rang. A moment of regret filled him. Then, Abraham rose and slowly extended his left hand. She took it and came up beside him. She looked off toward the sound with uneasiness. Her apprehension surprised him. This meeting seemed more important to her than he would have thought possible.

"Miss Rohann, I'll go answer the door. Perhaps you'd like to meet us at the chapel room."

She looked up at him with gratitude and turned abruptly for the door. He watched her straight back and proud carriage with a sudden realization that her confidence was hard won. Won over what obstacles?

He wanted to know.

The bell rang again, insistently. He kicked her builder's measuring tape as he hastened toward the front stairwell.

Abraham scooped it up and pocketed it for Sarah.

# CHAPTER EIGHTEEN

Having rung the bell several times, Mrs. Eleanor Whiting began to remove her Sunday evening gloves. She prepared to give the oak door a good thwack. Abraham opened it. Eleanor looked disappointed.

He was pleased to see her. "Eleanor, shall I close it, so you can finish hitting it?"

"I've mislaid my key. Young man, where have you been?"

"Fixing the kindergarten sink."

"Again? And I suppose you had your one good ear under the sink with the wrenches and whatnots, eh?"

"Not exactly. I could hear the bell. It's just that I'm slowing down – the lumbago you know, dear."

"Lumbago! I haven't heard that one for . . . Reverend Hallowell! Stop teasing this old lady and let me in. I want to see our architect and get things moving on this chapel!"

Abraham smiled and stepped back. As Eleanor pulled her arthritic knee up to the door sill, he slipped his left hand under her elbow, gave just enough boost and then withdrew to let her enter on her own dignity.

"I'm afraid we need to meet in the chapel space, Eleanor."

"The chapel! That's thirteen steps, young man!"

"Yes, but you're plenty early. We won't start without you. Promise."

Eleanor looked at him over her half glasses. The long and stony stare. His return was equal in severity, except for the slight twitch at the corner of his mouth – a give-away he could not control. She looked at his mouth and lost a bit of stoniness herself.

He cocked his head to one side. "I could offer you a pig-a-back ride, if that would help."

She harrumphed, linked her hand through his right arm and turned to the thirteen-step task before her. "I suppose this is going to be worth my while."

"Very."

"Good looking architect?"

"Exceedingly."

Eleanor knew very well how good Sarah Rohann looked, but she was very glad the reverend had also noticed. That was part of the plan she and Amanda had hatched during Amanda's last days.

"Exceedingly good-looking?" she parroted. "Then we shan't mind the climb so much, with a good view to soften the pain."

As they mounted the stairs, one slow step at a time, Eleanor Whiting took the opportunity to assess her pastor's well-being. She knew that the loss of Amanda Charles was as great a blow to this young man as it was to her. Reverend Hallowell probably would never know what a source of strength he'd been to Arthur Charles during Amanda's last illness.

Abraham Hallowell had become too damned humble to know his own worth, too aware of his flaws.

His congregation and his colleagues had grown aware of his power to lead. They'd also become alert to the compassion and penetration evident in his deep amber-green eyes. They were sensitive to the nuances of his compelling and resonant voice. They saw his physical power, too, especially in the face of all that had happened to his body some years ago. His agility and strength seemed amazing. To his friends, the physical flaws made him human.

From Amanda, Eleanor had come to understand that for Reverend Hallowell, his defect became a sign of his guilt. He deserved to have it and to be reminded daily of how he had gotten it. To him, it represented a gross failure in himself, making him monstrous.

Eleanor Whiting worried about the balance of Abraham's self-view now that his visits to Amanda's bedside had been cut off. Amanda's pithy wit and arrow-sure perception acted as an antidote to this young man's misjudgment of himself.

Eleanor knew herself well enough to know that she couldn't step into Amanda's shoes for him. She was too impatient. Amanda had always tried to soften Eleanor's impatience. Now, she'd have to work on her own flaws alone.

He'd have to go it solo, too. Too bad no one in the congregation could take a sharp needle and inject him with a little joy. Something had to make him lighten up. Laughing at life, even sometimes at yourself, made good medicine.

Well, she decided, it's time for the humorous and impatient Eleanor Whiting to feast her eyes on some exceedingly good-looking, and, of course, extraordinarily smart architect. Enough of stairs!

Miss Rohann turned toward Mrs. Whiting with a smile of relief. "I'm so glad you're first, Mrs. Whiting."

"Sarah! Nice to see you again."

The bell downstairs rang again. Eleanor turned toward Abe. "Find me a good stout chair Reverend and answer that bell – I shan't be running up and down those stairs."

Miss Rohann's puzzled look lasted until Abraham caught her eye. The barely controlled humor returned to her, bringing a dark shine to her eyes. Abraham turned away quickly, seeking a chair for Mrs. Whiting.

Eleanor Whiting looked at his back over her half glasses. She thought, "So far, so good, Amanda."

Sometime after the committee members had arrived, gotten their coffee, and greeted Sarah, who already seemed to be their favorite architect. They then gossiped about Mr. Glidden who never showed up at their meetings. They settled, (with the women mumbling about runs in nylons), around the ancient oak table. Chester Brown was, as yet, unwilling to let go of the subject of Irvin Glidden, but Myrtle Smithson squelched further gossiping temptations.

"Chester, if you continue to belabor Irvin's character, I am likely to say something about him which I will regret. Please desist!"

"Now Myrt," soothed George Wilkers, "Chester is understandable concerned. I mean, it's ushally the cruxial meetin' when Irvin shows up. Then you cain't get nothin' done for explainin' to him what he ought to of knowed from the beginnin'."

At this point, Eleanor, having successfully found the whitener for her decaf, called the meeting to order. "You have all met our architect. Now the Reverend has met her – and approves of her too, I must say."

\* \*

This last was said while staring at the Reverend over her half glasses. Abraham was glad to be at the back of the room at this juncture. He could see that Sarah did not know what to make of Mrs. Whiting's little aside. Mrs. Whiting barged on.

"Let us see what proposals Miss Rohann has for us. She had her work cut out for her after our last meeting. We gave her a long list of wants for a very small budget."

Abraham sat near the projector and admired the easy way Sarah seemed to have with this committee. She assured them that the list of wants was not a problem.

"It is always best for the architect to have all the wants in mind from the beginning. Even those things which cannot be afforded now, might be planned for in the future.

"I hope we've been able to provide for most of these wants. At the same time, I have been able to look at your beautiful building as an outsider, one who may recognize a few thorns on your rose bush – thorns that you've become used to. As we go through the photos of the building, we'll discuss the proposed solutions for your wants as well as a possible remedy for thorns."

She stayed near the committee table and used the remote control to play the pictures on the screen at the end of the room. At first, Abraham listened to the tones of her voice, but soon, he became caught up in her vision of what this chapel could be like.

Even so, he hesitated to approve of a beautiful chapel in an unreachable location.

With pews built for three instead of ten, she pointed out, they would have flexible seating, easily moved for other uses of the room. A simple wooden cross attached to the altar wall and a small stage with removable lectern and pulpit would encourage multiple uses of the room.

Abe began to imagine a youth group using this room.

In the slides she had of other chapels built by her firm, Abraham could see that she paid careful attention to details in the construction of the smallest elements. Coved ceilings hinted at the arched designs of more imposing rooms and added to the sacred feeling of a small room.

The photo of a baptismal font which she had made for another church showed joinery of such refined techniques that every member of the committee gasped. The cost of the font brought another gasp. All knew it was less than the simplest one they had considered from a church supply catalogue.

She showed a slide of her partner, master carpenter Miguel Salvador, with a cross he'd designed. The cross was exquisitely proportioned and beautifully made. But it was the sight of the young man that made Abraham Hallowell uncomfortable.

Miguel Salvador was a very young and darkly handsome man with long, sensitive fingers on graceful hands. Abraham's right arm found the depths of his coat pocket.

Abraham knew this young man disapproved of him, and that Sarah loved and listened carefully to this son. He swallowed hard around a sudden tightening in his throat.

The committee now had no doubts about who they wanted building their chapel and its furnishings. Abraham knew the chapel could be beautiful. He was still unconvinced that it was needed.

Sarah showed them a picture of her plasterer and stained-glass master, Ernst Schumacher. She proposed that the three windows of the Trinity be made as part of a class for members of the church – a workshop in stained glass construction taught by this leather-faced old man. The enthusiastic committee nearly began a sign-up sheet right then.

However, Mrs. Whiting had the reigns firmly in hand. "Sarah, you mentioned some thorns you might have seen that we have become used to. What are they?"

At that point, the door to the darkened room opened with a bang. The much-discussed Irvin Glidden arrived under full sail. "Had to use my key. Can't you hear the bell, Reverend?"

# CHAPTER NINETEEN

Eleanor Whiting was obviously peeved. "If you've a key to the whole place, why make the Reverend climb down and welcome you? This meeting started an hour ago Irvin, and it is the fourth meeting you have not attended. Sit down please."

Irvin was not to be intimidated. "Where's the blasted coffee maker?"

"Plumb emptied," George said.

Mrs. Whiting said, "Irvin, please sit down."

"Empty? Why?"

Chester Brown had had enough. "Glidden, the lady is talkin'. Sit down."

Reverend Hallowell stood up to smooth tempers, but it was Sarah who put things to rights. "I'm glad you came, Mr. Glidden. I am Sarah Rohann, and I have heard a great deal about you. Won't you please take my chair, I'll stand from now on, anyway."

"Who are you, young lady?"

"I am the architect for Rohann and Salvador. We're in the midst of a discussion, Mr. Glidden. Perhaps, while I finish discussing these slides, it would be helpful if you caught up with the rest of the committee. You may read my notes for this evening's meeting. They are not in complete sentences, since I was taking notes for myself, but a man of your quick mind can reconstruct the thoughts, I'm sure. There is better light near the exit sign if you'd care to move my chair over there."

Abraham was on his feet, ready to help Irvin move closer to the exit, but George Wilkers beat him to the draw.

"Good light," George said. "And good 'nough seatin'"

Irvin saw his chair disappearing to the far side of the room but was unwilling to give up dockside moorings so easily.

"Miss Rohann, I presume, since you claim to be an architect, that you can produce your credentials. Where did you get your degree?"

Abraham could see Sarah's back straighten, her shoulders square and her patience count to fifteen. When she answered, her voice was oil on water.

"I obtained my degree by a rather unusual route, Mr. Glidden."

"Thought as much." Irvin Glidden puffed about this revelation.

"It began with a degree in civil engineering from Princeton. I returned to Oregon to help design the tunnel which shortened the highway from Pendleton to La Grande."

Chester Brown whistled, "You designed the tunnel that avoids that long, steep hill east of Pendleton?"

"I was one of a team of three who did."

"It's a beaut!" Chester, who had driven freight trucks the last forty years, knew his hills and his tunnels.

Sarah went on. "Thank you. After the tunnel, I realized that I wanted to design buildings for people rather than cars. So, I obtained my architecture degree at the University here in Eugene while working as a contractor. I've been building homes and churches for the last twelve years – designing them for eight years.

Irvin Glidden was a man becalmed. He drifted from port to dry dock in drooping dignity.

Sarah smiled at Mrs. Whiting who raised one eyebrow and pursed her lips at her much-admired architect. Abe saw that Mrs. Whiting recognized a worthy colleague when she saw one in action.

"Now," said Sarah to the committee members at the table, "We come to the few thorns in the situation. First is access."

She showed slides of the entries to Wesley Church. "Six stairs to the sanctuary from the sidewalk to the front door, four more stairs just inside the door – ten stairs total to get in the front."

Another scene: "Eight stairs from the back door to the choir room below us and three more at the end of that hall up to the sanctuary."

A third scene: "Ten stairs from the side door, and the walkway here is only one and a half feet wide."

Fourth: "Thirteen stairs from the sanctuary level to the chapel. That makes about twenty-three stairs to get to the chapel. I think we'll have to suggest that grandmothers of brides not come to the wedding."

Chester Brown slapped his trick knee. "Some grandfathers won't even come, with that many stairs."

Myrtle studied the last slide carefully and raised a timid hand. "We better not put the chapel on this floor. We'll have to find another space. Oh, dear . . . "

George Wilkers said, "Now Myrtle, mebbe Miss Rohann here has a idea how we can fix it. Don't you fret."

Mrs. Whiting rapped the table to stop aimless talk. "Miss Rohann, the number of stairs in this old place is outrageous, I'll grant you that. But what can we do about it?"

Sarah showed another slide, a drawing of the portion of the church where the large rectangle of the sanctuary joined the square of the newer wing in which the committee was meeting. In the right-angle where the two buildings joined, she had drawn an elevator shaft. The facade of the shaft was finished with bricks and Tudor-like timbers similar to the sanctuary section. The area around the elevator had flowering trees and a bricked over patio. The effect was of a sunny, welcoming entry. Old and young would be able to come to worship without embarrassment over their infirmities.

Abraham leaned forward, fascinated. Never in his wildest fantasies would he have been able to turn the stair problem to their advantage. He'd thought of stairwell chair elevators – an embarrassing device for the user. He'd measured for ramps – clumsy and space consuming at best. He'd thought of elevators inside the building – difficult to locate and build. He'd even pursued these ideas with other architects.

Sarah had seen the problem and offered a beautiful alternative. She'd changed a liability into an asset. With an elevator, he easily could bring his children to his church. Amanda Charles would have been spared many agonizing steps each Sunday, had she lived long enough for this.

Abe knew they needed at least the elevator. Working together on a chapel might become a way to galvanize the congregation into other works.

And Amanda Charles had provided the initial funds for affording this solution. She and Arthur had talked over the use of her stock as a legacy. "Do something that will help the old people of the church. And get the young people involved in helping the old people. You'll have a better church family if you can see how to do both, Abe-boy."

Abraham had her trust fund – not yet announced to the congregation. His ace in the hole. He would wait and see how this committee reacted to Sarah's idea. Abraham watched to see who would ask the pertinent questions.

Myrtle Smithson wiped her clean hands on her handkerchief and made bold to speak. "Miss Rohann, that is wonderful. But won't it be expensive?"

"Yes. It will cost as much as the chapel itself."

Irvin Glidden was moving his chair back from the side of the room. "That's outrageous. Why, we could build a ramp for around a thousand."

"That's true," Sarah changed slides. Now on the screen was a ramp to the sanctuary. The drawing was equally carefully made, equally landscaped, but not equally satisfying. "In fact, Mr. Glidden, I played around with the idea of a ramp for several days before I tried the elevator. This was probably the most efficient and least intrusive ramp I could design. Still, any ramp only gave access to the sanctuary level."

George coughed and entered the fray. "That means that nobody who cain't take a goodly hike won't ever be able to visit the chapel or the Sunday school rooms of our church."

"And that, by God, isn't sociable!" exclaimed Chester.

Mrs. Whiting got them all back on track. "What are the costs of the elevator?"

"Sixty thousand dollars total. There's a foundation that will have to be dug, machine housing and insulation goes below the elevator. The company I recommend salvages elevators out of old apartment houses that are being torn down. They provide new parts, check out all the parts and refurbish any that need it. They do a good job and provide a twenty-year guarantee on parts and labor. There's considerable savings in using a reclaimed elevator initially. Also, there is savings in working with these people who are prompt and skillful in installation and service."

Irvin had heard the word "salvaged" and didn't like it. "Reclaimed elevator, Miss? How safe is that? We can't use just any reclaimed elevator here at Wesley."

"I have a list of the other churches in the Portland area who've used this company. Why don't you call a few of these and ask them how they feel about the elevators?" She handed each of them a copy of a list. Coming to the back of the room, she handed one to Abraham. He was surprised at the attention until she whispered, "How'm I doin'?"

"You've got 'em hooked. Reel 'em in."

"I will, if Mr. G. doesn't swamp the boat." She turned back to the committee.

In the half light of the room, Abraham felt safe watching the sway of her skirt until he caught Mrs. Whiting's clear eye on him.

As Sarah answered their questions – calmly respectful of the pushy Irvin, encouraging to the timid Myrtle, and playfully creative with George and Chester – the Right Reverend Abraham Hallowell felt the tug on his own line. He'd let himself be reeled in, far closer to her boat than he ever intended.

To break the line between them, Abraham took his eyes off the meeting. He began writing a note about having a source of funds which could be matched by the congregation in order to pay for the elevator and at least part of the chapel. And, he knew the Methodist funds that would make borrowing for the elevator possible.

*This might be a good idea after all.* He didn't bother to ask himself why he wanted it to work. It would be good for the church.

And that was all. At the end, he knew he would have to accept mere friendship with the architect.

When Sarah's presentation was over, she prepared to leave while the committee deliberated. Abraham handed his note to Mrs. Whiting, saying, "I will be glad to explain this after a decision has been made by the committee."

Abraham packed up the computer and carried it out for Sarah. Following her, he could once again feel the draw of her energy.

Outside the church, she stopped at an old Chevrolet truck. When she turned to help him hoist the briefcase, he blurted, "You drove the truck?"

"An old and battered truck. I need it to carry building material."

He laughed at himself. "Sorry. It's just the contrast with the suit . . ." He dared not continue into golden hair, dark eyes and all the other items the truck contrasted with.

Sarah bit her lip, seemingly undecided about plunging into something. He waited. Indecision looked so good showing through her usual poise. Evidently, she decided to go for it.

"Reverend Hallowell?"

He started at the caress her voice gave his name. Did she do that to all names? Salvador, Hallowell and everyone else?

"Reverend, if they go for the elevator, I want to enlist your help in taking them a step further."

"A step further?" He cast his mind over his own hopes for the congregation. "Let me guess. After we provide a way for the congregation to get more easily into the building – I hope you think along the same lines as I do – we make the building more accessible to the public."

She leaned toward him, excited. "Yes. Serving meals for lonely people in the dining hall near the church kitchen. Your kitchen is already up to code for that." She saw the mischievous smile on his face when she mentioned codes. "Ah . . . It was you who made sure it was up to snuff, didn't you?"

He grinned. "What else could we be doing, Miss Rohann?"

She laughed. "I suspect you are way ahead of me – and far ahead of your congregation. How about providing clothes for people in emergency situations, setting up high quality day care, having public day and night access to the chapel for people in spiritual need . . ."

She saw the gleam of laughter in his eyes and caught herself in mid-sentence. "Of course, this isn't my church, but so many churches could serve. Yours has begun by using the parsonage for homeless families. Now, you could look around and see what to tackle next."

"Do you believe in spiritual need?" Abraham fiddled absently with a tape measure in his pocket and waited to hear how his calling fared in her beliefs.

She said, "People are in need of a great deal more than food and shelter. When those are taken care of, they still need a sense of direction – of their place in the scheme of the universe."

"And you think they might be helped by having access to a church all the time?"

"Certainly, a sanctuary could help."

"Even when I am unavailable?"

"You can't be available all the time – God has to take over for you sometimes. You have needs, your family has needs. . . "

"My children" He smiled.

Sarah felt herself freeze. She glanced at him and decided to say the difficult thing. "Yes, and your wife."

His smile faded abruptly. "My wife died four years ago."

"Oh, I'm sorry." There was a long silence while her thoughts connected something, and she looked up at him again. "The bomb?"

He took a visibly deep breath and looked at her directly. "Not the bomb – parts of the silver chalice I held when the bomb was thrown at me." The muscles around his mouth went taut.

She frowned. There was something about the way he stated the facts that left the story incomplete.

Stirring himself, he retrieved their conversation. "You think the congregation could be convinced to leave the chapel open at night?"

"Eventually, yes. I could help you make the chapel wing separate from the rest of the church, to minimize the possibilities for theft."

He smiled. "You look on your art as something more than just building nice spaces, don't you?"

"Architecture should help the people who live with it."

"Help them improve?"

"I guess I do sound like a lecturer."

"You sound like a minister."

She smiled, then reached out her left hand. "It's been a pleasure getting acquainted with you as a pastor as well as a chaplain, Reverend

Hallowell. I like your style in meetings. I can't tell you how many ministers in supposedly democratic congregations just can't let their leaders do the leading."

He shook her small hand and held it. "Mrs. Whiting does a good job of keeping this committee working toward the general goal. There are some committees where the leadership takes a long-time surfacing. In those, you would think I was an autocrat."

"In those, I bet I'd see you teaching leadership skills." She looked down at their hands and up at him. He dropped hers and reached for the door on her truck. The pleats on her skirt swung out as she climbed into the seat.

He held the door open long enough to thank her especially for the elevator idea and to say he must get back to the meeting. He felt the weight of the measuring tape in his pocket. But he merely closed the truck door and waved her off. As she drove away, he held in his mind the image of a long and smooth leg that her climb into the truck had given him. These recent weeks, for the first time in years, he had developed a sharp sexual appetite.

Abe thought that Irvin Glidden, if he made this meeting tediously long, was in line to be torpedoed.

# CHAPTER TWENTY

The next morning, on the third-floor tower of Wesley Methodist, Sarah hesitated before the dark, heavy door, making the habitual tug at her skirt zipper. The worst he could do was tell her to go to the church office for her measuring tape. Of course, Mrs. Stevens, his secretary would have a very organized lost and found system.

Sarah took a deep breath and knocked with what she hoped was a business-like authority.

"Come in."

She thought he sounded tired.

The door hinges were well oiled, so he didn't hear her enter. Heavy draperies darkened the room and beat back the strong spring sunshine. He still concentrated on his writing. In the light of his desk lamp, his burnished red-brown waves stood in disorder caused by his thought habits. He ran the pencil through them once more while she watched. The lump in her throat turned over.

On his desk, she noticed a photo set to face Abe.

"Come in, Mrs. Stevens." He spoke a little louder. "I'm not quite through with the letter to Miss Rohann." When he looked up, his deep-set eyes took on a darker hue.

"Sarah!" This whispering of her name seemed harsh, pushed out.

Sarah was abashed to see frown lines deepen between his brows. She had interrupted something important again. Hovering near the door, she apologized. "Sorry. I always seem to barge in and disrupt you. I'll just go to the office."

"Wait, Miss Rohann." He half stood, dropping his pencil and pushing back his chair. "What can I do for you?"

"I left my measuring tape in the kindergarten room last night. It isn't there."

Abraham came around his desk, his left hand kneading his right shoulder. "I found your tape. Were you just going to retrieve it and leave?" He faced her squarely. His voice softened. "Can you stay a moment? Please . . . sit down."

She nodded, wondering what letter he'd been writing to her. Did he have to tell her she'd lost the bid? Was that why he seemed so agitated when she came in?

He pushed the overstuffed chair toward her with an inviting gesture. She sat down and then wished she hadn't because he stood over her, still kneading his shoulder, still frowning and working the muscles of his jaw.

She made herself look up and meet his gaze. The darkness under his eyes evidenced either a long illness or a long sadness. The piercing green of them focused on her face, yet she felt his thoughts exploring hers. Even through signs of illness, the strength in his mind manifested itself in his probing gaze.

She made herself return his gaze despite her fears. Did he see her shameless nature? Surely, he sensed that the tape measure was only a transparent excuse to speak to him again. Why had she allowed herself to be drawn back to him. Why didn't she put up her usual barriers? Why him?

Suddenly he blinked as if coming from a half-conscious state. He turned away, retreating to his chair. Watching his fluid motions, Sarah grew distressed at the direction of her thoughts.

He fell into his chair as if exhausted. His head leaned back into the worn leather. His whole body relaxed as he smiled. "That was a marvel – what you did last night. For two years I have tried to get through to that committee on the need for better access."

"I was presumptuous last night. Last night . . ."

His smile was gentle. "Last night, they needed your lecture. In the end, they knew it – they knew you were right. Except Mr. Glidden. He thought you were a snippet. 'Pretty, mind you, but a young snippet.' was how Glidden put it."

They laughed together, and Sarah watched the green of his eyes become lighter before the frown returned. His left hand again massaged his right shoulder. An habitual gesture, she guessed.

Abraham looked at her deeply for a moment. "How old are you?"

She jerked her head up. She hadn't thought her age would be an issue for this job. "What's that got to do with architecture?"

He looked down at his papers. "Absolutely nothing."

"I'm thirty-four. That's old enough to vote, pay taxes and design buildings that withstand earthquakes. Why?"

"Your cast is gone already?" His voice was intent, his hand unmoving on his shoulder.

Sarah controlled her concern. "It hurts a little if I turn too quickly, but I'm basically fine."

"And your hands?"

She glanced at her palms where the scars of the fire were fading. "They are healing. Really, Abe, my children don't get cholic or keep me from working. I fulfill contracts. I get plans done before deadlines."

Abraham stiffened as if he'd been hit. He stood up, pacing. His jaw worked hard when he stopped abruptly and wheeled toward her. "I'm sorry, Sarah! I wasn't really asking about your work habits."

"Then what were you asking?"

He shook his head, puzzled at his own actions. "I don't know. This last two days I've been abrupt, even rude too many times with too many people. Last night I was rude when you arrived."

Sarah stood to block his pacing. He halted a hair's breadth from her.

She spoke with a calm she didn't feel. "When I met you, I knew you had been through a bad time. You've lost someone vital to you."

Abraham looked at Sarah as if suddenly seeing more than he had expected to find in her. "Yes. Amanda Charles was a beloved friend."

"Amanda? I loved her, and Arthur. Did their kitchen two years ago and can't tell you how it hit me to find she had died, and I hadn't even known it."

He glanced off at the closed curtains. "Yes, she was a light in this world, and a wonderful grandmother to my kids." He pulled the photo set around so she could see it.

"Meet Deborah, Andy and Peter."

The children she saw there were very different from each other and not one of them looked like Abe.

"Goodness," she said, "Amanda must have loved them very much."

"Boy was it mutual," he said. "They miss her a lot."

Sarah said, "That is very hard on children. But on you, as well. You've been so busy doing things for others, you've had no time to grieve yourself."

He was suddenly busy, standing, moving away to straighten a book, pick up papers, replace his pen in its case. "I did that at the hospital, all those three weeks. I can put that behind me and get on with the work. It's what she would have me do."

Sarah watched all this activity and swift talk for a moment before she interrupted it. "If I'd been thinking at all, I wouldn't have come so early last night. You had a right to be upset with me, or anyone else who came when you needed time to let down."

"Nothing gives me the right to ask your age, or anything else personal. I should not speak as I did to you just now."

Anger at himself brought a thin tautness to his voice. If she remained in the tension of his grief, she would be tempted to reach out to him – a gesture she couldn't allow herself to begin. Obviously, something painful surfaced when he was with her. Any gesture from her risked a break in his brittle mask as well as her carefully made armor. For both their sakes, she should leave.

"Reverend, I accept your apologies," she said levelly, forcing herself to look him in the eye. "But remember, you have a right to be human, to be irritable and hurt by death. You even have a right to cry. Now I'll get out of your hair." She turned to the door.

"No wait! Please!" His hand caught her shoulder. His hand dropped immediately when she turned back.

Sarah was beyond prudence. "Why do I make you angry one moment and not the next?"

Abraham's eyes widened. "You don't make me angry, Sarah." As if trying to understand the conflict within himself, he spoke slowly. "I guess I'm angry at circumstances. You came into my life at low tide – when there are things I regret, things I can't ever change, things I'll never have again and that I'm just now realizing I want very much."

He took a deep breath and attempted a smile. "At high tide, I would have been a lot more fun. I really don't mean to be jerking you around."

"The moon," she said softly.

"What?"

"I came at the wrong phase of the moon." She wanted him to laugh and forgive himself for what he had said to her. But he looked at his right pocket where his missing hand should have been playing with change. And, she had noticed, he always faced her when she talked. Was he reading lips? Had the bomb affected his hearing as well?

She realized that it had been four years since the bombing. The loss of something so significant would be devastating, but she couldn't believe he'd let it still control him. He was far from self-centered. Was it the loss of the hand or the way he lost it that dragged at him?

All those children and his wife? Their deaths weighed on him, heavily. But what did those deaths and his missing hand have to do with his reaction to her? She could not see any connection.

Could she help him get beyond this Low Tide, as he so aptly put it? Did she want to? What would reaching out to him cost her?

It didn't matter. Last night, as he had talked about his hopes for his people, she had known that there was something compelling about this man. She'd known that she would not turn her back on him as she'd done so many others. Right now, she wouldn't count the cost. He was a man of high convictions, of belief in the innate goodness of his fellows, and ready to forgive their weaknesses.

He had stood up for her when she made absolutely no sense after the fire. He had put up with Miguel's suspicions in order to make sure she was safe.

Yet, he was a strong man in need, unable to forgive himself. She couldn't walk away. She had no idea what would be asked of her. She just knew that when the time came, for him she would do it.

She sat down again, slowly, deliberately looking at him. She would take a new approach and start this conversation all over.

"Did you need to discuss the chapel work with me, Reverend Hallowell?"

That question startled him. He seemed thankful for the sudden change in the direction of their encounter. "I . . .Yes. I was trying to write a letter to you when you arrived."

Standing next to her chair, he reached across her for the stationery on his desk. He straightened abruptly away from the near contact with her. "The committee voted almost unanimously, to recommend your firm . . ."

"Almost unanimously?" her voice carried laughter.

He smiled, loosening up a little. "With the exception of Mr. Glidden, you understand."

"Understood." she grinned.

The signs of his earlier distress eased as he watched her for a fleeting moment and then he returned to business. "They voted to recommend to the board that your firm be given the contract for the chapel design."

"The chapel? That's wonderful." No sooner did she become elated than she began to worry. "Was there no discussion of the access to the chapel?"

Reverend Hallowell laughed aloud. "There was discussion all right!"

"And?"

"And access is included in the recommendation."

"The elevator? They agreed to that? Last night? In one meeting?"

"Must I remind you that Mrs. Whiting chairs this particular committee?"

"Oh, yes. No foolishness." Sarah eased into a lighter mood with him.

"Right. No foolishness and (your own words, Miss Rohann), no floundering." His eyes were again light amber-green. The frown and the darkness around them diminished. "Furthermore, this committee voted to recommend that your firm be hired as contractors to build the chapel."

"Goodness! No other bids?"

"Mrs. Whiting has already brought two other firms to this committee. She was tired of dithering and saw no reason to delay construction for such a formality as more bids. 'The outcome,' she said, 'was a foregone conclusion."

Chester Brown agreed with her. And George and Myrtle agreed as well.

"After that, there was no discussion other than the deliberate and contemptuous lighting of Mr. Glidden's cigar."

"She allowed a cigar?"

"Until he laid it on the ashtray. She removed it to the sink. Both Mr. Glidden and his cigar went out in sodden fumes." Abraham sát on the corner of his desk nearest her, his eyes gleaming with humor, one arm in his pocket, one hand resting on his knee, his leg swinging freely.

Sarah leaned forward to capture the moment. "I feel like celebrating! Have you been out in the sun today?"

"Is the sun shining?" He looked pleased and glanced toward the darkly draped window.

"It is. You should at least open these drapes in the spring, Reverend. I need to be in the sunshine to celebrate. Walk with me and see the daffodils and the daphne."

"Are they blooming?"

"They are." She smiled at how remote from the physical world he was.

"Already. . . again . . .." he mused and appeared to notice a thin shaft of morning sunlight that crept between the curtains into the room. "Yes, I will come out then."

From his perch on the corner of the desk, Reverend Hallowell leaned down and said, "This letter I was trying to write . . . This letter was supposed to tell you about the committee's recommendations. But my thanks for your boldness kept creeping into the more legal jargon."

"Boldness – brashness . . ." she tried to dismiss her part in the triumph. He touched her lips with his forefinger, stopping her jabbering.

"And my thanks for what you did for me, under the sink." He studied her face.

Sarah sat, stunned. The fleeting contact followed by his glance conveyed a very deep, firmly constrained passion. The brief knowledge of it filled her.

His hand pressed hers for a moment before he stood and pulled her to the door. "Our sun awaits, Sarah."

# CHAPTER TWENTY-ONE

Hours later, when late afternoon sunlight warmed the paper on her drawing board, Sarah leaned her forehead onto the softness of newsprint paper and closed her eyes to recapture the memory of her morning walk with Abraham.

In tired reverie, Sarah's mind slipped back to the image of Abraham's bent head and his wild copper hair being buffeted by the wind. They had walked together in a quiet peace for a long time. Abraham had stayed on her right, keeping his good arm and his hearing ear toward her. Over time, the distance began to tell on him, and a slight limp appeared in his right leg.

Not once had he touched her during their wanderings. His efforts to keep from it had made her more aware of his presence than if he'd maintained a constant contact. His right arm had stayed in its pocket hiding place. His left arm had been allowed only to point at small features of the neighborhood. One time, it had warned her of the sudden approach of a car. Even then it had not been allowed to touch her.

It was flung in front of her as a barrier.

"Sarah! The car! Watch!"

"I'm all right, Abraham. Really. It didn't even come close."

In that brief moment, she had seen his fear for her. It had been a fear far greater than the situation called for. He seemed to know he was overreacting too and tried to smile, but the smile was forced.

"I guess I still live with Lebanese terrorists in my mind. I thought the driver was trying to run you down on purpose."

"Not here in Portland. Here we run each other down by accident, and we say we're sorry afterwards." She exaggeratedly looked both ways and led out across the street. The smile lines creased a little next to his eyes, then they disappeared.

"Except for the man who killed Bruce," he said. "That man is still out there somewhere."

"Yes. I wish . . ."

"Me, too," he said and stuffed even his left hand into his Levi pocket.

His stoic's mouth relaxed when she pointed out the leaf of a trillium from the overgrown hillside lot. "I can't bring you the bloom," she said. "The plant needs it. There it is, see? It's down under the vine maple."

"I see it now. It's beautiful. Is it wild?"

"Native, yes. Wild, no. Rather timid really. But if we leave it alone, perhaps there will be two there next spring."

By the time they reached the railroad tracks, he was quietly asking her questions, hands still in his pockets, tense self-control visible in his face.

"Where did you learn so much about plants, Sarah?"

"My Grandfather. He believed a good cabinet maker ought to know where to find the wood she might use. He knew the companion plants that grew near any kind of tree we have here in the northwest – the trillium, the twin berry, the low red huckleberry – find those and you have found spruce and old lodgepole pine, alder. He taught me how to find them, and he taught me the qualities that would make one wood more useful than another for my work.

"Your grandfather must have been quite a teacher."

"Yes, he was. He died two summers ago. Oh! Look. Pussywillows down by the railroad tracks. Must be a creek run-off near there."

When she handed him the budded Pussywillow, the deep hurt that seemed always to haunt his eyes softened. He held the branch to his face, closed his eyes and enjoyed the kitten fur. When he opened his eyes, he seemed surprised to be doing such a sensual thing. He looked at her, perplexed.

"Is pussywillow good for anything?" he asked.

"For petting."

"Oh." He held it away from him slightly. "I see."

"Look, Abraham. Even the new plum leaves are about to open." Sarah pulled down a branch of the Thunder Cloud Plum. From somewhere up in the tree, a small object hurtled down into her hair. She ducked and then looked up in time to see Abraham smile, not just with his eyes, but with his mouth as well.

"What is it?" She tried to reach it, to no avail.

He seemed very amused by her predicament. "It has black and yellow stripes, but it crawls. Many legs. Very fuzzy."

"A Bumblebee Caterpillar." She still could not find it with her hand and was afraid of squashing it.

"Why don't you bend down, shake your head and let me catch it?" He was really laughing now.

She bent down and shook. She was almost sure that it was his hand that tugged the pin from her hair just before she stood up. But when she looked, the caterpillar was safe in his hand and his eyes watched her hair fall about her shoulders. The look of pain had re-entered his eyes. He swallowed hard and looked away almost immediately.

His voice was rough. "Spring is so sudden this year."

"Does it seem sudden to you?" Sarah did not look at him, trying not to intrude on his private distress.

*What gave him such sadness?*

She put the early caterpillar back on his tree and hoped that no frost would come between him and his metamorphosis. When she turned around, Abraham gazed at her. The morning slant of the sun emphasized the lines of tension in the muscles of his neck and jaw. The dark, almost bruised look below his eyes was a startling contrast to the wash of bright color in his copper hair. They stared at each other, sharing a moment of wistful regret.

"Everything seems sudden – unlooked for," he said.

"Put the pussy willows in water. In the warmth of your office, they will burst forth."

"If I touch them, will they fall apart soon?"

"They are for touching. If they fall apart untouched, they've bloomed for nothing."

He closed his eyes against a sudden thought and then looked away. "I must get back to my sermon. I'll walk you to your car."

"Truck," she'd corrected.

Abraham again had laughed.

# CHAPTER TWENTY-TWO

The sun-warmed drafting paper stuck to Sarah's forehead. The effort to sit up and work seemed too great. Her hand with the pencil and compass rested in her lap. The other hand gripped the top of the drafting table. Behind her lids, her eyes followed the motions of the image in her mind, coming to rest on the quietly dignified figure she had seen in her rear-view mirror as she had driven away from the church. The image of Abraham Hallowell became hazy, and she slept.

In her dream, she saw his children as he had described them. Deborah who was hard to stop even though she had spent her life in a wheelchair. Andy, who had spent many years with a father who had tried to hide his existence. Peter, doing his best to live life fully and with humor despite a disease that continued its slow ravaging attack.

Sometime later, Sarah awoke with a start.

"Mom? You must be more bushed than I thought to go to sleep on a stool with your legs crossed."

"Miguel? Oh, I'm so stiff." Sarah stretched and rolled her neck around. "Ahh. That is just what I needed." After another minute's stretching, she sat up and turned toward her grown son. He leaned a hip on the wall and grinned at her. She tried to look secretive but managed only to look triumphant. "I have good news," she said. "Can you guess?"

Miguel's mustache twitched. "I don't need to guess. We got the job, and you sold that church on the elevator idea, right?"

"How did you know?"

"You left here last night with all our elevator brochures and returned with only a few. They were at least nibbling on the bait when you left the meeting."

"How did you know we got the job, too?"

"If they were nibbling on elevators, it means they grabbed the design idea, hook and all. And if they were tempted by the design, who else would they want to build it?"

"You're such a smart kid."

"You don't raise no dummies, lady."

Sarah corrected him. "Teresa didn't raise dummies. I just took the good son she raised and sanded him smooth.

Miguel wobbled his head rhythmically from side to side as if he were a cool dude. "Yeah, Big Mamma. I'm smooth all right. Just ask the ladies on our street."

Sarah punched his arm playfully. "Ladies on our street think grease and tattoos are smooth. What kind of character witnesses are they?"

"They used to admire grease until they got a whiff of sawdust. Now they're educated for sure. They know Miguel has what it takes. Sawdust is where it's at, Mamma. They learn fast."

Miguel rolled his eyes and batted his eyelashes in gross imitation of ladies eager for his attention.

Sarah laughed with her twenty-three-year-old son and thought of her older friend who had given him birth. How Teresa would have loved to be with him. He was so light-hearted and funny at times like this.

And at other times, when his soul was sad, he would live in a cloud of sawdust – sanding, planing, smoothing until she thought the wood might disappear. At times like that, Sarah knew he was feeling the sudden, violent loss of his father and the long painful death of his mother. Sarah could offer him her love and understanding, but no one could take away the hurt of those early miseries.

*    *

Miguel ignored the "remembering" look on Sarah's face. He had gotten used to her storing up memories for two mothers. Without comment on her state of mind, he got to what was nagging his own curiosity. He'd not missed the meditative and handsome face she had sketched near an unfinished floor plan.

"Mom, where'd you go this morning?"

His change of topic surprised Sarah. "I went back to the church to retrieve my tape measure. Left it there last night." She hadn't intended to worry him but hadn't left a message about her plans either.

"That was a good excuse to learn the outcome of last night's meeting." he teased. "Who did you talk to – the church secretary?"

"No, the minister."

"Ah-hah! Did he finally make it to a meeting last night?"

"Yes, and he was a big help. The other time he missed the meeting because he was home with a sick child. That's hardly shirking . . . "

"Sick child probably likes to watch basketball."

"Miguel! That's not fair."

"Sorry, Mom. Nice guy?"

"Yup."

"Married, huh?"

"No . . . Miguel . . . "

"No? Sick kid but no wife. He tell you that?"

"No. The chairwoman of the committee . . . "

"Ah, she's the matchmaker."

"Matchmaker! Cut it Miguel. Jealousy doesn't look good on big guys."

Miguel was chagrined. "Sorry, Mom. I'm usually the one trying to match you up with someone nice. I just don't want it to be someone nice who's all religious and has six kids."

"It's three kids. End of topic, okay?"

"I'll back off." He threw his hands in the air. His capitulation was fake. The next moment he was following up on a hunch he needed to verify.

"Mom, after you got the measuring tape, even assuming that took an hour and a half, (what with his children to talk about and all) where else did you go this morning?"

Sarah shrugged her shoulders. "I thought I was the mother here."

"You were. But I'm the concerned son. You were out looking for Kevin again, weren't you?"

She picked up her pencil and began sketching carefully. "Yes, I was."

"Don't, Mom. Just don't go there."

Looking up from the drafting board, she felt the stubborn set to her jaw. "I do only safe looking, Miguel. Kevin may be dying out there. Like Bruce. I can't let that happen. I'm not going to give up on him just because he might be in some low-life hotel."

Miguel's frustration surfaced. "Let me visit the hotels and joints. You saw too much. You're his prime target. He has warned you often enough. The graffiti keeps reappearing."

"Miguel, I'm not sure that's Kevin who's been leaving all those hate messages. Kevin's just wanting me to prove I care enough to go after him. If I give up on him, that will only prove what he always believes about the people in his life. They don't care."

"Mom, with Kevin it's more complicated. He's not hoping you'll be stronger than his mother was. The alcohol habit is too far gone for your love to mean anything to him. He just wants to sell the drugs, buy his drink and drown in it."

"And I'm not going to let him." Sarah was defiant.

"You're not even his mother. He killed her."

Sarah rounded on him. "You don't know that for sure!"

"Everyone but the courts knew it before he came begging you to take him in."

"He was clean here for months. He was never violent. . . "

"Except that time you caught him with Akesha, trying to get her to sell her stereo for ten dollars."

"Yeah, that. But he got over it soon enough."

"Mom! You had to belt him in the mouth to get him to stop breaking things. And if I hadn't come in just then, no telling what he would have done to you . . .. He was out of control."

"One time. But that doesn't prove he would kill his own mother."

"The neighbors heard him fighting with her. Two hours later they found her dead, cut up and bled to death. He killed her because she used his stuff to get her own high."

"That's just street rumors. Nobody ever proved it."

"You want proof? The proof will be when he kills you for coming after him – trying to dry him out. I don't need proof. I want you safe, Mom." Miguel turned his frustration on himself – banging his thighs with balled fists. "Mama! Stay away from him."

Sarah's own anxiety made her blind to her son's. Worry and strain were written in the small lines around her mouth. She tried to explain her small hopes for Kevin's recovery. "He was doing so well – going to school. He had almost finished building that beautiful cabinet. And then he just leaves . . ."

"Face it, Mom. Alcohol and drugs have more power over him than you or I ever will."

She wrung her pencil, round and round in her fingers. "What could his father have written to him?"

"One letter and the guy goes back to gang life," Miguel said. "Not much commitment to sobriety there."

"Even now," she said, "he might be wanting out. But the drink keeps him there. If we could get him dry for a while…"

Fear crawled up Miguel's back, but he tried to control his voice, to sound reasonable. "Kevin went willingly. He saw the life you offered him, and he chose to go back."

"His disease took him back."

"Those scrawls on our wall were in his handwriting. It's him threatening to get you."

"That's just testing – do I really care enough?

"No! He means 'you stay away'. His threats are serious. Promise you'll let me look in the hotels and shelters."

"I don't …"

Fear stabbed his heart. "Mama, I can't lose you, too!" His voice came as one long wail.

Sarah's head jerked up. She'd finally heard it. When he was most afraid, he called her `Mama', as he had Teresa. She saw Miguel's fear in its starkest form. A father, a mother and then her – it would be too much for even a grown man. At twenty-three, grown as he might appear, he was a boy in need of an anchoring love. And right now, she was his anchor.

"I promise, Miguel." Her arms slid around him.

His tears, he hid in her shoulder. His fear, she could feel in the shudder of his swallowed sobs.

# CHAPTER TWENTY-THREE

Downstairs, the office door banged shut. The chimes rang once, then twice as the door banged again. Miguel and Sarah heard a scuffle and then a rush for the stairs. The sounds of laughter and shoving filled the stairwell.

Miguel straightened, rubbing his sleeve across his dark face. Sarah put an arm around his waist for a quick hug before they both walked to the hall.

All this noise could only mean one thing. Their sixteen-year-old apprentices, Jeff and Akesha, were still heavily into competition, racing home from track workout. Winner had the privilege of picking the afternoon snack. Loser got to bake it.

"That's no fair, you turkey! I won to the shop. You din't say nothin' 'bout to the kitchen!" Akesha was indignant.

"It's always t...to the k...kitchen. I ch...ch...choose applesauce c... cake."

"Applesauce cake? That takes about a hour just to bake."

Coming down the stairs, Sarah decided to inject an element of cooperation into this competitive spirit. "Jeff, since you like a snack that takes a long time to put together, why don't we all work on it?

Who would like to cream the butter, eggs and sugar? Good Akesha. And the dry ingredients, Jeff?"

Jeff's face showed signs of balking.

"Want to use the sifter, Jeff?" Sarah asked.

Miguel smiled to himself. His mom had Jeff now. For some reason the kid loved to watch things get powdered through the holes of the sifter.

"Sh...sh...sure," Jeff agreed.

Sarah turned to smile at her oldest boy. "And now, Miguel, how about your favorite butter cream frosting with a little vanilla?"

Miguel's smug feeling died. Butter cream frosting was his 'Achilles tooth'.

"Sure, Mom."

"Good. I'll heat the oven and fix the pan. This should take no time. We can study for an hour at the table and then celebrate with cake."

"What we celebratin', Sarah?" Akesha asked. Always a quick study.

Miguel saw Sarah raise an elfin brow and put a finger to her lips. "Wait – a surprise for during cake." She led her troops into the refrigerator and hauled out butter and eggs.

An hour later, Akesha took a beautiful cake out to cool and resettled into her calculus text while Miguel and Jeff worked over Jeff's algebra problems. Sarah drew up work schedules for her son and her two foster children-apprentices. All three had a vested interest in working hard for the firm of Rohann and Salvador. They were stockholders and shared in the annual profits along with Sarah and old Ernst Schumacher, the plasterer and stain glass artisan.

By the time the cake had cooled and was frosted, all homework had been finished. It took cajoling by Jeff to get Ernst out of his plaster rosettes and up to the second-floor kitchen for their celebration. When they were at last gathered in the kitchen, Akesha stood poised over the cake.

"Okay, Sarah. Better tell us what we 'bout to eat this cake for," Akesha said.

"Tell f...fast. I'm hungry," put in Jeff.

Sarah made a show of shuffling papers as if organizing a long speech. Jeff's hungry eyes fastened on the thick corner of frosting. Ernst scratched his plaster covered arms and looked at all those pages. He inched toward the door to return to the work that was now his addiction. Sarah stepped in front of him and looked him in the eye with such a happy mischief that he was stopped cold.

"Ernst, we got the job at the church."

Ernst blinked. "Coved ceilings?" he asked gruffly.

"Yep, and three stained glass windows."

"You're kiddin' me, Sarah."

"Not kidding, Ernst. And a plaster rosette around the light fixture."

The old man grabbed her in his arms. "Oh, honey! They want a rosette, too? That's somethin'!"

Ernst had not been part of the Jackson home plans or the Schreibens' kitchen remodel. For him, this signified how important he was to the whole company.

The kids climbed over each other to join the hug, yelling simultaneously. "A new church job! Oh, Sarah, you did it! Can I stay on the track team? I don't have to work at Joe's Chicken no more. We gonna be real builders."

Miguel stood by, amused at the noise his family could make when it was happy. He folded his arms and leaned like an indulgent papa against the kitchen counter. Akesha jumped up and down, hugging her foster brother, Jeff.

Miguel laughed. Jumping was Akesha.

He knew they'd been close to no job when he finished the Schreiben's kitchen. The job for the Jacksons was important, but it only brought in a little bit every month. Working on the church would allow Sarah to get acquainted with a whole new network of people who might want a garage or a new porch or any of the small jobs that would keep them afloat as a family and a company.

In today's celebration, Akesha's exuberant dance brought her to her big brother Miguel. She yanked him back from financial worries into a celebration of the future and twirled him around the kitchen until they reached Jeff. Jeff's eyes shown, he put out his arms and joined the crazy dance. Ernst stomped his feet and clapped a polka rhythm.

Sarah beamed. Her family had grown willy-nilly, but there was nothing haphazard about the love they shared.

When her grandfather had bought this building and moved into it, there had been six apartments on the upper two floors and businesses on the first floor. Grandfather's construction business had slowly taken over the lower floor. The six live-in tenants had been barely able to make the low rent payments, but Grandfather had kept them warmed and covered. Only death had taken some of his tenants from him.

Death had taken Miguel's father by gun fire in the bar two blocks away. Death had taken Miguel's mother more slowly, giving her a long painful time during which she convinced the state that Sarah should adopt Miguel. The state had sluggishly fought the idea because Sarah had been single and so young. The strong presence of grandfather had been a deciding factor, bringing Sarah her first son.

Finally, death had taken her gentle, watchful grandfather. Then, at thirty-one, Sarah's life had consisted of an old building, a nearly grown son, three aged tenants, a degree in engineering, a license to practice architectural design and a large loan from the small business administration.

The dancers cavorted past Sarah, nearly pulling her into their maelstrom.

"Mom, have you forgotten how to dance?" Miguel spun out of the trio and rested breathlessly against the kitchen counter.

"Not forgotten at all. This kitchen will only hold one set of whirling dervishes."

Akesha and Jeff had slowed down. Akesha grabbed Jeff's head under her arm, let out her big-hearted laugh and rubbed Jeff on the noggin. "Sarah's got two left feet like old Jeffie. It's inherited. Small kitchen's just an excuse."

"Le' g...go my head, you girl. We gonna eat c...cake now and I get the c...corner piece." Jeff pulled his head backwards from the circle of her arm and headed for the table.

Sarah served up a corner piece with all its glorious butter-cream frosting to Jeff and divided the rest of the cake for Ernst, Akesha, Miguel and herself. Before Ernst took his cake back to his workshop, he stopped by Sarah's chair. His hug and now his hand on her shoulder were as close to affection as he had come in years.

"You got floor plans for the church that I can study, Sarah?"

"Sure, filed under `John Wesley' in the blueprint drawers."

"I still gonna teach a stain-glass-making class for those three windows?"

"The committee is hoping you will."

His leathery face broke into a smile. "Good. They'll be good." Gruff as he seemed, there was nothing he did better than teach other people his art. Students and windows were his posterity.

And plaster. If he had his way, every home would have plaster gods and satyrs staring down at dinner guests and grape leaves encircling the chandelier and archways.

"I know they will be beautiful," said Sarah. "I can hardly wait to see them."

"Humm." He retreated to his taciturn mask and shuffled toward his shop.

She watched his slow movements and thought about his role in their family. When she had inherited this building, one of her tenants was a drunk named Ernst Schumacher. Occasionally he had been sober enough to make stained glass windows or do plaster work for her grandfather. Sarah convinced Ernst that he was essential to her company. She cajoled him into Alcoholics Anonymous and she joined Al-anon for families. There, she learned to stop propping up his habit. As she withdrew her enabling and excusing, he began to stand on his own. As the company succeeded, his part in it grew until Ernst knew he was important. The dying arts were making a comeback and with them came back the artist.

As her family trooped down to their jobs in the workshop, Sarah smiled after Ernst, unaware that her son was watching her. When everyone else was gone, she turned to the table to finish her piece of cake. Miguel leaned on the counter, deceptively nonchalant, picking his teeth.

"Mom? Have you ever known how to dance?"

"Sure. I think I learned the polka in gym class back in the Middle Ages. Why?" This line of thought was new from Miguel.

"Never saw you dance or even get dressed to go to a dance. Never saw you go out at all."

"Too busy building things. Nobody to go out with."

"That's a crock. I intercept enough of those phone calls from guys to know there are a lot of builders, plumbers and electricians who want your time and company."

"Yeah, well . . ."

"I used to think you turned 'em down because you were too busy being my Mom. Then I got to thinkin' about grandpa and how angry he got over those calls. So, for a while, I thought it was for him you didn't go out."

"Miguel, there wasn't anyone I wanted to date."

"How would you know? You never let yourself know any of them."

"Vibes, son. The wrong vibes."

"From them or from you?"

"Miguel! Bug off." She felt the red anger burning her face. He had never talked to her this way before.

His head dropped and then rose again defiantly. "I'm sorry Mom, but I think you ought to have a life that isn't all tied up in "doing" for us.

"I am perfectly happy with my life. Doing for you is a great pleasure."

"It isn't right for you to not be interested or have someone who wants to spend time with you."

"Why are you pushing this theme, Miguel? I thought I made it clear that I would find someone when I was ready."

"I don't know why I push this right now, except that you spent all morning with some preacher with three kids, and I think that's the most time you've spent alone with a man since I can remember."

Sarah was hot with embarrassment. How had he put it together that she might be interested in Abe Hallowell? She had said so little – evaded on purpose.

Miguel pushed on, propelled by his awareness of how improper such a topic was between a boy and his mother. "Mom, I don't mean that it was bad to spend time with this guy, but why some mealy-mouthed minister with a lot of holier than thou ideas?"

Suddenly Sarah saw the picture and could fathom Miguel's worry. "You mean why someone who would disapprove of you and the kids?"

"Sure. You wouldn't be happy with him after a while either . . ."

She covered her mouth to hold down the relief and laughter that swept through her. "First, son, he is not mealy-mouthed or holier than thou. Second, I am not involved with him the way the builders and electricians would like to be. Third, I'm not lonely. I don't need someone. That's a myth they feed you with your fairy tales."

"I don't believe that. I want someone, someday. That's why I keep . . ." He waved his hands to indicate a whole range of activities.

Sarah supplied the list. "You keep going out with Susan, Carol, Shannon, Maria, Louise. . . "

Miguel poked her in the shoulder. "I didn't start this conversation to hear about my problems."

"These are not problems. They are nice girls, most of them. It's just that you tend to tackle looking for the right person and I tend to wait. It's two different styles. I'll stick to mine, thanks."

"And this preacher?"

"Is not mealy mouthed. That's all you get."

"But why all morning?"

"Did I ask you why the movie with Carolyn was six hours long?"

"No, but. . . "

"Well then," she started.

"Butt out, huh?"

"Yup."

He raised his hands as if calling it quits and backed toward the door. His glance dropped to the near-empty bowl of buttercream frosting. He grabbed it up and exited with it under one arm. The forefinger of the other hand was already running around the insides looking for leftovers.

*    *

Sarah sat at the table, toying with her fork. Why had she spent all morning with Abe Hallowell? What was it about him that made her want to be in his company?

And was Miguel on the right track? Was it for grandfather that she had never dated, except a few times when she was at Princeton where grandfather need not know? Or was it the disinterest in each man that she had always told herself it was?

She knew the answer without having to dig very deeply. She had loved her grandfather. He had been hurt by her mother and grandmother. Sarah was not going to leave him, or ever give him cause to worry. She was not going to be just like the other women in his life. When he was alive, she had been afraid that dating would worry him.

After his death, what had she been afraid of?

She would think about that when she wasn't so busy. She picked up her plate and began cleaning the kitchen.

# CHAPTER TWENTY-FOUR

Late Wednesday afternoon, Abraham Hallowell hitched his tired leg into the fire station, looking for Bob Chappell. He rubbed his leg and thought about how ambling through town with Sarah seemed to wear it out faster than running at the high school track. He supposed it was the frequent standing in one place to study nature that caused the wear. Running was a whole different kind of exercise.

"Yo, Hallowell," Bob's voice boomed. "What's up?"

"I'm still looking for this kid," Abe said as he pointed to the photo of Kevin he'd hung on the stationhouse wall.

"That's the kid that young lady was looking for at the fire, no?"

"Yes, 'tis. Evidently, he was doing well, and then, back into alcohol once during the last year. Seemed okay again for four months or so. Then he gets a letter from his dad, who's in Sheridan for selling heroin and the kid disappears."

Bob shook his head, "That alcohol is bad to get off of. We've had a guy working here who had to take the time to get off and stay off. Couldn't hire him back because he never stayed off long enough to build trust."

"What I don't get," Abe said, "is that Kevin left pretty soon after celebrating Miss Rohann's birthday by giving her a set of wooden beads he'd made himself. A boy cares that much and the next thing, he takes off. That doesn't make sense."

"Letter from Sheridan?" Bob asked.

Abe nodded.

Bob said, "Does she know the content of that letter?"

"No."

"Kid cares about her. I bet it was a threat."

Abe stopped cold. Why had no one ... why hadn't he ever thought this clearly. "A threat against her."

"Yeah, maybe," Bob said. "I'd be following up on this down at the prison."

"Right."

"Reese knows the ropes. He'll help you."

"Thanks, Bob. I'm outta here."

Bob smiled, "Anything, pastor. And since you asked, no need for counseling at this station. Just little fires and toy collecting for Christmas going on here."

Abe shook his head. "Yes, I should've asked. But you don't look stressed enough to remind me."

"Find that kid, so I can stop worrying about you."

Abe laughed, "See you soon."

*    *

At the police station, Reese put in a call to a friend in the offices at Sheridan. Then he asked Abe to attend a training for the force.

"See is this trainer worth the money and are the guys ready to hear what he has to say about how to de-escalate a situation."

Later, Abe reported to Reese. "The guy has good, specific suggestions. Your fellows asked good questions, but there are two men who scoffed, sat in the back and then mimicked the trainer afterwards."

"Good to know. I want those two names."

"Officers Bailey and Clarence."

"Okay. I know what to do about that."

"Will it help them sluff off attitude? or just make them angry?"

"Our speaker gave me some role playing to do among the guys that will help separate the two of them and make them start thinking about why they might want to de-escalate for their own health as well as for the person on the street."

"I hope that works, but my experience in Beirut has been that soldiers or police who are ruthless or trigger happy have life-long reasons for dismissing the value of others."

"Yeah, and justifying every action with 'he started it' like some six-year-old. And I'll be watching for that."

"Will the union obstruct or help you?"

"New leaders. We'll see."

# CHAPTER TWENTY-FIVE

As Abe left the police station, he became aware that a blue Chevrolet followed him. The car was about nineteen eighties design and had no license plate. He remembered the two guys, Langren and something, who had once tried to sell heroin to Miguel.

Abe turned left. The blue car turned left. Right. And they turned right.

Finally, he rolled north to Alberta Street and turned left. They were still back there, two cars back, but always there. He pulled over near a guitar shop and locked his doors. They pulled ahead three cars, but then over to the curb. He sat there for a time, then pulled out his phone and called Reese.

"Hallowell?"

"Those two, Langren and ..."

"And Templeton. Where are they?"

"They followed me from the station. Now they pulled to the curb on Alberta and 30$^{th}$ just ahead of me. They're not getting out."

"Don't go to the church or anywhere else you want to be safe. Maybe stroll into a shop near there and see what they do."

"I'll go into the guitar shop called Fretworks."

"Right. I've got a black and white about ten blocks away. Let's see what happens when he cruises by slowly."

Abe got out and walked into the shop. The young man at the counter said, "Be with you in a minute."

Abe nodded and stood near the window, just far enough back not to be seen.

Minutes went by as he studied the sheet music options in a nearby rack and watched the blue Chev. The fellows in the car twisted around, trying to see into the shop, but the sun glanced off their car window, blinding the man on the passenger side.

That door began to open. A tall fellow got out, turned to slam the door, but saw the police car coming. He swung into the car and closed the door again.

The black and white slowed in front of the guitar store and inched past Abe's old Buick, then seemed to go even slower past the Chev.

The clerk came to Abe's side. "What can I get for you?"

Abe hoped he hadn't put this clerk in danger. He said, "I was hoping you had some trumpet music, but I see you are strictly guitars and lutes here."

"Yeah. Trumpet music . . . maybe Classical Vibes down on McLoughlin Boulevard."

Abe saw the black and white go around the block again, inching past the Chevy.

"Thanks," he said. "I played coronet as a kid. Thought maybe I'd try it again."

"Good idea," the man said. "Music can be a fun hobby." He glanced at Abe's arm and his mostly empty pocket. "You know you can have them put a trumpet together so that you can finger the notes with your left."

Abe really looked at the man this time. The man saw the trouble and gave a solution without embarrassment. Abe was impressed.

"Thanks," he said. "I'll see what I can do about that."

Just then, the Chev took off down the block.

"I'll look up Classical Vibes. I appreciate your idea."

He left the store and got into his car. He edged into the traffic, drove half a block and turned right. He waited only a couple of minutes when the Blue Chev drove past on Alberta. So, they had gone around the block and come back looking for him. He wasn't just paranoid.

But why follow him? He wondered. Did Langren and Templeton think he was a policeman? Or did they know he had a connection to Miguel and Sarah?

Next time he was at the police station, he would park and walk in and out the back door. But he also needed to talk a little more to Miguel about these two.

After ditching Langren and Templeton, Abe went to the Triangle Motel where the desk clerk, Don Alvarez, knew him.

Out front, he passed the patch of grass and playground equipment that had replaced six infrequently used parking spaces – another Crowd Funding effort by Deborah and her club at the high school.

He opened the office door.

"Hallowell," Don said, "What's up? Almost got that room ready for the Richardsons. Bringing up the kitchen pans and dishes from the storage today. Anybody else need housing?"

"Yes, in fact, but today I'm also looking for a missing kid."

"So, I heard. Pair-a-Dice Motel guy, Samuel, you know, he called asking about that kid. What's his name? Kevin?"

"Yes. Kevin. Reddish-blond hair, freckles, might be drinking. Here's a photo of him when he was well."

Don looked over the photo. "Heck, Abe, none of the guys in your motel network seem to have seen him."

"Well, I'm glad they're looking. By the way, I do have another family at the shelter that will need a room until an affordable apartment comes up. Probably won't have the funds for a while, but they are in the same family group that works together, so I'm thinking they'll be ready one of these days."

"Bring 'em on in. I've got a unit that's second floor, so no noisy kids, if you can help it."

"Aren't all kids noisy?" Abe asked, "And aren't they all fun, just to see how new ideas enter their heads and how they learn new things every day?"

"Entertainment isn't what most people want in their motel stay — well, I take that back. There's some that rent that way, but I try not to rent to that kind. If you can bring me a family, I'd rather them than that other kind."

"Okay, Don. The Richardsons have two small ones. I'll pick them up from the shelter and bring them by Friday afternoon. And the way the high school kids are raising funds, you might want to save the upstairs set of rooms as well."

"What about apartments?"

Abe shook his head. "Getting harder and harder to find."

"Don't I know. Motel business is turning into long-term rental and that's pretty expensive for the renters."

"Wouldn't your owner rather have a stable clientele?"

"Lives in Las Vegas. What's he know about stable?" Don said.

Abe waved toward the swings. "I bet he knows nothing about the playground either."

"Keeping that for a pleasant surprise if he ever visits. So far, he only visits his bank statements."

"Good. See you Friday afternoon. Keep an eye out for Kevin."

"Will do."

*    *

On Friday, at the shelter, the manager, Everett Ranson, had not seen Kevin, but knew who he was, because months before, Sarah and Miguel had picked him up from the shelter and taken him to rehab.

"That kid has had all kinds of chances to make good. I don't know why he'd fall back into the habit."

"It may not be the habit," Abe said. "The timing makes it look like something threatened him."

"Well, I hope he's safe, then," Everett said, "I'll call the Richardsons down. They'll be mighty glad you've found a place where they can be together."

The family came tumbling into the shelter living room with several shelter inhabitants following them to give one last hug to the toddlers and their mom and dad.

Frank Richardson said, "I got a job at Wendy's, just janitor at night, but better than nothing."

Abe smiled. "That's great. Which Wendy's is this?"

"Northeast Sandy. I take the number ten bus from that motel you found."

Abe nodded. That's great. Got a bus pass still?"

"Yes, and so does Mary. She's signing up to assist in day care if the kids can be there with her."

"I hope that comes through. Meanwhile, we'll be hunting an apartment. The motel will be sort of crowded."

Mary said, "As long as we're together, motel-schmotel."

Abe lifted one of the twins. Frank lifted the other. And each of the adults plus Everett carried a suitcase out to the car.

"Oh," Mary said, looking through the window, "Car seats."

"Yes," Abe said. "Gift from a family whose kids outgrew them. We can store them in my garage for whenever we need them."

"That's really nice," she said, and Abe could see she was about to cry.

Frank put an arm around her and said, "People do what they can . . . most people. We'll make it yet, Mary."

She turned into her husband's arms, hugging him and the twin he held. "I know. It's just sometimes . . ."

"It sure is," Frank said. "Let's plug these little guys into the car seats and get on the road."

# CHAPTER TWENTY-SIX

Coming out of the motel and ready to head for the church, Abe noticed a chill in the air.

"Maybe some rain coming for those daffodils of Sarah's," he thought. He hadn't had time to think about Sarah or his unrealistic fantasies since early this morning. He reached in the back and grabbed his corduroy jacket. Throwing it on, he noticed an extra weight to it.

He thrust his right arm in his pocket and felt the solid square of Sarah's forgotten measuring tape. A slow smile invaded his eyes and then his whole face. This tape was good for at least one more visit with the mysterious Miss Sarah Rohann. Much as he ought to fight it, he knew he wanted that one more time. Next, he would seek her on her own turf.

Then he would stop this foolishness and get back to his lonely reality. A woman like Sarah needed a whole man. She deserved better than the Reverend Abe Hallowell.

His late afternoon had been set aside for editing his sermon. Ignoring the sermon, he turned the car north and headed into the seedier part of town, watching all the way for that blue Chevrolet.

Abe had her address memorized. Yesterday morning he had doodled over and over the street name as much as a hundred times while he tried vainly to compose a letter that sounded business-like and cool.

Atfalati Street was definitely an interesting place for such an urbane woman. He wondered how she fit in there. He was pretty sure her truck would look comfortable.

Abe had long ago recognized that Portland's slums did not look like the bomb targets of Beirut or the tenements which had surrounded his hospital in New York, yet plenty of misery existed within their confines. Jobs with unreasonably low pay and no hopes held the same bitterness no matter how old or broken the buildings in which the poor sheltered.

There was enough bitterness to lure the young toward violence and to make their grandmothers its victims. Yet, every once in a while, one could spot a ray of hope – The Knott Street Community Center, the Unthank Park Concerts, the Saturday School, The Reading Tree school in the park and Father Lee Owen Stone Preschool – they each represented a way this community was helping itself, reaching out and offering hope.

And with hope came pride. A house or two with new paint in isolated blocks, a repaired porch, a small business that answered the community's real needs for groceries or music fun – these were good signs, as long as the paint didn't signal wholesale gentrification.

Abe saw one of those good signs the moment he turned the corner of Atfalati Street and Eighteenth Avenue. A three-story building distinguished from the rest of the block by its neatly maintained exterior. The dark tan was trimmed in light blue. Very carefully outlined doors and windows hung straight within their frames. Blue numbers near the garage door showed that this was Sarah's home.

Abe pulled over to the curb and looked for the battered truck as he got out of the car. It was not in sight, but Abe decided to knock on the office door anyway. He waited for some time and was about to turn away when the door opened. A handsome, dark man, covered with a sawdust film, stared out at Abe.

Miguel.

"Yes? May I help you?"

This young man has grown up, Abe thought. His mustache and longer hair made it hard to pinpoint his age, but Miguel's agile youthfulness made Abe uncomfortable.

"I'm looking for Miss Rohann."

Miguel opened the door a little wider, more to study Abe than to ask him in. "What's up, priest?"

"Minister."

"Oh yeah. The kids. I forgot."

Abe was disconcerted by the direction of the conversation, if that's what it could be called. "Is Miss Rohann here?

"No actually, she's out at the moment. May I help you?"

He had not thought what he would do if Sarah were out. Scrambling quickly, he blurted. "May I borrow some paper and leave her a message?"

"Sure. Come on into the office." This time the door was opened wide. Miguel stepped back.

The office Abe entered was immaculate. Perhaps to keep it that way, the man crossed quickly to the door which led to the workshop and closed it before he rummaged in the desk for a sheet of paper. Hanging on the wall over the desk Abe noticed an old hand axe, much too long in the handle for Sarah, but perhaps the right size for the young man.

"Is that your priest smacking axe, Miguel?"

The man glanced up, "Only bad priests."

Abe took a deep breath so as not to reply in kind. "Well, do I need to dodge?"

"Can't tell yet. Sorry."

"It's all right. All preachers look alike, I suppose – priest, minister . . ." He shrugged in mock red-neck fashion.

To his credit, Miguel laughed. "I may be wrong about you, but that remains to be seen.?"

"Meanwhile, you'll stick with your prejudices, eh?"

"Hard to get rid of them overnight," Miguel said. "Especially when there's real experience to back them up."

Abe studied Miguel's back. "I'm sorry you've had such experiences. I'm afraid I have seen that kind of righteousness, and its destruction."

Miguel turned and looked directly at Abe for the first time. "You can't know . . ."

"No," Abe said. "I don't pretend to know what has hurt you. I only know what has hurt my family."

Miguel glanced down at the paper in his hand and said, "But you're one of them."

"Yes. I am one of them because, like many priests and pastors, I hope to be one who helps and not one who wields God like a sword."

"Sure, man." Miguel handed him the paper. His voice was still cold.

Abe added somewhat grudgingly, "She speaks very highly of you."

An awkward silence lay between them for a moment before Abe broke it.

"By the way, you can help me understand something. I was followed from the police station by those two crooks who have a grudge against you."

"White guys?"

"Yep."

"Langren and Templeton."

Abe asked, "Are there more guys who have a grudge against you?"

"No doubt there are. What did you do about them?"

"I evaded, but they stuck until a police car passed them twice. Then they went around the block again, looking for me, I think. But I had dodged them up a side street."

Miguel frowned. "They see you coming from the police station, right?"

"They did."

"I hope they are following you because they think you are police."

"That's what I'm hoping, too. Is there any way they know your company is working at my church?"

Miguel looked thoughtful. He shook his head. "I don't think they could know yet. I've been dismissing them as useless."

"Yes, but we don't want them near Akesha, or Jeff, or Sarah."

"Right," Miguel said.

"Well, I'll write and be on my way to work. Abe bent over the desk and drew a pen from his right shirt pocket. Miguel retreated to lean against the closed door to the workshop.

When the brief note was finished, Abe folded it awkwardly and reluctantly fished out the measuring tape to lay on top of it. Just to fill the emptiness before he reached the door, he made idle conversation.

"The axe. Is it very old?"

"Yes. Grandfather Rohann. He brought it from the old country."

"He must have been a very big man."

"The biggest, and the best."

Abe let that sink in – a gratuitous comparison between Sarah's grandfather and any other man. Finally, he said, "Well, the best to you, Miguel."

* *

In the office, Miguel Salvador stalked toward the desk, but drew his hand back from the note at the last minute. "Damn preacher! Probably just as judgmental as all of them. 'God's will be done. If your father was in the tavern fighting, what could he expect?'"

Miguel spit. " 'Your mother would smoke, you know. It's God's way with sinners.' "

He hit the desk with his two fists. "Sarah is worth three of you, and so was the mother I had before her. Sin or no Sin, she didn't deserve to die like that and be told that God wanted it. Take your judgements to hell with you."

He hit the desk once more and swiped the note and the tape to the floor before he pounded out of the building. He turned right and walked past Abe's old Buick without ever seeing anything but his own long pent-up anger at those who had twisted his mother's trusting heart and made her die in fear.

# CHAPTER TWENTY-SEVEN

"**B**ob!" Abe called as he entered the fire station.

"Yup?" Bob came out from under the hood of engine 3, asking, "Whatcha got?"

"You met Frank Richardson, right?"

"Sure did. Like the man."

"Well, he got into the training for the fire department, but to earn money he's gotten a job as janitor at Wendy's"

"So, he's doing both?"

Abe nodded. "He is. So, I hoped maybe ..."

"I know what you hope," Bob said. "Bring him on over. I've got plenty to teach him while he learns to clean up these behemoths and this station house. He working at night?"

"He is. But day would be better if he can get the late afternoons to go to his classes."

"Better for me, too," Bob said. "Let's start today."

"Benefits?" Abe asked.

"Firemen and apprentice firemen get benefits. Union package."

"Great. I've got Frank in my car."

"Boy, you take a lot for granted."

"No, I know Bob Chappell and I know what he'll do for a man."

Bob shook his head and laughed. "Just bring him in."

*     *

At the SUN Daycare, Abe filled out the forms to pay for two small children. The cost was halved by the fact that even before Abe showed up, LaShanda Schmidt, the SUN director had decided to hire Mary Richardson.

"Abe you can't afford this,' LaShanda said.

"It's not me." He pointed at the line for the source. "The funds are coming from a savings account started for the families in the self-support group. The families figured out that the biggest obstacle to getting a job was that somebody needed to care for the kids. So, they started saving for that need."

"Anybody else contribute to this fund? It's quite an expense. Your group has five kids in here to date. And now it will be seven."

"Yes, the alliance of churches in the neighborhood contributes every month – matches what the families contribute."

"Brother, have you been busy!"

"Not just me. Henry Frazier's church, Jason Halverson's company, which goes through his church funds, the Rose Villa Presbyterian Foundation .... A lot of people contribute a little to support this fund."

"Well, we appreciate them. These kids are really picking up the skills and the attitude. It helps us deal with the children who come feeling unloved. Your kids feel the love right from the get-go."

Abe smiled and signed the bottom of the form. "Shanda, I can't tell you how happy I am that you're hiring Mary. She's patient, kind and persistent."

"She showed that in her child-care classes from the very first day." LaShanda said. "Her teachers at the community college really liked her, wrote great letters for her."

*     *

Later that day, Abe entered the police precinct, unsure whether he had the energy to help anyone besides himself. He desperately needed sleep.

But Captain Reese greeted him from way down the hall.

"Saw your car drive into the back lot. Come to my office. Got news."

Abe walked down in a daze, trying to think what news Reese might have for him.

Reese closed the office door.

"That kid, Kevin?"

"Yeah?" Abe stiffened with fear for Kevin.

"His dad escaped. Two days before that house fire."

"The man leaving the burning house ..." Abe started.

"Probably Kevin's dad," Reese finished.

"Kevin left because of the letter," Abe said. "He knew his dad had escaped."

"So, the easy answer is he left to work with his dad again," Reese said.

Abe started to talk but Reese held up his hand to stop and continued. "But there may be other possible answers, I get it."

"And that would help explain the graffiti – Kevin and his dad trying to scare Sarah away from looking. But she and Miguel ..."

"And you," added Reese.

"Keep looking anyway," Abe finished.

"So, Sarah's family is in danger," Reese said. "She said he saw her at the attic window after he set off the fire. Can you get her to leave town for a while?"

"I don't know. They depend on being in town to finish work they do, and the kids go to school. Let me think about this."

"Better think fast, that old man is a big danger, probably Kevin is as well."

Abe said, "Reese, how about a security detail?"

"Too few guys here to sit and wait for action. You'd have to contract with a firm. Better to deal with people you know."

"Okay. I'll tell the family, but first I need to get Peter and make a phone call to the bank."

# CHAPTER TWENTY-EIGHT

A be held the phone tightly to his good ear in order to drown out
the lawn mower at the parsonage next door. He didn't want to stop
Samuel Downs from doing his assigned house chores.

"Sarah, I've important things to talk to you about. Can you meet
me at my house? I've got kids coming home from school."

She said, "Can I bring Miguel? He's . . ."

Abe heard the long hesitation and decided to make it easy on her.
"I know what he is, and I know there's probably a reason. Bring him
along. Here's my address."

\* \*

Abe saw that Sarah and Miguel were already on the porch when he
drove up with Peter. Miguel stomped on the old ramp watching it
wiggle while Sarah ran down the stairs to help get Peter's wheelchair
set up.

At that moment, Dick drove up behind Abe. His van side door
opened, and Andy drove his wheelchair onto the van lift. Deborah,
behind him, locked the wheels and flipped the leashes into place to
hold Andy's chair as it rode down.

Abe watched Miguel stand up and stare at this process. Deborah didn't seem to be doing anything more than taking care of business, but Miguel was a frozen iceberg in Pete and Andy's way on the ramp to the house. Abe got out to see what caused the traffic jam on the ramp.

Andy stopped. Sarah stopped. They all watched Deborah bring back the wheelchair lift and get herself out of the back of the van.

*     *

Inside the driver's side, Dick watched the apparent freeze frame in front of his window.

"What's going on, Deb?" he asked.

She looked up and saw the crowd waiting to get on the ramp and said, "No idea. I'm almost down. Want to bring the lift back up while I figure out what's the problem?"

"No. I'm coming out too." Dick checked his emergency brake again and turned off the motor.

Deb rolled around back and cranked down his wheelchair from the open back end.

Abe took over, pushed it around to Dick's door, where he helped Dick into the chair.

"Somebody should design a completely accessible van," Dick grunted as he straightened his clothes and himself. "Why don't they assume a driver as well as passengers with disabilities?"

Abe said, "I think you know that's got to do with probabilities."

"Yeah," Dick muttered. "We're an improbable bunch all right. Now what's going on at the front door?"

Dick watched as Deborah approached what appeared to be a dumbfounded young man who blocked the way to the house.

Dick could see the cause and the emotions, right off.

Deborah looked up at the young man and said, "Step aside, sir, or you'll be run over."

Miguel said, "Ping pong."

Deb stopped. "Yeah. So what?"

"You beat everybody at the tournament."

"Did I beat you?"

"Wasn't there for ping pong, but the guys said I should come from the basketball court and see this. See you."

Andy said, "You blocking the path to tell her that?"

Peter said, "Have to pee."

"Oh," Miguel said. "Sorry." He jumped over the rail to get out of their way.

Abe chuckled and pushed Pete up the ramp and into the house. Sarah followed him, but Dick stayed outside to watch the next moments.

Deborah said, "Off the ramp and into the daffodils."

"Oh, sorry." Miguel tried to take one long step out of the garden. He succeeded in skidding on the mud at the edge of the grass. He righted himself quickly, but not before he had mud on his left thigh.

Deborah said, "Sorry. I left the sprinklers on the long cycle. Bad for walking around and probably not good for the grass either."

Dick watched Miguel approach her, gingerly. He didn't seem to know Dick was there, only had eyes for Deborah.

Miguel said, "You had such fun that day, but not rubbing it into anybody. You kept telling them what they did well. You enjoyed the other players. You . . ."

"Hi," she said. "I'm Deborah."

"Um … I'm Miguel Salvador."

"Oh, Rohann and Salvador," she said.

"Yes. Cabinet maker."

"And basketball player."

"Well, actually, just a hoop lobber. Play for fun."

"That's the only way to play anything."

Dick decided to cough before the two of them completely forgot where they were.

They looked up, both startled.

"I'm Dick Street," he said. "Deborah's occasional sparring partner. Want to see the bruises?"

Deborah laughed. If she hadn't, Dick was pretty sure the guy would have taken him seriously.

The guy smiled, a tentative sort of, maybe-that-was-funny sort of smile and turned back to Deb. "You spar?"

Deb glanced at Dick and winked. "Ping pong only. Why don't we all go into the house?"

"That ramp is shit," Miguel said.

"Yep. But not a one of us wields a saw and hammer," Deb said. "Gotta use this one or the even worse ramp at the back door."

\*   \*

Inside the house, Abe had already taken Pete to the bathroom and gotten Andy and Pete an after-school snack of Tillamook Mudslide ice-cream. He was in the process of dishing up for Deborah, Miguel, Sarah, Dick and any other folks who walked in the door.

Sarah handed out the bowls to those that Abe named for her.

Dick said, "Abe, is this a meeting I should be in on?"

"Yes, in fact, come to think of it. We're all going to need to know what I just found out from Captain Reese."

"Okay," Sarah said, "We should all sit and pay attention." She glanced at Miguel who was still hovering near Deborah's wheelchair. "Sit, gang," she said.

Miguel leaned on a counter, which moved a little and distracted him. Sarah glanced at him again and shook her head.

He leaned on the refrigerator instead.

Pete said,

"Information coming.

We gonna need to sit.

Half of us sit anyway,

so, the rest gonna have to shift

For Themselves.

Please pardon all our wobbly things.

Our chairs were made by elves."

Abe smiled at Pete and said, "Thank you for the poetry, Peter. Now to the news. Captain Reese has told me that two days before you found Bruce and got out of the fire, Kevin's dad had escaped from Sheridan. How he did that, I don't know, but it puts a whole different perspective on why Kevin disappeared so soon after the letter. It also means that there is a different form of danger for your family, and you need to know about that."

Sarah's eyes had grown wide. "He threatened Kevin."

Miguel said, "Kevin rejoined his father's business."

Abe studied his children and decided they ought to hear this too, since he had a plan that might make them targets of Kevin or his dad as well.

"Why," he asked Sarah, "Do you think he threatened and didn't just ask Kevin to rejoin him?"

It was Miguel who broke in. "He never said anything bad about his dad, even though his dad beat him. His dad did that so much that Kevin always feared me and even Ernst. He thought all men beat kids."

Abe wished he'd sent Andy and Pete to their room, but it was too late. Andy already had his head bent over, trying hard not to look like he was crying.

Miguel caught on fast. He knelt a foot away from Andy's chair. "I'm sorry . . ."

"Andy," Deborah supplied.

"I'm sorry, Andy," Miguel said. "I never touched Kevin and Ernst wouldn't hurt anything."

Andy looked up at him. "My Daddy Abe doesn't beat anybody."

"I know," Miguel said. "I know." He reached out a hand and Andy flopped his hand toward Miguel's. Miguel held it a moment and said, "You're safe with me, too."

"Yes," Andy said. "But your Kevin. How can he be safe?"

Miguel said, "I have to say, I don't know what to think about Kevin. He always went along with what his dad told him, so I'm thinking he's been pulled back into all that. We need a plan to keep Sarah safe and find Kevin and his dad."

Abe watched this interchange, and he noticed that Deborah also watched, and she seemed amazed. Nobody got through to Andy on this wavelength except Peter. Miguel's connection with Andy was amazing.

But something … some contact was being made between Miguel and Deborah, and Abe wasn't sure he approved. Miguel was older than Deb. He was at least four years older, and that made Abe very nervous.

He plunged on into the plan.

"I have an idea," he said. "I talked to Reese about protection for your family, Sarah. He said we could hire security contractors, but it would be better to rely on people we know. Well, I suspect your plumbers, your electricians and your concrete guys are a better protection than any contracted security firm."

"Yes, they are," Miguel said, "But we don't have them every day, just on days we're working them."

"Here's my proposal," Abe said. "As Miguel has noticed," he glanced at Peter, "and Peter has so eloquently put into verse, our house needs help."

"It needed help when you bought it," Andy said.

"Yes, it did."

"That's what made it affordable," Sarah added. "So, what's the plan?"

"And what's the house got to do with protecting Sarah?" Miguel asked.

"Well, I hope it's a plan that will help protect all of you. I went to the African American Cooperative Bank last month, with a proposal which they approved today."

"Last month?" Miguel asked. "We didn't know you last month."

"Right. And last month, I didn't know who I would ask to take on this job, but it seems to me, the more you are around plumbers, electricians and all those contractors I met at the hospital, the safer you all will be."

Sarah stood up. "No."

Abe stared at her. "No? I know you have this house in Southwest, and the Jackson home, and the church project, but . . ."

"It's not that. It's Andy and Peter and Deborah. We're not bringing our problems to them."

Abe smiled, "Thank you. I appreciate that you saw that problem. The second part of the plan is that Arthur Charles has offered to take our tribe into his house and he's hiring help for us while we're there."

She sat down. "If we're here and you're at Arthur's home, we can be safer."

Miguel interrupted, "Safer until Kevin's dad finds us."

"Which I hope will take quite a while," Abe said.

Sarah said, "And I appreciate that you want us to be safe."

"And I want that ramp to be safer," Miguel added.

"Me, too," Peter said.

"But," Sarah said, "Andy is right. Kevin is still out there with that dangerous man."

Miguel said, "Mom, here's what I know. I've got Booky Kerns and our grocer, Muhammed, looking for Kevin. You know Kerns has this network of book lovers. He's taken the photo to all of them. And Muhammed goes to worship and to all these immigrant groups."

Miguel glance at Abe and continued, "I've been everywhere, and most of the places I go, Abe has been there before me. He has some sort of network of motel people, park workers, street people, shop people, street news vendors and police on the lookout for Kevin. If Kevin can be found, almost the whole town is looking for him."

Andy glanced up at Abe with a new openness in his eyes. "You did all that, Dad?"

Abe sat down next to him. "I tried. We haven't found him yet."

"That's somethin'," Andy said. "But maybe Miguel is right. Maybe he doesn't want to be found. Maybe he's trying to get his dad to love him."

Everyone in the room stood in silence, each one thinking what it would be like for Andy to want his dad to love him.

After a long moment, Deborah said, "So, Dad, how about if you and Sarah and Miguel go through this house and figure out how to spend that money the bank is loaning us. Pete and Andy and I will make dinner for everybody."

"Plan for three more," Miguel said. "I need to go get my brother and sister from track practice and our plasterer from the office. Mom, you and Abe make a list of repairs. We can go over it later tonight."

Dick interrupted all the planning. "How are you and your family going to be safe at night? If you're at home, isn't that where he'll be most likely to get at you?"

Abe nodded and said to Miguel, "Can't this be your night place and we'll all be at Arthurs's while we hope to flush out this guy?"

Sarah looked flustered, "Wow, I guess we can plan that."

Miguel said, "Akesha, Jeff and I will do some packing and then come back with clothes and tools. We'll have to shovel Ernst out of his plaster work, but we'll do it. Don't worry, Mom. We'll figure this out."

Abe smiled and said, "Tell him we want plaster gargoyles in the ping-pong room."

Even Miguel laughed at that one. Then he rattled the keys out of his pocket and strode toward the door.

He turned and said, "One hitch in this plan. Abe has been followed by those two who tried to sell me heroin. They've got a vendetta against me, and maybe also against Abe because he comes out of the police station all the time."

Abe said, "I'm going to be going in and out the back and parking well away from the station. I'm hoping they followed me because I seem to be police, but there could be a connection to you."

"So," Sarah said. "You park as far back in Arthur's driveway each night as possible, and you take different routes to pick up Peter."

Dick said, "Just in case, I'm going to roll to the front and repark the van a block away. I'll lock the van, hoping I can eat dinner here."

"Good idea, Dick," Sarah said.

"You sure can," Deb said. "I'll get your wheelchair in and out of the van and then we can wheel back. Want to call your roomies and tell them you're not coming home until about eight or nine?"

Dick said, "Sure thing, boss. Then you can put me in charge of shelling the beans or something."

Andy said, "Beans. Yech."

# CHAPTER TWENTY-NINE

By the end of dinner, Abe felt certain that Miguel had fallen in love with Deborah when he had watched her win the ping-pong tournament. And Abe wasn't too happy about that.

Deborah wasn't going to be eighteen for another three months. She needed to go to college next year, not be in love.

The rest of the family had had a wonderful time eating around the dressed-up ping-pong table. Andy went quiet every once in a while, watching Jeff and Akesha talk about track practice.

And frequently, Andy glanced at Abe as if he'd found a new person inside a known person.

Abe noticed this change in Andy, but he also noticed a quiet calm about Sarah.

Toward the end of dinner, the kids cleared the table. Dick said he'd take the family to Arthur's in a half hour and then get on home.

Miguel and Dick walked and rolled out to the van, getting acquainted. They brought the van back to the driveway.

Inside the house, the ping-pong table was revealed. Deborah began teaching the rules to Jeff and Akesha while Peter and Andy played a game of UNO in the den.

Sarah took Abe's arm and pulled him into the living room.

"I hope you'll stay here, tonight," Abe said. "Art is expecting us."

She sat a moment and then she said, "Abe, I can't thank you enough for how you've been looking for Kevin, setting all these people on that problem."

"You've got the contractors looking. I've got my network. I sure hope we find him before anything . . ."

She put her hand on his. "Thank you," she said simply. "And for being patient with Miguel."

He smiled, but then he said, "Deborah is only seventeen."

Sarah nodded. "I think Miguel knows that, Abe. And Miguel is always careful of others. But she is a gem of a girl, isn't she?"

Abe nodded. "Always was. Her family loves her. Her county doesn't have enough medical service for her, but her parents come here when they can. They miss her a lot."

"I bet they do. Now, let's make a tentative budget and then you get your kids to Art's for bedtime."

He nodded. "I changed all the sheets this morning."

She laughed. "We could have done that."

He glanced at her hand on his arm. "I wanted it perfect for you."

"Thank you." Then she removed her hand and got out paper and pencil with their list of changes to make.

\* \*

Outside, Miguel sat on the running board of the van next to Dick's wheelchair.

Dick said, "Abe showed me photos of the work you and Sarah have done, and of the kitchen at the Jackson house. Pretty impressive."

"Thanks. It's work I really enjoy. I hear you're going to Reed College."

"Yes, Math and Physics. I wanted to be an environmental studies major, but..." he slapped his knees. "Easier to push a pencil than a wheelchair."

Miguel nodded. "I guess we all have to figure what we can do and set new goals based on dreams mixed with reality."

"Sure do. By the way, Deborah's eighteenth birthday is late next summer."

Miguel smiled and said, "Are you warning me that she is under-age?"

"Yeah. Guess I am. But also that she has a birthday coming and besides that a scholarship to the University of Oregon."

"Wow. That's great for her." Then Miguel looked Dick in the eye. "How do you feel about her?"

"Greatest little sister a guy can have," Dick said. "My family is down in Corvallis. Big brother, little brother. But Deb has filled in that sister role for me, and for Peter and Andy, too."

"You seem to be part of this family, too."

"You're right. Abe's only been in town for about three years, but he's great and his foster kids are pretty wonderful. I've also got a physics teacher and his wife, good friends of Abe's and mine."

"How did you get to know them all?"

Dick looked back toward the house, where warm light shown from the dining room and kitchen. "Well Abe and my physics teacher are good at solving problems – really creative. That's what gives him this network you found."

"What problems has he solved for you?"

"He and Dr. James, that's my physics professor, they went in together with my folks to buy this van. I deliver Deb and Andy to high school. I take students at Reed on field trips, and usually they are field trips where there's wheelchair access – out to the lighthouse, up to Mount Hood. It's given me this whole new life."

"You're the driver and everyone needs you, eh?"

"Something like that. Meanwhile, I can get to my physics classes and to concerts and out on dates."

"Dates? Man, that *is* a whole new life."

Dick laughed. "Not easy to get into some restaurants and many movie houses are a bust, but I can find places to go."

"Well, let's change that, about the movie houses and restaurants." Miguel said.

"You're starting here," Dick waved at the rickety ramp behind them. "Boy, do they need it. Abe Hallowell can barely afford the utilities and the mortgage. It'll be great to be able to get Andy into the bathroom on his own steam. A big improvement."

*    *

After Abe and his family left in Dick's van, Sarah's family settled down.

Miguel sat with Sarah in the living room. "I locked the offices up, checked the fire-escape door. Left lights on timers and doubled-locked the garage door."

"Thank you, Miguel. I love our house, but it has become a target."

Miguel shrugged. "Let's see that list and the draft budget for this house," he said.

"Miguel?" Sarah said, her voice tentative.

"Yes?"

"What have we learned today?"

"I've been learning it the last two weeks. That guy . . ."

"Abe," she said.

"He's not like the priest at all."

"True. Anything else?"

"I'm beginning to think I owe Kevin an apology, and I hope we find him safe and soon."

"Me, too. And thank you, Miguel, for looking for him, even when you thought it was not worth the effort. You made the effort."

"Mom, I hope he's still out there to find. I think his dad threatened you, Mom. That makes the most sense. He left to keep you safe."

She took a deep breath and nodded. After a moment she said, "Now here's the list and the budget."

# CHAPTER THIRTY

Abe stood in the upper hallway of his church and watched the construction crew put up sheets of plastic to contain dust. Demolition soon would rip out a wall on three floors, so that the elevator framing, now installed outside the building, would have access to the basement fellowship hall as well as the main floor and this second floor. A hole had been excavated, and concrete poured for the entry into the basement and beneath that a small room for elevator motor and gear.

Thank goodness the western conference of the Methodist churches had money to loan for such renovations. The speed at which it became available had astounded him until he realized the Bishop knew the work of Rohann and Salvador from other congregations in the Northwest.

"Best in the business," he'd said. "Careful, thoughtful and efficient."

So, then he knew that Sarah was famous. It appalled him that he'd leaned on her to do his house. There must have been some less intrusive way to keep her safe from Kevin and his father, but he didn't have a good idea how to undo that rudeness.

Sarah had planned this elevator to be the first part of the project so that the elevator would become a useful tool for the rest of the renovation on the second floor. Equipment, sheetrock, lumber, everything would come up in the elevator.

However, some work had already begun in the space where the chapel would be. Every evening after track practice and dinner, Akesha and Jeff had been whacking down the wall between the small kitchen and the chapel space. Smashing things seemed to give them a great pleasure.

In place of that wall there would be a half wall with a countertop and a pull-down shutter to keep the view of kitchen clutter out of worship. When the shutter pulled up, the room became a community playroom with an invitation to share bread.

"Share bread?" Akesha had asked the first time Abe put the sharing in Biblical terms. She had laughed and "Huh-uh! We're gonna share Tostitos and salsa here."

Abe knew she was joshing him, and he loved it. After the first two days here, she felt as comfortable joking with him as she did with Sarah and Miguel.

Jeff had not yet come out of his shell, possibly because around Abe, his stutter grew worse.

Today, Abe saw that Jeff had gotten up on a wobbly ladder so he could whack away at plaster in the center of the ceiling. Abe strode into the demolition area and put his foot on the bottom of the ladder and his hand and arm on the sides.

"Where's this ladder come from?" Abe asked.

"You…You're ba . . . basement," Jeff said.

"My basement?"

"Ch. . . church ba . . .basement."

"Well, this one's headed for the trash. Too shaky. Want to help me find a better one?"

"Sh …sh . . . Sure."

"Good. Come on down, Jeff. Let's go hunting."

Miguel said, "Okay hunters, could you take this one to Sarah's truck and bring up the six-foot ladder she's got under that lid?

We'll take this to a recycling place later after we fill the truck with demo debris."

Jeff took off his eye protection goggles and lifted one end of the ladder. Abe reached down with his left hand and lifted the other. Jeff glanced at the arm in Abe's pocket and said, "I lead down the stairs."

He turned around to lead and had begun walking toward the stairs by the time Abe realized two things. One, Jeff had spoken as clearly as anyone, and two, Jeff had realized Abe needed guidance since he couldn't grab both the ladder and the stair rail.

Jeff was sixteen, Abe knew. He'd just given a whale more attention to another human's need than Abe expected from a boy. Impressive.

Abe used the wall as a help all the way down and then wished there were a wall next to the twelve outside stairs leading to the truck, because there, Jeff showed his age by hustling down the steps. Abe hustled right after him, and, at the bottom, dropped his end of the ladder to grab his right leg.

Jeff dropped his end and ran back. "I'm sor...sor...sorry."

Abe stood up, put his hand on Jeff's shoulder. "You were great, Jeff. The leg is a bummer. Thanks for leading on the steps. That helped a lot."

Jeff looked at Abe carefully, decided he meant it, and then said, "Wooden ladders are heavy."

"Yes, they are. Let's hope Sarah has an aluminum one in the truck."

Jeff smiled. "She does."

Great, thought Abe. Not a stutter in sight.

"Well, let's get that one upstairs so you can whack at the ceiling. Is that where Ernst is going to raise the roof?"

Jeff laughed. "Raise the ceiling. Make it look like a cathee ...thee ...cathedral."

"Fool the mind, if not the eye," Abe said, quoting Ernst, and they both laughed.

"Her car is in the lot behind the ch . . . church, so Keh . . . Kevin's . . ." Jeff waved, a gesture that symbolized the whole situation.

"Good planning," Abe said.

They found the truck and excavated the ladder from under other tools.

Jeff said, "Light ladder. You…you…open doors. I carry."

"Deal," Abe said.

*  *

Moments after setting up the ladder with Jeff, Abe swept debris as Sarah came into the room.

"Abraham Hallowell," she said, "I happen to know you have a sermon to write."

"I do," he said.

"Deborah let it out that you are doing your writing at night, because you are helping to move this project along in the daytime. And I also know you were doing visits to several hospitals this morning and several places of ill-repute where one might find a graffiti artist."

"True."

"So, hike up those stairs and write so you can sleep tonight."

"Sir, yes sir," Abe said, imitating his Marine days from before Beirut.

"Chaplain Hallowell," Sarah said, mock saluting him, "March double time."

Abe grew aware that everyone in the room turned to watch them – Jeff, Akesha, Miguel and the contractors out in the hall. So, he saluted her and said, "Sarge, yes sir. Moving now, sir."

"Ma'am," she said.

"Yup," he said, and turned around, heading toward the stairs up to his tower writing room.

He smiled as he climbed the stairs, pulling his bum leg up with a hand on the pants crease.

Now he was glad for his blunder of asking her to work on his house. Rude, it may have been, but he knew he wanted to be near her for as long as he could get that nearness.

She was the thoughtful teacher of Jeff. She was the enthusiasm builder for Akesha, and, he was sure, she was the reason Miguel had finally accepted him – sort of. She was a treasure of a human being – out of bounds for him and for the kind of thoughts he kept at bay, but she was his to appreciate for this time. And his to keep safe.

He wished he could find Kevin. But now, every motel and dive in his network also had a photo of Kevin's father, Aaron, to watch out for.

\* \*

Three hours later, he had the draft of two sermons, one on Paul's letter on the body being nothing without all its parts. Amazing to him came the realization that he'd only noticed the parallels with himself at the end of writing the draft. He glanced at his missing hand and went on to sermon two.

That was, perhaps the first time he had forgotten his hand and just been himself. It had happened because, as he wrote, he had been thinking about families and how they functioned – Sarah's family, Kevin's family, gangs, his family, the family of the friends of Arthur and Amanda Charles, the church family.

His church family was even now signing up to learn to make stained glass windows for a space where presently there stood only an ugly blank wall.

His second sermon was on the need to care for self – to know when to ask for help. And the knowledge that each of us should not be too buzzed about our own independence to realize that when we ask for help, two people benefit. Giving is receiving in so many ways.

He steered clear of using Akesha and Jeff as examples, even though he'd learned how Akesha had asked for help mainly because she knew Jeff wished for the safety of Sarah's home. Using that example was too easy to identify.

Instead, the examples he gave were from his experiences in the Marines, and in Beirut and finally from the streets of Portland, where Street Roots, the local street newspaper, represented a leg up and a supportive community for its vendors, and where many of the stories were written by the people of the street with excellent research and stunningly persuasive realism in the writing.

Finished with his drafts, he put his head down on his desk and rested, knowing it was almost time to pick up Peter and meet Andy and Deborah at home.

Fifteen minutes later, he heard his door open. He sat upright.

"Ah," Sarah said, "I'm glad you've removed those dark curtains."

Abe rubbed his eyes. "Mrs. Steven's was delighted to help me pull them down. We both sneezed for about twenty minutes after we took them to the cleaners."

"They are going back up?"

"The cleaners claim they disintegrated in the bath. But I think Mrs. Steven's suggested that demise for them."

Sarah smiled as she looked out. "The light on this north side is beautiful. Enjoy. But right now, it is time to get Peter and get home."

Abe stretched, then he lifted his laptop. "Two sermon drafts. Am I dismissed?"

"Dismissed," she said.

"Ma'am, yes ma'am," he said as he rose, a bit slowly after cramping his leg for three hours. "Are you getting out of here too?"

"Not quite yet, we've got two truckloads of debris to dump, my truck and the contractors' bigger truck."

Abe stopped her by holding her shirt sleeve. "You go to the dump with Miguel. Nowhere alone."

"Sir, yes, sir."

*  *

As Abe and Peter drove away from Pete's school, his Bluetooth phone rang. His read-out told him it was the manager of the Richardson's motel. "Don Alvarez, what's going on?"

"Abe" Don said, "You've got to give up on this Kevin kid."

"What's happened?"

"Somebody took a gun to the office at Pair-a-Dice Motel."

"Samuel?"

"In critical at Emmanuel. Three other motel owners called to say they've been threatened. Three men with semi-automatic pistols came into their offices and tore down the photos, said if they kept asking about missing kids, they'd be dead."

"Did they come to you?" Abe asked, fearful for everyone in the place.

"No, and I've warned the families. I've taken Kevin and his Dad off the wall and have locked my doors. Kids aren't playing outside today, or until I'm sure no one has us in their crosshairs."

"Thanks, Don. I'm taking Peter home and then I'm on my way to Emmanuel Hospital. You've called the police?"

"Yeah. They know the connection to the search for that kid."

"Those who threatened – did they say there was a kid with the men?"

"No. They were sure he wasn't with them, or in the car."

"Car. What kind of car?" Abe asked.

"Blue Chevrolet with no license plates."

"Damn!"

"You got that right, Reverend. Be careful."

Abe hung up.

From the back seat, Peter said," Dad, you watch out for those guys."

"I will, Pete. I watch all the time."

After delivering Pete home to Arthur, Abe pulled over long enough to call Sarah, then drove to Emmanuel Hospital to find Samuel's condition.

Langren, Templeton and someone else, Kevin's dad, maybe, knew he was searching. Did they know where he lived and worked? Yes, they knew he worked with the police, but what about Charles Wesley Methodist? What about his home? What about Sarah and the kids?

Had he put them in harm's way, just as he had done to Samuel?

# CHAPTER THIRTY-ONE

That weekend, Sarah's crew awoke in Abe's house. Sarah came out of Deborah's bedroom talking about how clever Deb had been in choosing furniture.

"But," she said to Miguel, "In the other bedrooms, we are definitely going to have to find less clunky and sturdier beds."

The family puttered around having breakfast and studying the work schedule they'd laid out for themselves. All the time, Miguel and Sarah seemed preoccupied with something besides building, but they didn't mention the shooting at the Pair-a-Dice motel.

They waited for Abe to call with news about Samuel. Dick had stayed the night with Abe's family while Abe spent the night next to Samuel's bed.

While they planned, Miguel recognized that Sarah wanted to save as much money for Abe's family as possible. He knew that feeling – he looked around and saw that the house had been beaten up by wheelchair accidents. For Deborah's sake, he wanted to wipe out most walls and just have an open space, but he also recognized that Andy and Peter lived here.

Teenage boys need privacy, he remembered.

Well, probably girls needed that, too.

After breakfast, he found himself standing in the doorway to the room that belonged to Deborah.

While they worked here, and hid out here, Sarah was using this room, but the room was totally unlike Sarah. Green, light blue and hints of rose colors were in every bed pillow and curtain flounce.

Deborah's room – after seeing what a difference the fabric made in how he felt, he'd gotten onto the internet and looked up drapes, then curtains and found the word for that frilly thing that surrounded each pillow and the bottom of each curtain. A flounce.

His mother, and his mom, Sarah, had never used a flounce in their lives.

Coming to terms with how it made him feel was a lot harder than figuring out what to call it. The decoration choices made him want to take care of the girl, yet he knew how independent she was.

Still the flounces on the pillows were in keeping with the frills on her blouses and the puffs in her sleeves, the slender belts at her waist and the colors she wore that made her green eyes shine.

Everything about her said feminine. And everything about her said, "Don't even try to push my wheelchair for me."

She made him want to know more, to see her tournaments, to understand what she studied and how she thought.

He stepped into the room and studied her desk. Neat, note paper for writing to friends and her parents, pens next to note paper, a book – the Silmarillion of Tolkien, and The Gene by Siddhartha Mukherjee – a book you wouldn't want to land on your nose as you fell asleep.

Miguel heard Sarah's footstep and backed out of the room quickly, but as he turned, he saw he hadn't been quick enough.

He decided to bluster it out. "Any changes needed here? Better storage? Closet?"

Sarah smiled, "No. It's the boys' room that needs those things. But we'll tackle that later after we do the main bathroom."

"Main bathroom?" Miguel asked. "There's only one."

"A big problem for this family. We'll demolish the wall between the boy's room and the bathroom, take out this closet and end up with a bigger door straight from Pete and Andy's room into the bigger bathroom."

"Are we doing another bathroom?"

"Yes, out of the L shaped space at the end of the living room. There's room there for a shower, sink and toilet in a place where Deborah can get ready while the boys get ready. And directly above the boys' bathroom, another for Mr. Hallowell."

Miguel knew these other two bathrooms were spendy, but he also thought Sarah had an idea where to get good used showers, sink and toilets.

He bet she hadn't even brought the third bathroom up with Abe. He would have nixed the idea because he was focused on getting the kids into comfort, but hardly himself.

At that moment, Sarah's phone rang. She clicked into it.

"Abe?" she said, "How is Samuel?"

"He's alive but has a lot of damage to his lung and his intestines. The recovery will take a lot of time. Don Alvarez is here and offering to take him into his motel while he recuperates."

"How about his job?"

"That motel won't be open for a time. The owner is hopping mad, saying that Sam got into an unnecessary argument and caused the problem."

"So, setting up to fire him."

"Yes, but the police are also cordoning off the location for their investigation. They believe the event may not be related to Kevin at all. The shooter never mentioned Kevin."

"But the threats to the other motel owners . . ."

"Yes, a couple of them picked Langren and Templeton out of a photo lineup. Reese is out searching for those two now."

Miguel asked for the phone. When she handed it over, Miguel said, "Abe, Langren used to live with his dad on Weidler Street, somewhere in the block near the Lloyd Center. His dad may still be there. A good place to hide out."

"Okay, I'll tell Captain Reese. Thanks, Miguel."

When Sarah hung up the phone, she and Miguel just looked at each other. Finally, Miguel said, "Reese knows Kevin may be a victim. I think he'll make that clear to his officers."

"I sure hope so." Sarah said. "All we can do is keep on working."

They moved from the living room space back toward the kitchen. "Well," Sarah said, "Akesha and Jeff? Let's get the sledgehammers out and bash a few things."

Miguel laughed. He knew those two loved this part of the job. At this point in a renovation, he was always the one at the hardware store and the lumber yard.

"Where's my list," he asked Sarah.

"On the breakfast table," she said. "Let me get the gang started here and then let's talk about what to get first. We don't have room in the garage to store all we need at once."

"How about that room at the back of the house for storage?"

"Yes, I'm thinking that can be a space later for a caretaker as Peter gets less able."

Miguel stopped cold. "Peter will get less able?"

Sarah looked up at him, tears hovering. "Yes. His disease is degenerative. Over time, he'll need more care."

"Hell!"

"Yes. Hell for everyone," Sarah said.

"Well," Miguel said, trying to get back on track. "We can use that room for storage, but it won't hold long lumber."

"So, we'll have to spread out the buying."

Miguel smiled, "Starting with three toilets?"

"No. They are already in there."

"You've been to Hippo Hardware without me?"

"I was there with Arthur Charles."

"He's not a good bodyguard, Mom."

"No, but he's alert for trouble, so we were all right."

* *

The work at the church and the work at Hallowell's' home went smoothly for a week. Separately, Miguel and Abe drove by the Jackson's home twice that week and found no more graffiti or any sign that Kevin's gang had been around. The police and the networks gave Miguel and Abe updates on Wednesday and Friday. But some of the motels were no longer checking in, afraid to be involved.

Either Kevin's gang no longer existed, or every member of the gang had gone to ground, left the area or died.

Given Bruce's death, the 'died' explanation was terribly possible. Abe saw Sarah deflate as if punctured when she heard this news. He started toward her, but it was Ernst who put his arm around her shoulders and glared at Abe.

"There, girl," Ernst said. "That Kevin is his son. Aaron wouldn't kill his own kin. You know that. Kev'll be all right. Maybe a little mixed up, but not hurt."

She whispered, "But the other boys . . ."

Abe glanced at Miguel, who shook his head and said, "Let's get back to work. There's nothing else we can do until they show up."

* *

Once, during the second week, Abe dropped Peter off at day care and found himself following his son into the building, reluctant to let go of him.

At the last minute, he watched the caregiver adjust the tower that was newly attached to Peter's chair, and then Abe turned back to the car.

Peter needed his friends, not his dad today.

Last night, Abe had called Peter's parents in Malheur. They were set to visit this weekend, a drive of several hundred miles. Peter's doctor had set them up with a social worker who found them an apartment for the five days that they could afford to take off from work. Peter's little brothers and sisters, who hardly remembered him, would stay with their grandparents. Abe would try to be a good host, but he wasn't sure how to do it.

Abe drove around, wandering and without thought, until he realized he was at his own house, and it seemed empty. He decided to get some of his lighter clothes, since the weather was warming toward summer.

As he walked toward the side door, he saw the truck at the back of his driveway. He was glad the drive curved so the truck couldn't be seen from the street. Sarah's truck. Or maybe Miguel. But he thought Miguel was sheet-rocking the church walls today.

He let himself in the back door and heard her upstairs. That surprised him. He knew of no plan to do anything up there.

He hitched his leg up the stairs quietly, because she hummed as she worked. From the sound of it, she rhythmically attached plastic sheets on a wall with a staple gun.

He stood in the hall until she seemed to be done with the staple gun and was fiddling with the plastic. She still hummed a tune he didn't recognize.

He thought maybe a Finnish folk tune – something her grandfather had taught her.

He stepped into the room and found her bent over with her back to him. Her overalls hugged her bottom and her thighs.

He swallowed hard and stepped back into the stairway hall outside of his attic bedroom.

"Hey," he called.

"Ahh!" she cried. "Who?"

He moved back into the room. "Just me. It's okay."

She faced him, the staple gun in her hand, her eyes wide.

He put up a hand. "Please lower that thing," he said.

Her hand lowered it. "Sorry," she said, a little breathless.

"Didn't mean to take you by surprise," Abe said. "I just couldn't figure why you'd be up here."

"Umm," she said. "Needs sprucing up, don't you think? Paint and stuff?"

He looked around at the dark rafters and the one small window. "Well, it wouldn't hurt, but you could just toss the tarp over the bed, not tape it up so carefully." He pulled back the edge of the plastic sheeting.

"What's that hole doing there? And that pipe?"

"Exhaust pipe venting the toilet from the boys' bathroom," she said. "Let's go downstairs."

"Isn't that pipe supposed to go out the roof?" He looked up and saw the hole where it had always done that, a place where he'd hung notices to himself about things he needed to do.

The hole above was bigger than it had been, and it was now covered with a tarp.

"Oh, it will continue up," she said. "It just needs some adjustments."

He frowned, trying to figure the adjustments, but she already headed down his stairs.

"Paint rafters?" he asked.

"Well, maybe not. But to get our permit, we had to promise to insulate under the roof and in the walls. All else depends on the budget," she said. "Do you like looking at rafters?" She asked. "We can leave them available and just cover the insulation with sheet rock."

"I like rafters if that is cheaper."

She stood on a lower step and looked up at him. "Come see what we've done so far."

After a whirlwind tour of the boys' room demolition and the gutted kitchen, Sarah took him in the living room where the L-shaped end of the room had been turned into the framing for a wall and a wide door that opened into the hall back toward the bedrooms.

She waved her arms. "Your main bathroom, sir."

"Wow!" He said. Abe stepped inside and studied the markings and the piping.

"Sink?" he guessed. "Toilet with turn-about chair space, drive in shower with drain. Drain to where?"

"Drain to hook up with drain from boy's bathroom and angle, at a slope, into the pipe in the basement that takes effluent from all the drains."

He nodded. "But the exhaust vent pipe from the toilet?"

"A little harder, but there is space next to the living room chimney for it to go up through the attic and out."

"Oh. That's why the toilet is here instead of there," he said.

Sarah smiled. "Yes. Closer to the chimney by about three feet, so no need for a sharp angle out."

He looked at her, studied her, and saw his angel, problem solver, kid saver, and he collapsed to the floor.

"Abe," she said, down on her knees beside him. "Abe, what is it?"

He tried to stop, but he couldn't. He cried, his hand and his arm to his face.

"What's happened?" she whispered. "What?"

He knew he was beyond blubbering, but he couldn't help it. "Peter . . . Peter has to use oxygen. At . . . at night this year. But now also in daytime."

"Oh," she said, "That lovely boy." She took Abe's hand.

He gripped her hand and tried to wipe his tears with his arm.

She pulled out her bandana and wiped his face for him.

He stuffed his arm back in its pocket. "I'm sorry."

She shook her head. "I'm sorry, too. He is such a sweet and thoughtful and funny boy, but I know he is very sick."

"Duchenne Muscular Dystrophy," he gulped out. "No stopping it. Only holding actions."

"Oh, Abraham. What does he know? What does Andy know?"

He glanced up at her. She'd seen it then, how Andy needed Peter.

"Peter knows. His doctor talks to him."

"And you. All of you will take this hard."

"Deborah understands. I've tried to talk to Andy, but he shouts me down. I don't know what he'll do, and we haven't very long."

"Will Peter get to live here?" she asked.

"I. . . I don't know."

"Then we have to show him the progress, often."

"Yes. Thank you. I'll bring him this afternoon."

She nodded and touched his arm, "Good idea," She said.

He pushed his hand deeper into its pocket.

# CHAPTER THIRTY-TWO

A half hour later, Sarah watched Abe walk out the side door to his car. After he got into the driver's seat, she saw him pull his arm out and wipe his face again. But he noticed her still at the doorway and dropped his arm out of sight, waved with his left and started the engine.

When he was gone, she slumped against the door jamb.

That arm, she thought. He hates it, hides it.

She knew that hiding habit from having moved the clothing in his closet in order to get at the bathroom exhaust pipe. He had five suit jackets, and every one of them was worn on the right pocket, a pocket designed so the arm could go straight in deeply.

He still felt the loss of his hand, and now he was going to lose his sweet boy. Of course, the doctor had told him this would happen. He knew it when he took Peter in, but the oxygen tank in the daytime, that was a blow, another big step toward the end. More and more trouble breathing because his lungs couldn't be forced to work.

Abraham Hallowell and Andy and Deborah were working their different ways toward grief. And Sarah could only hope to make any of it better for them.

\* \*

At three thirty that afternoon, Sarah saw that Abe had pulled up to the driveway. She waited and watched from the living room window. Abe got out Peter's chair, set it just behind the car's back door, set the brakes, attached the tower for the oxygen tubes, and then lifted Peter into it.

She heard Peter say, "A new ramp!"

Abe smiled. "Longer, wider, smoother."

"Andy will love it."

Sarah saw Abe hesitate at that, and then he started pushing.

"Yes, he will," Abe said. "Let's go see what else has changed."

Sarah made a note that they needed to change these windows, but that would have to wait. The place was a sieve for dirty air and for sound, but she couldn't fix that this year, or maybe for a couple of years.

Instead, she answered the doorbell.

"You put the doorbell down low," Peter grinned at her around his green oxygen tubes.

"Miguel did that. Deborah suggested it."

Peter whispered, "Deborah suggests

Miguel does.

Deborah smiles.

Miguel turns red."

"Not a rhyme, Peter," Abe laughed.

"Free verse," Peter said, as quick as a wink.

Sarah laughed with them.

"Okay," Peter said. "I'll work on it."

Abe said, "What do you notice here in the front hall?"

"A shoe rack. A coat catcher. A bench for Dad."

"How do you know that's for Abe," Sarah asked.

"He's the only one that isn't always sitting down already."

"Oh…"

"Besides," Peter turned toward Abe. "Sarah is always thoughtful, so she'd notice what you need."

Abe glanced up at her. Sarah felt her face heating. Abe smiled.

"Peter, you are an observer," Abe said. "Yes, she is thoughtful."

"Next, down the hall," Sarah said quickly.

So, Abe pushed him down the hall.

"Wow! A new room." Peter glanced in. "Pipes everywhere. Must be a bathroom. And look, Dad. You can push me in at any angle."

"Yes, I can. But there is more." Abe pushed him toward the boys' room.

As soon as he saw the demolition site, Peter sang out,

"A mess,

A mess.

You can't invade our mess.

A board here.

A pipe there.

And now you must confess.

You can't invade our mess."

"Better than clothes all over the floor, eh?" Abe said.

"Is that a bigger bathroom?"

"Yes," Sarah said. "With a toilet room that's closed off from the shower and sink room."

"Why?" Peter asked.

"So Andy can be on the toilet by himself while you are in the shower or sink," Sarah said.

"Oh . . ." Peter looked up at his dad. He didn't say anything more for a moment, and then he said, "Andy will love it."

At that moment, Sarah knew that Peter knew.

She walked on down the hall into the kitchen, breathing fast, so as not to cry. She heard Abe behind her describing to his son how the two beds and nightstands would fit and where the wheelchairs would go at night. And then she heard Peter trying to be cheerful about how it all would finally work.

A few moments later, they wheeled into the kitchen.

"It's going to be beautiful, Sarah," Peter said. "Thank you."

"My pleasure," she managed. And then she let Abe describe where the refrigerator would go and how its door would open all the way, so the drawers could come out easily.

After the kitchen tour, Sarah took them to the back door and showed Peter where the ramp would lead to the back deck and another ramp would take him to the back yard.

Peter looked up at Sarah and said, "Did you know my mom and dad are driving up here from Malheur, right now? They will be here tomorrow."

"That will be wonderful."

"Yes. They'll get to stay five days, and then they have to drive back. That's a long drive, diagonally across Oregon, except there aren't any diagonal roads, so it's even farther when you have to zig-zag."

"But they don't mind. They get to see you," she said.

"Yes," he fingered his green tubes. "I love them."

"Yes," was all Sarah could manage.

Abe said, "Well, Pete man. You need a nap before dinner, so let's get over to Arthur's."

Pete looked up. "See you, Sarah. This will all be great."

"Thank you," she said.

As they got into the car, Sarah heard Peter say, "Grandma Amanda would love this house. It would have been perfect for her."

Abe said, "Grandma Amanda was happy anywhere that you were, Petie."

Peter smiled up at him.

Inside the living room, Sarah could not stop the tears that streamed down her face.

*     *

Peter's mother, Laura, and his father, Grant, clearly were surprised by his rail-thin body and his effort to appear normal while breathing with the aid of tubes.

They stayed near Peter as much as possible while he introduced them to his school friends and school caretakers. They sat in the school library while he slept, but the librarian brought them a lunch from the teachers' room.

Grant wanted to pay for the lunch, but the librarian said, "Peter paid for anything we can do for you. He is a gem."

Laura nodded. "He's pretty special all right."

"Not to mention," said the librarian, "he's pretty entertaining with his imitations of various animals he's seen at the zoo and in the wild."

His dad laughed at that, and then he buried his face in his hands and turned away.

Laura put her hand on his back and rubbed his neck. The librarian left them alone, finding some excuse to leave the room.

After a few moments, Grant and Laura ate the sandwiches. Laura peeled the small oranges and handed one to Grant.

"Sweetheart," she said. "Peter knows he's dying. We have to talk to him about it. He shouldn't be forced to keep hiding the truth from us."

"He doesn't want to talk about it," Grant said.

"No," Laura said, "He believes you don't want to talk about it."

"Why do you think that?"

"Because he's talked about it with Abe and with his teacher."

"They told you that?"

"Peter told me when we were in Arthur's bathroom this morning."

Grant stared at her. Then he stared at his hands. "What does he say?"

"He wants to know what we think is next."

"And what did you tell him, Laura? Was it all that stuff about Jesus?"

"Yes, it was."

"God, I don't know."

"Grant, not a one of us knows for sure. But losing Peter, we have to hope it is all that Jesus stuff, or something like it. And for Peter's sake, we have to believe it. Why would any creative force not want to take a child like Peter to its heart?"

"I'm a physics teacher, Laura."

"Are there things about the physical world we don't yet understand?"

"Of course," he said.

"Other dimensions we haven't explored?"

Grant just stared at her.

"Then why not, Grant? Why do we have to pretend everything is explained and explainable, when it isn't. We don't know. Isn't that important, too?"

"Okay. Can I say, 'Peter, I just don't know, but I wish I did'?

Laura nodded. "I think that's as good an answer as Peter might hope for. You don't know. You and I hope for more for him, and for all of us. And even though we also don't know for sure, an after-life is what a lot of people have believed. And they have believed it long enough that the oldest graves we have found on earth include useful objects that people may need in whatever comes after."

Grant took a deep breath. "We can talk about this honestly?"

"Peter does. We can, too."

# CHAPTER THIRTY-THREE

Late in their visit, Abe kissed Peter goodnight and left Pete's father and mother in his room. Abe started to put away the evening dishes, but soon sat heavily near the kitchen table. Arthur had gone up to his room in order to let the family say their goodbyes, because Peter's family was leaving early in the morning, before Peter would wake up.

Abe heard them murmuring. He heard Peter's voice rise in questions and fall in statements. He knew that Peter meant to talk to them about the possibility that he might be gone before they could visit again. As Abe and Peter had driven from his school to pick up his parents for dinner, Peter had practiced on Abe what he would say.

Abe admired Peter's honesty. He must have talked to Arthur and Amanda before she died. Amanda believed she would see Jesus, and someday, she would see Peter and then Arthur again. Amanda had a lot stronger faith in the teachings of her New Testament than anyone Abe knew, including himself.

So, he hoped Peter's parents had the same optimism but also the same honesty.

After a few minutes, Abe heard Laura's voice singing a simple tune. She sounded just like Peter, making it up as she went along, a poem about the next life.

She sang clearly, softly.

When Peter goes to heaven
He'll have the fastest wings
When Peter goes to heaven
He'll be the boy who sings
He'll run and play
Most every day
He'll breathe and shout
And help God out,
When Peter goes to heaven.

When Peter's up in heaven
He'll look down on Malheur
When Peter's up in heaven
He'll smile on Portland fair
He'll see we all know of his love
And we are glad he's free above
Because his lungs
have easy air
He'll sing to us,
"I loved it there."
When Peter's up in heaven.

And then Abe heard Peter say, "Safe journey, Mommy and Daddy."
Abe put his head down on the table and stuffed his dish towel into his mouth so he could muffle his tears.

*   *

After the weekend with Peter's parents, Abe seemed worn and on edge. He'd driven to the house to try to work off the memory of Peter having to say goodbye to his parents. Each of them knew that, with luck, there might be one more trip out here for them.

Abe had tried to find a way to afford airplane tickets. Child services couldn't afford it. Finally, he'd asked Arthur – Arthur who did everything for them. And the answer was yes. So, as he said good-bye to Grant and Laura, Abe handed them tickets to come again in two weeks. He sent those fine people off in tears. His tears and theirs.

Peter was at his school, where he now slept about half the time in a room for napping children.

The other kids were at school. Miguel and Ernst worked at the church, but Abe came to work with Sarah at the house looking over the plans and choosing bathroom light fixtures.

As Abe glanced through a confusion of catalogue choices, Sarah used his stove to boil water. He spent most of the next five minutes watching her pull leaves off the weed she'd found in his backyard.

"You're sure that's edible," he asked.

"Mint. The most prolific weed in the Pacific Northwest."

"Okay."

"In Lebanon," she said, "the main weed would be oregano or sage or…"

"I didn't know plants there either," he said. "I lived in the city. If a family was very lucky, they had a roof garden with tomatoes. But roof gardens were dangerous because of rockets."

"Well, here, our greatest danger is Kevin's father and his goons," she said.

Abe saw that worried crease come between her eyebrows. He stood up and walked toward her. "Let's hope the police find them soon."

218 Those Who Curse You

"And let's hope the police don't kill them," she whispered.

He took her leaves and put them in the tea pot. "Mint smells good," he said. "Let's take this to the living room where we can mark the demo lines on the chimney wall for that bathroom pipe."

They relaxed with the peppermint tea, Abe sitting on the sawhorse, and Sarah on a ladder rung.

"Trust you," he said, "to make something delicious out of one of the weeds that pervades my garden. Anything you can make out of morning glory root?"

"Only nightmares, as far as I know."

Abe's smile dimmed. He gazed out a window at the green and purple backdrop of trees in his old yard. Nightmares he had plenty. But he would not say so to this woman.

The trees outside swayed in the early summer breeze, drawing his attention again from his inner turmoil. The soft green of apple trees and voluptuous darkness of the flowering plums were a stark contrast to the thrust of blackness in the ancient fir.

The fir would not die. Winter damage left it lopsided and broken but its power and insatiable desire for life overshadowed the more gentle trees, curtailing the expectations of those nearest it. Its roots sucked life from their ground and its tattered arms denied them much needed sun.

"Abe, where is your daydream taking you?"

His reverie broke. He sought to cover his thoughts with light humor but was unable to succeed. Instead, the image of the trees intruded strongly, allowing the worry to slip out unguarded.

"Sarah, I use too much of your time. I impose on your goodness and concern for the children."

"You're not imposing on me. I got into this project with my eyes open and I don't begrudge a minute of it." She stood, fiddling with the level, watching the bubble, not looking at him until she was directly in front of him. Her dark brown gaze caressed his copper hair and then his eyes.

Her attention made him uncomfortable. "Is my hair sticking out in all directions as usual?" he asked.

"No," her laughter seemed a quiet, loving sound, "Your hair is doing its usual dance in the air – every curl for itself." She suddenly looked puzzled.

He sat up straighter, putting his hand behind him to keep from reaching for her waist. "What is it, Sarah?"

"You went to Lebanon because it was your homeland?"

"Yes. I was born there." Her question baffled him: she didn't usually indulge in non sequiturs. "My mother was Lebanese," he added, hoping it was relevant.

Sarah leaned over his head as he tried to sit up straight without touching her. "Red hair. And not a black curl in the bunch." Her mischievous gleam was barely concealed.

He grinned but did not relax. She was so close, her breasts so softly traced by the fall of heavy twill fabric. He forced himself to look up at her teasing face. Did she know just how much of him she was teasing?

He tried to keep his mind on the banter. "My mother's hair was long, curly and dark red. My father was a blond."

"Mom had red hair?"

"The crusaders left more than their religion in my mother's land." He raised his hand in a shrug.

She had the grace to blush.

His gesture had brought his hand dangerously close to forbidden fruit. He put his hand behind him again. If she stood there longer, he would have to move, or fall backwards off this sawhorse. He longed to take her by the waist and pull her hard into his body. But how did one hand do that effectively?

It didn't.

Suddenly she stepped back and held the level upright. The bubble rushed to the top of the glass. A bubble of anxiety filled his throat. The beat of the pulse in his throat became unbearable.

"Sarah," he blurted.

"Yes," she whispered, as if she knew the urge he fought.

"I can't . . ."

"Why not?"

He stared at her. Yes, he thought, we both want it.

Despite his long struggle, he took her question as assent. He grabbed her hand and pulled her with him out the back door and to the shade of the apple trees.

When he looked at her face, he saw how much he had startled her.

"I'm . . ." he started.

"Don't say it." She was vehement.

"Say what?"

"Don't say that you're sorry you grabbed my hand. Abraham Hallowell you are too much sorry and never enough spontaneous!"

He flung himself on the ground, barely catching himself with his hand before he landed. Her obvious annoyance loosened something more spontaneous in him.

"Sit down." He ordered. He started to soften it, then didn't. "Sit."

As she sat, her face beamed with approval. He reached over and pulled the one pin from her hair. "This golden brown does not appear often on the streets of Beirut."

His attention followed the swing of her hair. He remembered doing this before, twice. He could admit he wanted her. Why not? Just as she had asked.

He closed his eyes to veil the hunger he felt. But his hand remained in her hair, pulling her toward him.

\* \*

Sarah thought briefly that grandfather would think her immoral for wanting Abe to want her. Thoughts of her grandfather's admonitions faded as Sarah saw Abe's subdued desires finally made evident. She came willingly, watching his lips part to allow a ragged breath just before he took her mouth.

His kiss was gentle only in its first seconds. Then his consuming need took charge of their bodies. With an urgency he no longer tried to control, he pulled her beneath him, pushing his right arm inside her overalls and across her back. He lifted her back toward him with his arm while his left hand pushed the shoulder strap aside. The heavy fabric descended. She felt the hardness of his chest against her breast and the insistent exploration of his lips on her eyelids, her cheeks, her throat.

She wrapped her arms around him, offering him her desire to feed his.

His hand pulled the scooped neckline of her t-shirt. He buried his face in the soft flesh above her bra, kissing the curve of each breast. His right arm found the waist of her shirt and pushed underneath it, caressing her silk-smooth flesh. His lips nuzzled aside the lace and found her sensitive nipple, taking it greedily.

Her entire body responded strongly to his passionate kiss.

Even as she trembled with the sensations his mouth aroused, his arm brushed across her back.

Suddenly, he pulled up, breathing heavily. "No. Oh no." He looked at her flushed and bewildered face. "I didn't mean to let it touch you."

She reached up, taking his face in her hands. Holding him still she asked in a shaky voice. "Why?"

"It just ... I can't keep it from you ... Oh Sarah." Swiftly, he pulled the strap of her overalls onto her shoulder.

His eyes darkened just before he looked away. "My scars. You felt them. Your whole body jerked away from my arm. I thought I could keep it away from you."

"Why would you even think that? Have I ever said `I love you, but not your arm'?" She sat up quickly, holding him by the shoulders so he could not leave without listening. "Why do you let it come between us so much? You act as if it were poison and could kill me."

"That's just it." His voice choked on the self-condemnation. "I am here, and they are not because of this. You are right to pull away from it."

He was making no sense to her, except that she recognized the recurrent theme of the children who died in his church. Children and women – his wife, Elani.

Sarah whispered, "I know. I know." He glared up at the apple tree above them, but she pulled his lonely and broken body into her arms, cradled his head on her shoulder and whispered, "Tell me about your wife, Abe. Tell me about Elani."

At first, his arms tightened around her. His whole body stiffened before he expelled a long shuddering breath and sat up. He looked for a sign that what he needed to tell her would be accepted.

"Please, Abe. It weighs on you so much. Tell me."

She thought he would tell her about how they died. She had heard parts of it but never all of it. Maybe if he could get rid of all of it, the guilt would not be so great a burden.

Instead, he told her about an even older guilt – an earlier, instinctive form of self-defense.

# CHAPTER THIRTY-FOUR

"**A**t twenty-eight, I went home to Beirut expecting to be the assistant pastor in the Christian Community Church. I had been a member there until I was twelve years old. When I arrived, I found that the old pastor had been murdered the day before. I was alone, scared, and responsible for the lives of many families.

"Beirut was no longer my home. Life there was entirely upside down – not like the life of the cosmopolitan city I had known. People used to live in harmony, side by side, vastly different cultures co-existing in relative peace. Or so I thought in my childhood. Now, it was one seething cauldron of hate.

"And the Christian and Muslim ideals I had come to believe in were over-ridden by the age-old tradition of vengeance which drives everything in the mid-east. I was at the helm of a ship with a broken rudder, fighting the storm with no hope of anything beyond survival of the next wave."

Abe shifted his body off his right leg. He studied the grass between them carefully as he continued.

"I worked day and night, sometimes successfully, to keep the neighboring communities talking to each other. I believed that if the people talked on the street, sold and bought from each other, invited each other to weddings and dinners, no outsiders could convince them to kill each other. I was not alone in this work. Leaders of most of the religious communities were doing the same thing all over the country.

"But always, there is a group that preaches chaos as an easy solution. And there is a discontent with life that makes it attractive to believe chaos and war would be better.

He looked at Sarah briefly where she sat in the grass beside him. His mind took solace in the sunlit honey color of her hair. He did not look at her eyes as he embarked on the next part of the story.

"When Elani's father and brothers began inviting me to share the hospitality of their home, I was grateful. A few hours, once in a while, with warmth, laughter. . . And each time, Elani served the meal and poured my tea, tended to my needs. I was glad when a marriage with this dark, graceful daughter was proposed. I did not even want to wonder why they would pursue a marriage for her with one who might be murdered at any time, or who might take her back to America when he gave up the ship.

"I did not look beyond the fact that I needed someone, and she was gracious to me."

Abe moved Sarah's hair behind her shoulder and left his hand on her throat. He watched her expression while his thumb caressed the smooth underside of her jaw and the delicate shape of her ear.

As always, "Come and Go" were at war in his mind and body. His right arm was carefully held to his side as he continued his story.

Abe dropped his hand and looked away. "I needed someone so badly, I chose to believe we would be happy soon. But she was used to being a princess and I was not a prince."

Abe looked down at his arm. The dark bruises had come back beneath his eyes. "It's just that I was so worn with care for others that I pretended our problem was not there. By the time I could not ignore it, she rarely let me even pretend to be her husband.

"On that last night, I did not know why she chose to be so loyal and follow me to the church service, to sit in the front row. Now, I think it was because of the baby. She knew about the baby, but I did not. I believe she'd decided to act like a wife so that the child would have a happy family. She sat near me in a show of loyalty, and she died."

Quietly, Sarah said, "They both died?"

"Yes. And others near her as well."

Sarah was silent for a long time, trying to see how his twisted, youthful marriage controlled their own relationship.

Or was he afraid he could not keep her happy sexually? How could he believe that? It was so blatantly obvious that she responded to his passion . . . it embarrassed her to think how easily he had just now made her want his most intimate caress.

Then what held him back? The arm? Did he really believe it repelled her?

Finally, she made herself ask him. "What have I done to make you think I don't want your arm to touch me?"

He looked at her in surprise, then anger. "Sarah, don't pretend with me. I felt your frisson . . . your shiver, while I kissed you. You cannot keep the shudder from your body when my arm touches you."

"But you were kissing me as well. How can you know which I was reacting to?"

"I don't know which caused it. I only know that my intimacy is unwelcome to your body, however much your mind wishes to deny it. I can feel the truth."

To admit blatantly that she wanted his loving was difficult, but she knew she had to do it now. "I was acting that way because I wanted you more, not less. You misunderstand . . ."

"Please, Sarah! Don't. I know how my arm makes you feel. Let's leave it at that." He rose, distancing himself, nearly losing his balance because of his bad leg.

Sarah followed him swiftly, "But what you think is not the truth."

He pulled his arm from her hand. "Sarah, please don't. I just want to salvage a friendship with you out of the mess I've created this afternoon."

"If you won't believe me, how can we even be friends?"

He turned on her with haunted eyes. "Don't go. I won't touch you. I promise."

"Abe, you're not even listening to me! I want you to touch me."

He backed into the deck. Unable to believe, afraid to risk total rejection, he chose not to acknowledge what she said. "I must go get Deborah and the kids. I think we better not work together tomorrow or over the weekend."

"Are you telling me to just get on with it?" Now she knew he thought her promiscuous. She had as much as told him she was – that she wanted sex with him.

"I just think we ought to cool down."

Embarrassment turned to anger. "Fine!" She flung the level at the grass, grabbed her keys and stalked toward the front gate.

* *

In a daze of self-loathing, Abe watched her walk out of his life. He wanted to stop her, but then what? He would want all the things he had wanted this afternoon. He would have to watch her shrink from him more and more as his wants became insistent. It was better to stay away altogether than to be the object of her disgust.

# CHAPTER THIRTY-FIVE

That afternoon, after looking like a loose woman and practically begging him to make love to her, Sarah didn't want to ask Abe to do anything, so she went to the hardware store to replace the blade on her saw and get tape for the sheet-rocking in various parts of the house.

On the way home, she kept an eye out for any person or vehicle that might be following her. She went around Abe's block and a couple of other blocks in order to lose anyone who might be related to Kevin's dad.

As she parked at the back of the house, she saw that Abe's car also was back there. Abe was inside. She nearly backed out and drove away, but she had work to do and kids to create a home for, so she decided to brave it out and pretend he'd never shunned her.

In the house, she was relieved not to find him right away. She put the new blade in her saw and took it and the tape to the new bathroom at the living room end of the hall.

And there, she found Abe on the floor with blood all over the back and side of his shirt.

Down on her knees, she tried to talk to him.

"What happened."

"Shrapnel," he gasped. "Lebanon."

She put her hand on the bloody shirt and realized for the first time that he had a bandage wrapped about his waist.

She pulled out her cell phone and called 911.

To the opening questions, she said, "Ambulance. 2608 NE 16th Place. He says it's shrapnel," Sarah glanced at him. "I think old wound and still in his back."

"Yes," he managed.

"Bleeding, but I'm afraid to put my hand on it because I don't know exactly where the shrapnel is.

"Yes, I'll open the door and show them where."

"Yes, that's the correct cell number."

"I'm his . . ."

"Wife," he said.

She stared at him. "Wife," she repeated.

She hung up and ran to open the front door, then ran back to him. She found him trying to sit up. "Lie still. Let them lift you. They are trained."

As he slumped back to the floor, she took his hand. He gripped hard as a spasm of pain took over. After it subsided, he said. "Wife, want you . . . Want you with me."

"Right. I understand," she whispered. "I'm calling Dick, Miguel and Arthur to gather the children."

Within minutes, others were ready to get Andy, Peter and Deborah to St. Joseph Mercy Hospital. And just then, the ambulance pulled up in front of the house.

Abe said, "Akesha . . ."

"Miguel is bringing Jeff and Akesha here. I'll call them to let them know. You stop worrying."

"Together."

"Yes, we're all in this together. You just need to get well."

# CHAPTER THIRTY-FIVE

The surgeon, Samuel Franks, told her that Abe was very lucky. When the shrapnel started to move, it moved away from his spine and toward the surface.

Dr. Franks said, "His internist, and I always knew where it was. We just couldn't get at it safely."

"Can I see him?"

"He's still asleep. I'll have someone from the recovery room get you when he begins to wake up, maybe another hour. He lost a lot of blood before you found him."

"Yes." She thought about how she'd almost driven away in order to avoid him.

"Mrs. Hallowell?"

That name surprised her. She hadn't thought that far into this 'wife' business. "Yes?"

"I've looked after Abe's situation since he came here from Lebanon, and I have to say I'm surprised to find he married."

She laughed. "He told me to say that. He didn't want to come here without somebody, and I was the only somebody around. I'm his architect."

Dr. Franks looked at her over his glasses, reminding her of the stares of Eleanor Whiting. "Pretty important architect, wouldn't you say?"

"Well . . ."

He said, "I think he didn't have his usual guard up, and now you know."

She sat back. Amazed to think how many people saw through Abraham Hallowell's defenses.

Dr. Franks smiled. "What is your real name, then?"

"Sarah Rohann."

"Well, Sarah Rohann, someone will come get you as soon as he wakes. Meanwhile, do you have the number for his children?"

"Yes."

"Thought so." He nodded with the smug look of a man who has finished a crossword puzzle in ink. "Tell them he is much better. That metal piece will no longer be bothering him."

"I will."

"Nice to meet you, Miss Rohann."

*   *

Sarah watched Abe wake up. First, he stared at the hospital ceiling, but he clearly had difficulty focusing.

"Abe?"

He turned first in the wrong direction, and then toward the sound of her voice. "Ahhh." He whispered. "Thank . . ."

And then he closed his eyes again. But his left hand moved toward her on the sheet. She held it.

"I'm sorry," he whispered.

She leaned close to him and said, "I almost didn't find you in time."

He squeezed her hand and slept.

Hours later, after the children had been allowed to visit, and after Miguel and Dick took them all to their homes, Sarah again sat next to him.

The nurse had propped him up with pillows. He seemed to have recovered from the anesthetic that his operation had required.

"How is Peter, really?" he asked.

"Deborah says he is using the oxygen all of the time, now, and his teachers are telling her that he is sleeping much of the time at school."

He nodded. "I want to be better so I can be with him."

"The doctor says you will be able to go home tomorrow."

He took a deep breath and nodded. "Good. I need ...him."

"Yes," she said. "And he needs you, so I'll leave and let you sleep now."

He reached for her. "No. I mean no, please. We need to talk."

Sarah sat down again, afraid of what the subject might be. So, she decided to tackle it head on.

She looked at her lap and tried to get it out. "Abe, I'm not ... I'm not ... promiscuous."

His eyes opened wide, and he sat back as if struck. "Promiscu ... how can you think I would say that?"

"I ... I let you ... no, I invited you to ..."

"Sarah, I wanted you. I started it this morning."

"But you ..."

"Sarah, why would you think anyone could believe that about you?"

"I don't want to be like my mother ... my grandmother..."

Abe tried to lean toward her but had to stay against his pillow. "Sweetheart, tell me about your mother."

She couldn't answer. And then he took hold of her hand. "Tell me, please."

She glanced up at him and then off at the window on the far side of his bed. "Grandfather always thought ... he waited to see if I would ... Mother, she left me for him to raise, just like grandmother had left my mother for him to raise. Both of them. They ran around with other men ... and he was so hurt and so good."

"Oh, Sarah. You spent all these years proving to him that you wouldn't . . ."

"He taught me everything, so I would be too busy. He taught and he worked, and he watched . . ."

Abe pulled her toward him. "Sit here, please."

She sat on the side of his bed.

He studied her face. "Everyone needs to love," he said. "You need to be loved and I need it. This morning – I think that was this morning, I risked, but I didn't stop because you . . . because I thought you were wanton. I stopped because I didn't want to hurt you . . . or be disgusting to you, with how I touched you."

She looked up at him, and she smiled. "Abraham Hallowell, we are so stupid."

"Stupid? Or . . .?"

"I loved how you touched me. But you didn't listen to me about that. You claimed you didn't want to hurt me. And when that didn't make sense to me, I realized you probably thought me a loose woman who let men do that all the time."

He stared at her. After a moment, he said, "As I remember it, I was grateful that you let me, and then . . ."

"And then you let that damned arm come between us."

"Well, it isn't the hand I want to have when I touch you, and I still want to touch you."

"It is the arm and the hand on the man I love. I've never wanted to love anyone as I love you. And the sooner you believe that the sooner we can be safe with each other."

"Safe?"

"When we get to the place where we can listen and believe each other, then we will be safe to love each other. Until then, my fears and yours are going to come between us."

"Sarah, please believe that I think you beautiful, loving, generous and the best of women."

"I can believe that when you realize that you are the best of men, with or without a right hand."

He stared at her. "Can I kiss you before I fall asleep again?"

"Please do." She reached across him and pulled his right arm out of the covers and put it to her face as she leaned toward him.

He hesitated and then, leaning on his left hand, he moved enough to touch her lips with his. His arm reached behind her head and pulled her more thoroughly into his kiss.

When they came up for air, she whispered. "Now, Abraham Hallowell, sleep and be ready to go home in the morning."

"Thank you. I will." He lay back.

She covered him with his sheet and blankets, kissing him once more, she said, "Work at believing in yourself. You teach that God loves all. All includes Abe Hallowell."

She turned out his bed light and left the hospital room.

# CHAPTER THIRTY-SIX

Abe came home to Arthur's house and slept in the den for almost forty-eight hours. When he woke up, Peter and Andy were sitting in their wheelchairs next to his bed.

"Hello, gentlemen," Abe said.

They both laughed. "Hi Dad," Peter said.

Andy just smiled.

Abe said, "Andy, what's up, man?"

"You dream a lot."

"About what?" Abe asked. He was afraid he talked in his sleep.

"You dream about falling, mostly."

"Oh? And how do you know?"

" 'Cause you grab the covers and jerk, like the covers are a rope."

Relieved that he must not have said anything, Abe bluffed. "Yeah, climbing is scary, and you sure do need a rope."

"Are you getting up?" Andy asked.

"Sometime soon, I hope."

Abe realized that Arthur stood in the doorway. Arthur stepped in and said, "Well, boys, shall we try to feed this guy the soup we made?"

"Sit up, Dad," Pete said, and then he added, "Can you sit up?"

"Let's test it," Abe said.

Arthur came into the room and pulled pillows up as Abe rolled to his side, winced from feeling the stitches in his back.

"Wow!" he said. "It feels like a big hole in my back."

"Pretty much," Arthur said. "But they got it all and it should heal over in a few weeks."

"A few weeks?"

Andy said, "Dr. Hoff sent you a page of exercises."

Abe looked at Andy. "Oh, kind of like the page of exercises he gave you a year ago?"

Andy glanced down at his feet. "Different exercises."

"Uh-huh. Make you a deal."

"Okay. I'll do mine if you do yours."

"Yes," Abe said, "but this time, we have to do them at the same time. After bathroom, but before breakfast and dinner."

Andy glanced at Peter who watched him carefully. Finally, Andy said, "Okay. Before breakfast and dinner."

"Together," Peter added. "Same room."

"Okay." Andy said. "Living room."

"Great," Abe said. "Now where's that soup. I'm starving, Gentlemen."

At that unlikely description of them, Andy and Peter laughed again. Arthur brought in a rolling cart with the lunch for four already laid out.

*　*

While Abe recovered, Sarah and Miguel worked during the days at the church and in the afternoon and evenings they worked with contractors and Jeff and Akesha to get Abe's room and new bathroom finished and the Jackson home further along.

The final payments from the Schreiben's kept them all going financially and brought new prospects from the Schreiben's neighbors and friends.

The plumber got all the fixtures into Abe's bathrooms downstairs. Miguel taught Akesha and Jeff how to install tile floors and backsplashes. They did the same tile work in bathrooms at the Jackson house while Miguel managed the last details on the Schreiben house in the southwest hills.

One evening after dinner, Akesha stood looking at Abe's kitchen and then she and Jeff began wandering through the house with Miguel, checking things out.

"There's lots of rooms in this old house, huh!" Akesha said. She came to the room off the back of the house where they had been storing lumber and fixtures.

"What we gonna do with this room?" she asked Miguel.

"Dunno," Miguel said. "Can't afford to do anything with it now. Maybe down the road. A den. A guest room."

"Or,' Akesha said, "A den that can be a guest room when needed."

Jeff said, "Abe's walking now, so ...so it doesn't need to be...be his bedroom."

"Yeah," Akesha said, "When he first came to Arthur's from that hospital, I thought he was never gonna walk again."

Miguel glanced off into the kitchen where Sarah washed pans while trying to keep water off the unfinished counters. He whispered, "I'm glad you didn't say that back then."

Now they all three whispered. Jeff said, "She wou … woulda freaked."

"Why were all those people at the hospital calling her Mrs. Hallowell?" Akesha asked.

Miguel said, "She explained that. He wanted somebody with him. Didn't want to be alone, so he said she was his wife."

Jeff snorted. "Didn't want to be with … without her, you me … mean. Not jus … just anybody, but Her."

Akesha punched him in the shoulder. "You let them be. We start teasing, they'll never figure out what they want."

Jeff turned toward Miguel. "Not so bad for a p . . . priest, is he?"

Miguel stared at Jeff. "You got to tease somebody, tease Jeff into doing his algebra."

"Wanna h . . . help me?" Jeff asked.

"Kitchen table. Five minutes."

# CHAPTER THIRTY-SEVEN

And then the graffiti reappeared, first on the garage door of Sarah's home and office, and then on the plywood covering over the church elevator shaft.

"He knows where we're working," Miguel said to Sarah and Ernst. "He may even know about Hallowell's house."

"I don't want that man around Abe's parishioners," Ernst said. "We've got new families in the house and they and their friends are now here on Sundays, as well."

"The police are here on a drive-by basis," Miguel said.

Sarah spoke up. "We need to hire a protective service at the church, and we need to stay away from our office."

They arranged to do just that, but the congregation decided also to protect the five families next door, so a security guard walked the property in methodical but unpredictable timing.

When Deborah saw the CX3 of the Coxwell Thirteen gang painted on the plywood covering the elevator shaft she said, "Let's turn it on them. That's an elephant sitting down, the C is his rump. The X is his open mouth and the three is the ears of a mouse pulling a thorn from his paw."

Miguel laughed. "Aesop's fables! Animal tales."

"Yes, except Aesop used a lion. We're not letting this gang think we believe they are lions."

"Give me a sketch," Miguel said. "I'll do it."

So, they worked upstairs in the church on the sketch. They created a sitting elephant with his big mouth crying over a thorn. That took care of the big C and the X. As they started turning the 3 into the mouse ears, they enjoyed listening to Ernst's stain glass class in the next room. They noticed that a lot of younger people were in the class along with the oldsters that normally came. Ernst was having a great time in there. People wanted his knowledge.

By the next day, both of their paintings were sketched out on their plywood surfaces at the church and on the garage door at Rohann and Salvador.

On the church plywood, Deborah painted the lower half while Miguel worked the upper.

"Our brush strokes are different," Miguel said, standing back.

Deborah studied the situation. "When we come to my upper reach, let's mix the strokes together at that level so there is a smooth transition."

Miguel looked at her. "I thought you only played ping-pong."

"You haven't been in my closet, have you?"

"Umm... wouldn't you say that your closet should be out of bounds for the builder?"

"Definitely. Don't go in there as the builder. Go in there as my friend. Back, left, behind the long and useless prom dress."

He stared at her. "There's a prom dress?"

"It used to belong to Grandma Amanda Charles' daughter. Amanda wanted me to have it."

Miguel stopped. "She wanted you to go to a prom?"

Deborah glanced at her paint job. "She wanted me to go."

"Is there a prom?"

"There is." Deborah picked up the paint brush and fixed a few things that Miguel knew did not need fixing.

"Deborah, would you go to the prom with me?" Miguel asked. "Unless I'm too old and you already ..."

She stared at him. "You're jiving me."

"Not. I bet you can do a mean twirl in that chair. Maybe you need a shorter prom dress, but when is this event? and will you go with me?"

She stopped painting, and he could see wetness at the edges of her eyes, so he started painting again.

"Maybe," he said, "you'd rather go out to dinner with me, or..."

"Yes."

He looked at her again and saw she had wiped those tears and put pink paint on her cheek. He reached his hand out, held her chin with his fingers and wiped off the paint with his thumb.

"Paint," he explained. "And which? Dinner or a prom?"

"Dinner," she said. "I'd love to go to dinner and just talk."

He smiled, and relaxed. He couldn't actually see himself at a prom for eighteen-year-olds. He'd been too old for that even in his high school days. But for her ...

Deborah laughed. "Can't fox-trot or waltz, so dinner."

He frowned, "Does anybody fox-trot these days?"

"No idea," she said. "Let's go do the other mural at your place."

"Can we get that chair in my truck?"

She studied his truck at the curb. "Possibly not."

"Where's Dick when we need him?"

"Studying chemistry, physics and biology at Reed College," she said.

"That settles it, I'm getting a van next time."

"Let's get over there when Dick can take me, then."

As they started inside, a blue Chevrolet pulled up beside them. Miguel got between it and Deborah.

"Get to the ramp," he whispered, and felt relief when she did just that.

He recognized that car, but it had acquired a license plate – probably stolen. The two men inside were the two who had been across the street from the police station three weeks ago. Matt Langren and Dorsey Templeton. Templeton rolled down his window, swiped his blond hair from his eyes and stared at Miguel.

Miguel remembered these were the guys who had followed Abe from the police station, and maybe the ones who shot Samuel at the Pair-a-Dice motel.

"Hey, Salivate, kind of pretty, that painting." That was Templeton, hanging out the passenger window.

"Glad you like it," Miguel said, ignoring their usual supposed humor on his name.

Langren leered off in the direction of Deborah's disappearance. "Kind of hard to get it on in a wheelchair, isn't it?"

Miguel just stared at him and hoped Deborah was out of sight, and out of hearing range.

In his head he said the license plate number over to memorize it.

Langren leaned over and said, "You seem to have a lot of cripples in your life all of a sudden. Wonder what would happen if they got dumped out on the road."

"Captain Reese would know to look for you," Miguel said.

"Oooh, Cap Reese," Langren said. "Salivate is suddenly friends with police."

"And many others who know to keep track of which little dive holds two flee bags."

Templeton rolled the window up and drove off.

Miguel stood there shaking. They threatened Deborah and her brothers, and he knew the police had lots of seedy motels to watch and not enough evidence of them selling. And he had been angry enough to hint that they should move.

He ran to the ramp and found her up the ramp, out of sight, in her chair, a long shovel in her hand and her chair turned to roar down the incline if needed.

Miguel fell on his knees beside her. "Where'd you get this shovel?"

"Construction leftovers," she said and set it down. "We need to call the police."

He pulled out his phone and typed something. "License plate," he said.

And then he called Abe. When he answered, Miguel said, "Langren and Templeton drove by as we painted. They threatened your family with getting dumped from their wheelchairs into the road. Where are Dick, Pete and Andy?"

He could hear Abe stand up. "Deb?"

"Here with me."

"Dick and Andy are on their way to Arthur's from school. Picking up Petey is my next job. I'll call his school."

Miguel asked, "Are you upstairs in your office? Can Deb and I come up and plan with you."

"Gotta get Pete. I'll meet you down there on my way to the car."

And then, as Paul, the security guard, came running around the corner, Miguel called Captain Reese. The guard told him where the Chevy had gone up Sandy Boulevard.

"Yeah," Reese said, "a plain car just spotted them near your security guard and is now following them."

*   *

Because of the renewed awareness of danger to both families, the next few days were a whirl for Sarah and Miguel, calling contractors, making work schedules, making certain Jeff and Akesha's coach and teachers were aware of the danger. The coach agreed to bring them home after practice each day. He planned to take a circuitous route and get Jeff and Akesha to watch for followers.

The hardest part for all of them was wondering what Kevin's father might be planning. The only help was that the Chevy driven by Templeton had hovered on Sandy near the church for long enough that an alerted officer in an unmarked police car saw them. Paul, the security guard, had run up to the next busy street, talking to police dispatch on his phone. He had pointed his elbow at the Chevy as if he were combing his hair back.

After the police car followed the blue chevy, Paul had returned to be sure the church and house remained safe.

The police said the license plate had been stolen, of course, but they had followed Langren and Templeton up Sandy Boulevard from near the church to an old motel just at the east edge of town.

Reese had the place staked out, but neither Kevin nor his dad had showed up there, yet.

The police decided to follow Langren and Templeton wherever they went, on the chance they would intersect with Aaron and Kevin.

And then, the coach at the high school took photos of a gang of boys who seemed to be hanging around the track practice for no reason. Sarah recognized many of them from Coxwell 13.

After this threat, and with summer vacation coming in weeks, Sarah and Miguel foresaw big trouble coming.

"Mom, I've got a plan." Miguel said.

"Let's have it."

"Methodist Summer Camp down at the coast."

"Methodist? You've got religion of a sudden?"

"There's a Quaker Camp right across the highway. Would that be less religion?"

"Doubt it. What's the idea?"

"I applied to be a camp counselor, teach the kids wood-working skills and get all of our gang out of town."

"All?"

"Peter and Andy, too."

"And Deborah, I suppose."

"If she wants to do it. I brought her an application to work with the athletic director. But the idea is that Akesha and Jeff will be safe, and Andy, Peter and Deborah, I hope. You and the contractors can work on the house and Abe can keep looking for Kevin with his police and fire and motel network."

"What does this camp cost?"

"Abe applied for scholarships for them."

"Wait a minute. You and Abraham cooked up something together?"

"Yes, after the Chevy guys made their threat. We are just hoping it works. Won't know for another week or so."

"Did this camp interview you?"

"Yesterday."

"Oh, that extra-long run to the grocery store?"

"Yeah, Mom. I didn't want to spring this until it was a real possibility. But I want the kids to be safe."

"I appreciate that, Miguel, but I'm a lot uncomfortable with you working this out with Abe and not with me."

"I didn't think you'd even think it possible until we had this much in the works, so I just took this idea to Abe because he's a Methodist minister."

"Not a priest," Sarah jibed him.

"Okay, Mom. I was wrong about him."

She smiled. "Miguel, let's hope this works."

"Yeah. The biggest problem is that it doesn't get you out of town."

"I'll be here and not at our place. Abe will be at Arthur's."

"Well, I guess that will be safer. But you've got to watch out, like when you go to the hardware store. In fact, let Abe do the runs to the hardware store, you just stay here until they catch Kevin."

She said, "You know Ernst keeps going back to his part of the shop," Sarah said.

"I know," Miguel said. "I told him I was going to change the locks if he didn't stop that and get the plaster forms built for the church while he was *in* the church."

"I'll try to keep him so busy here or at the Jackson's that he won't feel like going back to the house."

"That's best. Except I want you not to go to Jackson's either. They are not living there until next month. And Kevin or Kevin's father knows about that place as well. I've set the lights and everything there, so it looks like somebody is living there."

"But the windows," Sarah said.

"I got used curtains at the Goodwill and hung them on the downstairs windows, and paper on the upstairs windows that looks like shades."

"My goodness!" Sarah stared at her son. "You've been thinking a lot, haven't you?"

"I've talked to all our contractors. Muhammed, and Booky Kerns and anybody we know, all those people who came to the hospital, they are looking for Templeton and Langren. They're also looking for Kevin and they have photos of his dad. If they see any of that gang, they call Captain Reese. We'll get him, Mom."

Sarah sat down on the nearest step. "Whew! And I've just been here whistling and cutting wood while you did all of this."

"I hope you measured twice and cut once," Miguel joked.

"Yes, indeed."

After Miguel returned to work at the church, Sarah looked around Abe's house and studied all the things she wished to share with him: how the light fell differently on the chimney now that Ernst had plastered it over and she had put tiles into the mantle support; how the newly finished kitchen counters curved toward the doors so that wheelchairs could glide smoothly by; and how the ceiling of his attic room shone in the light from the new large window over his bed as its rays fell on the plastered sheet rock above the exposed rafters.

He might not see all of this again before it had been finished and painted. He was heavily involved in care for Peter, and Sarah had not seen him since their talk at the hospital.

She hoped he really meant what he had said about trusting her love. She hoped he didn't have time to think maybe he should write Sarah Rohann out of his life as a bad bet, too easy a conquest to trust.

# CHAPTER THIRTY-EIGHT

**M**iguel and Deborah had dinner several times at Cha Cha Cha and also at Pastini's where her chair fit into the table in an alcove. They enjoyed talking and laughing and touching – hands, toes, arms, shoulders, all the little nudges and caresses that meant affection.

At the same time, they never took it any farther, Deborah because it was all so new to her, Miguel because he was so aware that he was considered an adult out with a teenager. She might be nearly eighteen and very adult in attitude, but she was a teenager.

And he had no idea where this might go, but he certainly didn't want it to go downhill in any way. Finally, he asked about her scholarship.

She smiled. "Next August I'm going to go to the University of Oregon and major in art therapy."

Only a hundred miles away, Miguel thought, but he said, "Not athletic therapy?"

"Oh, I'll play ping-pong and I'll be on the tour, but my focus is on art. Didn't you get into that closet, yet?"

He ducked his head and said, "Way too personal."

"Okay, Mr. Do Right. I will have to come over there and pull the artwork out for you."

"I look forward to seeing it. Are you coming to camp with us?"

"I sent in that application you gave me. My interview appointment is Thursday morning."

"Want a ride there?"

"Got that van yet?"

"No."

"Dick will take me on his way to college."

"Tell me about Dick," he said, somewhat apprehensively.

She said, "He's a junior in college and according to friends, it's Dick's fault that his favorite physics professor, Dr. James, is married to the world's best violinist."

"Really?" No mention of a girlfriend for Dick, but the way she talked about him relieved one worry. He said, "How did I miss this famous violinist?"

"Wow! You missed that story? Scary and wonderful. Read the newspaper, Miguel. It's amazing what you can learn."

"Doesn't that depend on the newspaper?"

"You'd know more about that if you tried several. Try *Street Roots* and the local ones first, easier to see what's true there. Try the national newspapers after and throw out the ones that seem to scream a lot of fear into people."

"I'll go looking," he said.

"I'll help you," she said.

Miguel gave her a huge grin. He couldn't help it.

*  *

Deborah applied to work with the camp athletic director, and on Thursday, she discovered that the woman knew who she was.

Mrs. Kean said, "Deborah Applebaum, what a pleasure it will be to work with you. I watched you do an impromptu class in ping-pong at Eisenhower High after one of those exhibition tournaments. You are a very fine teacher."

Deborah smiled. "Those three kids just came up to me asking all kinds of questions . . ."

"And you were kind enough to answer them. Do your parents know we're talking about taking you away for several weeks?"

Deborah said, "It turns out that my foster dad and a friend were the ones who cooked up this idea. You've already accepted my foster brothers and their friends on scholarships."

Mrs. Kean looked at her over her reading glasses, "And your foster dad is . . .?

"Abe . . ."

"Oh! Abe Hallowell. Now this is making sense. I wondered how you knew about this camp."

"Methodist networking," Deborah said.

Mrs. Kean smiled as she put down Deborah's application. "Now, we get to the care questions."

"Yes. I can transfer, bed, toilet, shower." She waved a hand. "All that kind of stuff. I can repair my wheelchair and any other wheelchair that is in trouble. And I prefer a lower bunk."

Mrs. Kean laughed. Then she asked, "Meds?"

"Coffee, black."

"That's it?"

"It is, except in special circumstances, which haven't happened for two years."

"But these will be new circumstances, so . . ."

"I'll bring a sheet explaining for the nurse, and I'll bring that medicine just in case."

"Okay. One other topic. Abraham told us that he is anxious to get his family and this other family . . ."

"The Rohanns," Deb supplied.

"Yes, he's anxious to get them out of town until one of the Rohann foster kids is found, because of the threat to both families from the Coxwell 13 gang."

Deborah was glad to have Abe's words and his coaching to fall back on. He'd told her he didn't want Kevin's name in any discussions about this, but he wanted the camp to know the truth."

"Yes," Deborah said. "I think they are more of a threat to the Rohann kids, but since we're friends, Dad thinks we should all be out of town until the police get this sorted out."

"Well, we are looking forward to meeting all of you and having a fine summer. We'll hope that helps the police and your foster dad make some headway with this gang thing."

"Thank you."

As she turned her wheelchair to depart, Deborah said. "Oh! I help with the care for Peter and Andy at home, so they trust me. Could we bunk near each other, so night goes smoothly?"

"That is a very good idea."

# CHAPTER THIRTY-NINE

During the two weeks before camp, no more graffiti appeared, and no one sighted Kevin or his father. The blue Chevrolet was found trashed and abandoned in the parking lot at the Jantzen Beach Mall. So, they knew Langren and Templeton had probably stolen yet another auto and changed its license plates, too.

Both families kept a watch for any hint that the two thugs were cruising by the church or the other homes.

Sarah convinced the Jacksons to wait their move until later so that they were not part of the danger from Aaron's gang. Life seemed to be on hold for everyone.

During those same weeks, it became evident that Peter should not leave town. Miguel wanted Peter to see the camp, so he went to Arthur Charles's home and knocked on the door. He had been here last as an eighteen-year-old, helping renovate for Amanda's wheelchair.

Arthur opened the door and looked up in surprise. "Miguel?"

"Yes, sir," Miguel said, pleased to be remembered.

"My goodness. You're not a teenager anymore."

Miguel said, "I try not to be, but sometimes it's hard work, you know."

Arthur opened the door wider, chuckling. "I know. Only my joints remind me that I'm not twenty-five. Come in. Come in."

Miguel stepped into a living room where he could tell the furniture had been moved to widen the spaces for three wheelchairs.

Arthur said, "How long has it been since you remodeled our kitchen?"

"I think I was eighteen, so maybe five years. We didn't know that Amanda was so sick, Mr. Charles. I'm really sorry that you've lost her. That must be pretty hard."

Arthur glanced at a photo of his wife on a nearby credenza. "Yes. Amanda always made me laugh, no matter her pain."

"I liked her a lot," Miguel said. "She was so calm and yet funny. She made me look at myself and admit I could let go of anger, mostly."

"Mostly?"

"Yeah, well some anger dies hard."

Arthur put a hand on Miguel's arm. "Don't I know." He glanced again at Amanda's photo and then said, "But something brought you here today. You looking for Abe?"

"Yes, I am."

"He's out in the back yard fixing a leak in my garden drip system. Come on through."

Miguel followed him through the kitchen, which still looked pretty good, with its low counters and two sinks, one dish sink at wheelchair height. They walked out the den door onto the deck and found Abe on his knees, trying to rejoin two pieces of hose with a special joining piece.

Miguel got down and provided the right-hand push to get it all back together. Then Abe straightened and studied Miguel.

"You just happen to know I needed a hand?"

Miguel laughed. "Guessing. But really, I came to ask a favor."

Arthur said, "How about if you two brush off the dirt and sit on the deck out of the sun?"

They rose, Abe a little slowly. "Leg," he explained, "but getting better."

Miguel nodded.

Arthur said, "I'll bring us all some iced tea. Sugar, Miguel?"

Miguel chuckled. "You've got me, Mr. Charles."

Arthur went in his back door. From the deck chairs they could see him puttering around in his kitchen.

"What's your favor?" Abe asked.

"Is Peter at school?"

"No. He's still in bed. Not enough oxygen, even with the machine. He needs a lot of sleep, these days."

"That's not good," Miguel said. "I was hoping we could take him to see the camp. He can't go with the others, but I thought, maybe it would be fun for him to see the cabins and the ocean."

Abe covered his mouth with his hand and looked away. Miguel looked at his work boots. After a moment, Abe reached over and put his hand on Miguel's shoulder.

"Thanks," he said. "Yes."

They both sat there in silence. In Miguel's head ran the little rhyme he'd heard Peter use to describe their house "Gotta shift for their selves. Our chairs were built by elves." What a creative mind in a fun boy.

Arthur came out with a tray and three glasses which he set on the table nearby.

He sat down next to Abe. "You gentlemen planning something?" he asked.

Abe said, "Miguel hopes we can take Peter to see the summer camp. I think we'd better do it soon."

"Tomorrow?" Arthur asked. "Start early in the morning? Hour and a half there, hour and a half back, maybe he can last for an hour at the camp."

Abe looked at Arthur. "Probably about right. But what about Andy?"

Arthur asked, "Can Deborah help me take care of him?"

"Losing Peter is going to be as hard on Andy as anybody," Abe said.

"Yes, but you want camp to be a new space for Andy when he gets there. Just let Andy go to camp without that memory of visiting with Peter."

Abe sat still, thinking this over. Finally, he said, "Yes, I think you're right. We'll get Peter and Andy dressed, send Andy and Deb to high school with Dick and then we'll go to the beach. Does that work for you, Miguel?"

"Yes."

Arthur added. "We've got a caretaker coming in afternoons. With Deb home we should be able to handle Andy's needs until you return."

Abe nodded. "Okay. That's what we'll do."

Another silence followed. The sun rose over Arthur's cherry trees and shone on the roses – Amanda's roses, Miguel knew. He'd watched her pruning them often during the summer when they built the kitchen. Here Arthur had the perfect wheelchair house and, until recently, no longer any wheelchair. Everything in the house must remind Arthur of his missing wife.

Things went bad for some, Miguel knew. It went real bad, way too often.

*  *

Early the next afternoon, Abe lifted Peter into his wheelchair as soon as they arrived at the Methodist camp. He fixed the oxygen tank into its carrier on the side of the wheelchair.

"Oh," Peter said. "All green."

At first Miguel thought he was referring to the tube from his oxygen tank to his nose, but Peter seemed to be gazing up. Miguel looked up and saw that Peter must be taking in the spruce, fir and hemlock trees that surrounded the camp.

"Yep, Green right down to the sand." Miguel said.

"I hear the ocean," Peter sighed.

"Yes," Miguel said. "From here that's kind of a hike, but we can drive a little farther north and get to it on Minnehaha Lane. Let's see the cabins and lake here first."

"Minnehaha, like that poem about Hiawatha?"

Miguel stared at him.

"I like poetry," Peter explained. "On the shores of Gitche-gumee, by the shining big sea waters . . ."

"Stood the wigwam of Nokomis," Miguel said. "Daughter of the Moon, Nokomis. Dark behind it rose the forest . . ."

Peter glanced up and said, "Rose the dark and gloomy pine trees . . ." Peter laughed with glee. "Yes," he whispered and began drumming Longfellow's chosen rhythm on his wheelchair arms.

"I'll come back as Hiawatha," he said to the poem's insistent beat.

Miguel stopped pushing, "Why Hiawatha?"

"So, I can have adventures and fall in love," Peter said.

Abe had stopped walking. Miguel glanced at Abe and saw the startled look, so Miguel carried the conversation for both of them.

"Adventures are a great idea," Miguel said. "If you are Hiawatha, will you be by Gitche-Gummee, Lake Superior, when we come to look for you?"

"No, the big trees there are gone. I will be by Crater Lake."

"Great place to have adventures. We will seek you there."

Abe still stood behind them, trying to gather his calm.

Miguel said, "Here are the cabins. This week they're not used because school isn't over yet."

"But," Peter began, "when you all are here, where will you teach woodworking?"

Miguel pointed at a small shed at the end of the lane. "I'll be there. There are tables and tools in that building."

"Hiawatha would know how to build homes, and fishing nets and canoes," Peter said.

"Yes, he would. He could teach at this camp himself."

Peter nodded, and said, "Hiawatha taught peace to his nation."

Miguel nodded, pleased with Peter's choice of heroes. "He did that. He worked hard to bring peace to his tribes."

After a moment, Peter said, "But he and Minnehaha didn't play ping-pong."

"True," Miguel said, "However, he lived in the east. Some of the tribes in the east played a game where you run and toss and catch a ball using a net on a stick."

"That's cool. We'll do that game."

"I can hardly wait to hear about all the things you'll do when you are Hiawatha."

By this time, Abe had gathered his thoughts and caught up to Peter's hopes. He asked, "Peter, when you are Hiawatha, wear one special feather so we will know you."

"Gold finch," Peter said emphatically. "We'll make friends when they come through on their migration and my gold finch will leave each of us a feather."

"That will be special, and we'll be able to spot you and Minnehaha in a crowd." Abe said.

Peter smiled. And then changed the subject. "Where will Deborah be teaching ping-pong?"

It took Miguel a moment to come back from imagining Peter as Hiawatha and in love. After a beat, he said. "She'll teach in the main building here. It has a big room for games. A ping-pong table is coming tomorrow." Miguel said.

Abe said, "Want to go up the ramp and see where people eat and play games?"

*  *

A half an hour later, they had passed the fire pit for night meetings and singing. They passed the boat dock on the lake. As they returned to the parking lot, they noticed the Quaker camp across the highway, where there was an even bigger lake, and a diving board which Peter declared scary fun.

They packed themselves back into the car and drove two minutes north to Minnehaha Lane.

As soon as Abe had carried Peter to the sand, and Miguel had spread a blanket for him, Peter declared. "I've never seen anything better than this ocean. Look at those rocks. What made holes in them?"

"Waves," Abe said. "Years and years of waves."

"Oh, look," Peter said. "The water is still crashing out there, make the holes bigger every minute."

"Yes. Every minute."

Peter looked around at Miguel who put up an umbrella to shade them. "Thank you, Miguel." Peter whispered. "Please sit down."

Both Miguel and Abe sat on the blanket with him.

Peter let his toes push into the sand, which was dry. "Don't people make things with this sand?"

"Yes, they do," Abe said. "But they make it out of the wet sand closer to the ocean. Wet sand sticks together better."

"Miguel," Peter said, "maybe you could bring the kids down here and teach them how to build a house, maybe a house with sand and maybe a house with sticks and leather, like Hiawatha."

Miguel held a spoon for Peter – a yogurt for lunch because it had become difficult for him to swallow. Miguel stopped, yogurt spoon in mid-air and said, "That's a great idea, Pete. I'll do some research about how Hiawatha would have built his home."

While they ate, Abe and Miguel had to make the bites smaller in the little orange or the cookies that Miguel had made for Peter.

After a time, Peter asked, "Dad, did you have a beach where you lived in Beirut, Lebanon?"

"We did. Another beautiful beach."

Miguel glanced at Abe, thinking he'd never heard about living in Lebanon. He'd never thought to ask. He only knew that somewhere someone had thrown a bomb.

"Dad," Peter said, "Do you still have friends in Lebanon?"

"I do."

"Elani's brothers?"

"Yes. They write to me, and a friend named Saleh."

"And that guy who flew with you to the hospital?"

"Jean-Marie Biquet, yes, we write, too."

"That's good. Friends are good."

"Yes, they are. Tell me about your friends, Peter."

Peter sat and thought a moment, and then said, "My friends are afraid to be friends. They are all sick and they see me be more and more sick and they are afraid they will catch what I have."

"So, they stay away even at school?"

"Yes, but the teachers are friends who stick by me."

"The teachers are adults. They understand," Abe said. "The others are children, and it is hard for them to understand how they feel, so they pretend they don't feel and that it will all go away."

"That's what Mrs. Stamps says to me. She tries to talk to the other children about ups and downs and feelings, but really, they are just too scared."

"I'm sorry, Peter. It must be hard to see them afraid of you."

Peter leaned on Abe. "I try not to care, but I care a lot."

"Andy loves you. Deborah loves you."

"And Miguel loves me. That's why he knew this would be a good trip."

Miguel just reached over and put a hand on Peter's hand.

A few minutes later, Peter fell asleep. Abe stayed on the blanket with him while Miguel packed the car and then Miguel carried Peter to his car seat while Abe carried the blanket and the umbrella.

# CHAPTER FORTY

On the day after Miguel and Dick took the rest of the family to camp, Abe and Arthur had to take Peter to the hospital. Sarah met them there as the ambulance arrived.

Abe reached out for her. She took his hand and they rushed into the emergency entrance following Peter's gurney. Arthur followed them.

The nurses expected them and took them into a room.

Doctor Hoff met them, talking to Peter, who gasped for breath even though his oxygen tank was working.

"Peter, I'm giving you something to relax, so you don't have to work so hard to breathe."

Within moments, Peter's breathing relaxed, but Doctor Hoff glanced at Abe and said to Sarah, "Ma'am, could you and Arthur stay to help Peter? I want him to know you are here."

Sarah nodded and took Peter's right hand in hers. Arthur put his hand on Peter's shoulder.

"Abe," Doctor Hoff said, "Please come with me."

Sarah watched them go out into the hall. She turned to Arthur and said, "There is a chair behind you, Arthur. Pull it up. We're here for a time."

Arthur did just that and sank into it as if it were an old friend. She knew he had been in exactly this position for many weeks with Amanda, and that wasn't very long ago.

Peter stared at her as if he feared she might disappear.

"Peter, we are here," she whispered. "Close your eyes and think about the waves on the ocean. They will help you breathe."

"Andy," Peter whispered.

"Andy will be all right. We'll make sure Andy knows you love him. He will know we all love him."

Peter closed his eyes. Sarah crooned to him in the rhythm of Hiawatha, but in her grandfather's language. She crooned an even older story of a hero in Finland and Estonia. The Kalevala had been grandfather's favorite poem. Sarah didn't know Hiawatha, but she had recognized that rhythm the first time Miguel told her of Peter's wishes for his afterlife.

Arthur held Peter's feet and massaged them gently. It was clear he loved Peter, too, and Sarah remembered that Amanda and Arthur had become grandparents to Abe's children. What a difficult time this would be for Arthur, as well.

\*　　\*

Out in the hall, Doctor Hoff looked Abe in the eye. "This great little guy is on his last days. He is dying, Abe. He's now into the pneumonia we talked about. I know you've known this was coming, but, Abe, I'm worried about you and Arthur, so I want you to be aware. This is it."

Abe nodded, not certain he could speak.

"Is that Arthur's daughter in there with him?"

Abe shook his head. "No, my… my friend. Architect. Re-did Arthur's house for Amanda. Now my house for kids."

"Where's Andy?" Doctor Hoff asked.

"All the kids are at the Methodist Camp down near Rockaway Beach. Most of them know that Peter is too sick to continue."

"They know he's going to die?"

"Well, yes."

"Abe, you haven't been sugar coating this for Andy, have you?"

"What do you mean?"

"The words you use. He can't continue, for instance. That's not what we're talking about here. We're not hiking, and Peter can't continue so we leave him by the side of the road until we can come back."

Abe looked as if he'd been smacked.

"Abe, we talked about this. That 'he's passed on' kind of language is not helpful. Peter is dying and Andy is going to be hell broke for mad when he finds out. Bring Andy home from that camp. Deborah understands and Deborah has had a chance to say good-bye, but Andy hasn't had that chance and he needs it."

"All right," Abe said. "How long have I got?"

"You've got maybe twenty-four, thirty-six hours. We'll do the best for Peter, but go. And on the way back you tell Andy why."

"I'll work this out with Arthur and Sarah. I'll be back in three hours."

"Okay. And get his parents on the plane, now. I'm going in there and talk with Arthur and Peter while you explain to Sarah . . . what's her name?"

"Rohann."

"Oh," Doctor Hoff said, "Adolf Linder Rohann." He looked around the corner at Sarah. "Yes," he said. "I should have remembered. Tough girl."

"What!?" Abe couldn't believe this description of her. He felt like hitting any man who said such a thing.

Doctor Hoff put up his hands. He saw how Abe felt. "I mean, she can take what gets thrown at her. That kind of tough."

"Okay," Abe calmed down. "I'll tell Peter I'm getting Andy. I'll talk to Sarah."

Doctor Hoff nodded.

*    *

Within a little over an hour, Andy was in the car and very upset.

Back in Portland, Sarah and Arthur waited at the hospital. Peter's parents were on their way. Sarah had arranged for a male caretaker to be on call for when Andy came home. Abe and Arthur were not going to be able by themselves to visit Peter and take care of Andy.

But at the moment, Abe's problem was to tell Andy the hardest thing.

"Andy, I know you were enjoying that camp."

"They have a therapy pool. I feel good in the pool."

"That's a good thing to know."

Andy cut to the heart of it. "You said Peter was sick. What's going on?"

Abe took a deep breath "Andy, Peter is dying. He has pneumonia. We're going to the hospital to see him."

"Pneumonia? But he has that oxygen tank. People get better from pneumonia."

"Most people do, that's true, but Peter's muscle disease makes him just keep getting worse and now his heart and lungs are not working well at all."

"But Dad, I just saw him on Friday. He was fine on Friday."

"Andy, think about the last three weeks or so. We want Peter to be fine, but how has he really been?"

"Well, his nighttime inhaler stopped working, so he got that machine that gives him oxygen all the time, but…"

"And on Friday, he was not breathing well, really, was he?"

"No, but I wanted him to take a deep breath. If only he'd taken a deep breath …"

"I wanted it too, Andy. We all wanted him to be able to breathe deep and be well. But we can't force that. It just doesn't work."

Now Andy sat in silence. Abe hoped he was crying in the back seat there, but he didn't look in the rearview mirror so Andy could do that alone.

*    *

Andy flailed in Abe's arms. They both sat on the bed in the boys' guest room at Arthurs' home, but Andy's grief consumed both of them. Arthur had called Doctor Hoff, who recommended a trip to the hospital followed by a sedative.

"In that order," Arthur repeated to Abe.

"So, Abe put Andy in his wheelchair, called public transport and accompanied Andy on the special bus to the hospital.

Once in Peter's room, Abe rested against the door jamb and let the boys seem to be alone.

Andy grew quiet. He managed to wheel himself to Peter's bedside. Peter turned his head.

"Hi," Peter said.

"I'm sorry," Andy said.

Peter smiled. "You get to throw things," he said. A few breaths later he was able to say. "Don't throw at people or pets."

Andy laughed and then he sighed. "I want you home."

"I love you, too," Peter said. It took a moment for him to get enough energy to continue, but Andy knew to wait. Finally, Peter said, "Andy, I'll be in heaven, helping you."

Andy said, "Can I help you?"

"Yes." Moments later, he said, "Take my stuffed lion and be a lion with him."

Andy sat very still. "I'll be quiet like your lion, unless somebody threatens my pride."

"Your family," Peter said.

"Yes. My family is my pride."

Peter smiled. "Abe loves you."

"I know," Andy said, glancing over at Abe. "I beat up on him and he just keeps coming back."

"So," Peter whispered. "Stop beating. Laugh more."

"Can't be as funny as you."

"Can too, if you practice." Moments of breathing ensued as Peter closed his eyes. Then he looked at Andy and said, "Practice on Abe. He laughs at anything."

Andy glanced at Abe again. "Comes back for bad jokes. That's true."

"Andy, I'm glad you came." And then Peter's eyes closed, and he slept.

Andy put his hands over his ears and started rocking back and forth.

Abe moved into the room and rolled Andy out into the hall to a nearby family room. He knelt in front of him until Andy became aware. And then Andy reached for Abe, who hugged him and let him cry.

# CHAPTER FORTY-ONE

Peter's time awake now came in snatches and his breathing was difficult to watch. Andy visited two more times, and then Abe drove him back to camp.

When his parents came, Peter awoke long enough to smile and hum a little of his mother's tune. His father kissed his forehead and took Peter's hand. Then Peter went back to sleep for long minutes.

By the day that Laura and Grant had to return to their other children, Peter was hardly ever awake. His presence was only announced by the noise of his oxygen delivery and his monitors. Abe felt the heaviness of their hearts as he drove them to the airport. At the last moment, Grant turned to Abe and said, "I'm sorry we brought you this grief, too."

"Grant, I've been lucky to know Peter and both of you. I know this is hard, especially since the other kids barely knew him at all, but he has been a light for our household. I don't regret it at all. I'm mad that such diseases happen, but I'm glad to have been here with you all in this time."

"Peter wants to be cremated," Grant said. "And he wants some of his ashes to be near Amanda. And some of his ashes to be with us. Can we work that out?"

Abe reached for Grant's hand. He didn't trust his voice much, but was able to say, "We'll make it work."

"Thank you," Laura said. "We'll grab our suitcases from your trunk. Just sit tight."

Abe was glad for that offer. As soon as he waved them into the airport's revolving door, he drove down the road a hundred yards, pulled into the shoulder and sobbed.

*   *

At the hospital, Peter woke for a minute.

"Mom and Daddy are with your brothers and sisters," Abe whispered.

"Good," Peter said, and closed his eyes.

Abe sat in the chair and watched his little boy relax into his medicine. Suddenly, Peter opened his eyes. "Dad?"

"Yes?"

"Love Sarah."

Abe didn't want to be dishonest, but he remembered her reaction to his touch. "I know," Abe said. "I want to."

"She . . . love . . . you."

Abe smiled. "Peter loves Sarah," he said.

"That, too." And then he went to sleep for a long time.

*   *

The elevator doors near the hospital lounge opened and closed with such regularity that Sarah had stopped turning to see who was getting on or off. She was numb with hurt for Abe and Peter. Abe's visits to Peter's room always began with a squaring of his shoulders, a deep breath, and a wiping of his face to clear away the worry and tiredness.

In between visits, he paced. Occasionally he leaned over Sarah, grabbing the arm of her chair and talking about some insignificant part of the renovation that needed finishing. He talked until he ran out of adrenaline and then in mid-sentence, the words stopped, and he just looked at her. The pain of losing Peter darkened his eyes and deepened the lines around his mouth.

This evening, Sarah reached up to comfort him. He let her brush her hands over his face. He turned to kiss her palm. His right arm came out of his pocket and caressed her arm.

His eyes opened wide. Startled at what he was doing, he stood up suddenly.

"I'm sorry." He turned on his heel and strode down the hall to the men's room. When he returned, he sat across the lounge from her.

Before she had a chance to say anything, the nurse came out. "Mr. Hallowell, Peter is about to wake up again."

Abe rose slowly, squared his shoulders, took a deep breath, and felt Sarah next to him. She touched his arm and looked up at him, making him face her.

"Abe, don't be sorry. I care about you. Let me care, please."

He was acutely conscious of her hand on his arm – the arm that ached to touch her as it had on the afternoon in his back yard. He looked down at her face, so full of concern for him, so fresh and untouched.

"Sarah, I know you care about me and my children. I just don't want to overstep the bounds of friendship."

"Who set those boundaries?" She frowned up at him.

It was the first time he recognized the little lines between her brows. She too had gone through sorrow for Miguel, for Akesha and Jeff – even for Kevin.

Sarah's hand tightened on his arm. "Who said there had to be boundaries to our friendship, Abraham?"

Her insistent question brought him back to the present. "Circumstances. The boundaries are caused by our circumstances."

He was evading. He knew it and she knew it.

"Abe, you have enough on your mind right now. I won't press this. Just remember that I have set no boundaries to keep you out. I am here when you need me."

He swallowed audibly. The familiar look of regret and sadness deepened as he watched her earnest expression. "You are more than I deserve, Sarah. I'm grateful for your caring."

"Let me care then, Abe. Let me in . . ."

"I must . . .I won't . . ."

Sarah knew that Peter's illness and Abe's need to hold himself together taxed his waning strength. She gave him permission not to finish this difficult conversation. "Go to Peter, then. And take my love with you. Just hold his hand for me."

He squared his shoulders and ran his hand over his face briefly. "Thank you, Sarah." He went through the door to cardiac care like a man going to wrestle bears.

Sarah's heart twisted. She wanted to hold him and Peter in her arms, comfort them and go on this difficult journey with them. The tears spilled over her lids and trickled down her cheeks unheeded.

"Sarah."

She didn't hear the low voice at first.

"Sarah."

Dick Street sat at the edge of the lounge, his wheelchair still in the passageway. Sarah realized that she had dimly heard the elevator doors open and try to close several times during her conversation with Abe.

"Dick! I'm sorry I wasn't there to hold the door open."

He smiled gently. "All things to all people. . .? Sarah, you can't have a confrontation with Abe Hallowell and rescue me from elevator doors at the same moment. It just isn't possible."

Sarah felt rattled.

Dick understood. "I didn't hear anything I wasn't already aware of. Would you take me for a walk? I want to talk to you somewhere else for a few minutes."

Sarah was ready for any distraction. She walked alongside Dick in uncomfortable quiet as he wheeled himself down the long hall. An occasional moan or cry interrupted the silence of the night. The rooms sat near the intensive care unit. In one room, a nurse helped a patient cough. The cough was dry, tired.

Dick looked up at her, sharing sadness for these people.

When they passed a small alcove with two chairs and a potted plant, Dick stopped. "Here. Please sit down, Sarah. No one will bother us."

Sarah sat. "What can I do for you Dick?"

"You can listen and not tell me to butt out until I've had my say."

She frowned and asked, "What is it? I need to clean the sawdust out of your van?"

"It's Abe's van, too. And no, I like the smell of sawdust. I... well I need to talk about something rather personal. I want you to know I do it because I care about both of you."

Sarah brushed a stray curl back into her knot of hair. "I'm listening."

Dick leaned forward and touched her hand. "He loves you."

Her throat went dry and tight. "He doesn't want to."

"He can't believe any woman would ever want him to touch her. He is afraid to trespass – afraid to face rejection and lose you entirely."

She looked at the potted plant, the tweed rug, the wheel spokes of his chair. She pressed her lips tightly together and stared at the light bulb overhead, fighting back tears.

Dick continued in a low voice. "He sees himself as a monstrous piece of a man for whom physical love is no longer possible. He believes his hand, his ear and his limp are God's retribution for the murders he caused."

"Murders he caused? How can he believe that?"

"At the time, in spite of the threats, he knew that if his church stopped holding services, they would lose their strength as a group. They would disintegrate into weak and easily beaten individuals."

Sarah spat out her defense. "His congregation agreed with him. That's why they were all there that night."

"Yes," Dick continued firmly. "In spite of terrorist threats, they needed to stand solid in their faith and with each other. But after so many died, he condemned himself. He was arrogant to insist on holding the Maundy Thursday service."

"And for that God took his hand?"

"For more than arrogance. He was holding the chalice when the bomb was thrown at him. He warded off the blow with the chalice, raised his right hand and sent the bomb ricocheting down and to his right – toward the front row of the church – where the women were seated."

"A reflex action . . ."

"Cowardice. That's what he believes it was."

*    *

Sarah could only sit in shock. She looked beyond herself and Dick to the misery in the soul of the man she loved. Replaying the scene over and over in her mind – understanding both the innocence of his involuntary reaction to the missile and the condemning interpretation he had given that action ever since.

At last, she whispered, more to herself than to Dick, "How can I help him forgive himself?"

Dick spoke slowly, hesitantly. "He doesn't believe he is worthy of you."

"He's always telling me he doesn't deserve me. I never knew how deeply he meant that."

"He needs to know you love him, deserving or not. But you'll have to do something alien to you. You must force him to see how much you love him."

"Alien?"

"He needs you to touch him – to make him touch you. I know this is not like you, Sarah, but he needs to know beyond doubt that you love all of him – want all of him."

Sarah felt the power of her desire for Abe and turned from Dick's scrutiny.

Dick watched the flush of passion light up Sarah's features and soften the lines of her slender body. His own loneliness surged into conscious thought. "Someday for me… Someday there will be such a one for me."

When Sarah composed her shameless thoughts, she saw that Dick's head was bowed in his hands. She reached to reassure him. "Thank you for having the courage to butt in. I know you took a chance, telling me this."

He dragged up a smile. "Abe needs you now more than ever. He is taking Peter very hard."

As they returned to the ICU, the door swung open. Abe emerged. "They have to… they're aspirating him again."

Sarah remembered Teresa's last days. A constant build-up of fluid in her lungs. More and more, she had to have the fluid removed. And the noise of the process alone was frightening. A good nurse would hold Teresa's hand while they worked on her – a small connection with something outside her failing body, some loving touch. Sarah had to know if someone was doing that for Peter.

She pushed in the door and for the first time appeared in the room that was off bounds for any but family. The nurse looked up, startled, and accusing.

Sarah blurted out, "Hold his hand. Please hold his hand. He's so frightened."

The nurse's eyes grew red rimmed. Her voice shook. "I am holding him. I talk to him all the time. Are you Sarah?"

"Yes."

"He talks about you to his dad. Come hold him with me."

Sarah moved to the far side of the bed. Looking down at the frail little body with Peter's eyes, she took his dry hand. A momentary pressure was all the recognition Peter could muster, but it was enough.

Sarah talked to him of the house, the sunshine, the postcards from the kids, the apples appearing on the tree outside his bedroom window at home. When the nurse was done, she signaled Peter's need to sleep. Sarah kissed his damp forehead once for herself and once more.

"That kiss is from Dad. I'm going to take him home for some sleep too. Dick is here when you need someone."

Peter tried to wink. His eye lashes were wet and left a tear on his cheek. Sarah reached to wipe it before it ran down into his oxygen mask. She smiled at his brave trembling face. "I love you, Peter. Sleep well."

The nurse walked her to the door. "That's your voice on his story time tapes, isn't it?"

"He has those here?"

"They help him a lot. He relaxes when we play them. Patients in the other beds seem to relax too. I hope you don't mind if we copy your voice for other children."

Sarah was surprised. "Mind? No, please do it."

The nurse looked sheepish. "We did. They're being used in the peds ward right now."

As she came to the door, through the long glass window she saw the face of Abraham. He smiled at her. With tears running down his face, he was smiling at her. He opened the door and stood back. "Thank you for helping Pete . . .," he began, just before she put her arms around his waist, laid her head on his chest and cried. Slowly, his own arms encircled her. Leaning against the wall, they consoled each other.

Dick's chair clicked off down the hall, leaving them alone.

# CHAPTER FORTY-TWO

After work and dinner, Deborah and Miguel sat in silence on the steps to the main lodge at the Methodist camp. Miguel had returned from the beach with his half of the campers just before dinner. They had built Hiawatha's Onondaga longhouses and Navajo hogans, or as close as Miguel could figure with the little information and material he had.

The main purpose of his excursion was to get the kids to talk about how the material you had, the weather in your land, and the traditions you live with determined the design of the homes you create.

The truth was, Miguel inched his way toward the idea that much of life was determined by materials available, the needs and traditions in your region. He wanted these kids to think, to be open to change and to new ideas. He silently thanked Peter for this idea.

Tomorrow, flutes from alder bark and later, noise makers from maple seeds and dried squash skins. Peter's one idea had given him a direction for this summer camp that could prove much deeper than just teaching children how to carve animals or faces or construct boxes.

And he'd watched Deborah approaching ping-pong with something similar in mind. She used physics lessons and lessons in how to think about self-progress as the foundation of what she taught. It all appeared to be ping-pong, but it was really lessons in angles, momentum and speed. And each game was laced with lessons in measuring against yourself and not against another person, including noticing what you could learn from the technique of the person who just beat you.

Sometimes, that lesson was in noticing their skill. Sometimes it was in noticing what they did to distract or rattle you.

Miguel looked at Deborah and said, "That Peter is a genius."

Deborah glanced at him. "Yes. I'm glad you brought him down here, Miguel. I don't think he'd ever been to the ocean."

"Do you think Abe will bring Andy back to camp?"

"Abe told me Dick is bringing him. He thought those short visits gave Andy a chance to tell Peter what he needed to say. He didn't want Andy there when Peter died, but when Peter could still communicate a little."

"Coming back, Andy is going to need a lot of time in the therapy pool, I think," Miguel said.

"Yes. And he'll need a lot of time pounding on things, so be prepared."

Miguel nodded, and then he stood and said, "Can we go for a walk?"

"Sure. This path seems pretty smooth."

"Let me give you a push, too. Don't want to wear out the motor here."

They walked along a path that paralleled the ocean below. Soon, Miguel stopped pushing at an opening between the trees that gave them a view of the night sky. "See that planet?"

Deborah answered, "Venus setting after the sun. It does that for a few weeks every year and a half or so in our hemisphere."

Miguel mused. "Don't the old myths talk about Venus rising from the sea?"

Deborah nodded. "She does that near Greece and Italy, or maybe New York, places where the ocean is east of where you stand."

Miguel laughed. "Yes, but here she rises from a mountain range and sets in the ocean."

"She is bright and beautiful whether setting or rising."

Miguel said, "You could probably watch her rise from the east coast of Spain, too."

"Spain, eh? Oh, Señor Salvador! If Spain watched her rise, she would probably be called Maria . . . Let's see, Maria del Agua or Maria de las Aguas Grandes or Maria de las Aguas Sanctas or ..."

Miguel whispered, "Deborah, you talk too much."

She continued to tease him. "It was you who mentioned Venus, Señor. I just think we should explore her every aspect – or do you tire of her beauty?"

Miguel said, "Never. I brought her up because I wanted to distract you. You didn't notice that I was wheeling you so far from everyone else, right? I want to spend some time alone with my own Venus."

"I noticed. It's cold out here near the ocean. Your own Venus! Quit pulling my leg!"

Miguel took off his coat and covered her shoulders. She stuffed her arms into his sleeves.

He said, "I wouldn't pull your leg. You are bright and beautiful when you smile . . ."

"Miguel! Stop!"

"You don't want to hear it? Okay."

His silence lasted about thirty seconds, and then he finally had to ask the question he had planned. "Deborah, why can't you walk? What happened?"

"I was born this way. My spinal column was not closed. It was unprotected and there was permanent damage to the nerves in my legs."

"Just in your legs?"

"Everything else works. Is that what you're asking?"

"Yes," he said, and then added slowly, "But also, is it safe for everything else. . . I mean, Deb, I love you. Someday, can I love you without . . . without hurting you?"

"I . . . I don't know."

"You never asked?"

"Miguel, how can I ask my doctor such a thing?"

"That's what he's for, for God's sakes. Is he a he?"

"Yes."

"Would you ask your doctor if she were a she?

"I suppose I could. It would be lots easier."

"Deborah, this is something you need to know for you – not just for me. I mean I'm sure I'm not the first or the last guy to hope that someday you can make love – or make babies. You gotta know all about yourself. Otherwise, you might be cutting yourself out of some part of life when it isn't necessary."

Deborah looked away, silently and he could see she was holding back tears. After a moment, she said, "What if I can't. What if everyone says, 'No way!'? What do we do then?"

"Then I learn to love you in a different way. Let's face that one only if it is true. And the truth is, it may never be me you love, but someday, you will fall in love, and you should know. Debbie, ask!"

"I'm afraid."

"So am I. But without asking, we don't have much to go on."

"It's just so embarrassing."

Miguel said, "This whole damn conversation is embarrassing, but we have to

have it, or we'll never get beyond ping pong and elevator rides in our friendship. I want to go so much farther – not now, but someday – after you go to college, or whatever else you want to do. You will want to love someday."

"Miguel, I already love you."

He sat suddenly on the hard ground in front of her. "You, Deborah Applebaum, are wonderful. I want you to have adventures like our young Hiawatha, but I'm hoping you'll come back to me and still be in love, because I'm not going to fall out of love. I know this full well."

She looked at him. "How can you know?"

"Because the moment you sent that little white ball caroming off the green board and into that guy's chest, I knew you were the girl for me."

"That was a lucky shot."

"Huh-uh. I saw you do that in three different games that afternoon. It is a shot that says, "Take that, arrogant jerk!""

"Really?"

"Yes. Surely you know those are the only opponents you use that shot against."

She laughed, "I know. So, watch out, Buster."

Miguel smiled, and then he looked at her.

She nodded, "I'll ask."

He took her hand in his and kissed her palm.

# CHAPTER FORTY-THREE

Abe had to get outside while Peter slept, if only for a few minutes. *My little boy. My little boy.*

He pounded down several flights of stairs and came to a back door. He knew he shouldn't go out that door. It would probably set off alarms, but he took a small testament from his pocket and put it in the door jam.

As an alarm went off, Abe looked at the end of the short sidewalk and saw someone. Crumpled, but someone. He ran to the lump of clothing and found a pulse, heard labored breathing, and turned the person face up.

Stunned, he whispered, "Kevin?"

"Help me." Kevin gasped. "Wrong door."

Two security men came running out.

"He needs help. Get emergency," Abe said.

One security man pulled out his cell. The other yelled at Abe, "You shouldn't a opened that door."

"This boy needs help. He can't go any farther. Get him help."

Abe turned back to Kevin. "Kevin, what's wrong?"

"Cold turkey."

"Oh God. From what?"

282 Those Who Curse You

"Cocaine."

"How long?"

"Yesterday. Left Dad's motel. Decided best. Can't. Cramps."

"Yes. I know. I'm glad you left Aaron. Sarah and Miguel, they all look for you."

"Dad wants to kill …"

"Kill you?"

"Pro'bly. But Sarah."

Abe froze. "Where is dad's motel?"

"Grand Avenue, north, near river."

Abe pulled out his cell and dialed Reese. "Found Kevin, trying to get off cocaine. At St. Joseph Mercy. Dad is in motel, Grand near Columbia River. Wants to kill Sarah. Kevin left him yesterday, so probably out looking for vengeance."

Reese said, "You stay at the hospital. I'll check on Sarah."

"And Ernst." Abe said. "He goes back to office. Ignores danger."

"Okay. Stay where you are. Take care of Peter and Kevin."

By the time Abe got off the phone, medics had Kevin on a gurney and rolled him toward their ambulance. The emergency room was on the far side of this very large building.

Abe ran after them, jumped into the ambulance. Medics looked at him.

"Related to him," Abe said. "Can check him in."

They nodded and took off around the building.

He glanced back at the door and saw the security people. They picked up his testament and pocketed it before they closed the door.

As they rushed Kevin into the emergency ward, Dr. Hoff came out to greet him.

"I heard communication. Knew you were down here. I'll check Kevin in. You go to Peter. It is time."

At the elevator, Abe couldn't punch buttons enough times. He was so afraid. "Shouldn't have left him. Shouldn't have left him. Shouldn't have left him."

After a moment, he opted to run up the five flights. By level four, his leg dragged some, but not like before the shrapnel came out. He renewed his efforts, passed the elevator as it arrived on five, and ended in Peter's room out of breath.

The nurse glanced up at him and waved him over. Peter barely breathed. His eyes lay closed, but he whispered "Dad, Daddy, Mommy, Sarah."

"I'm here, Peter," Abe whispered. "We all love you."

"Safe journey," Peter whispered. And then he lay still.

After a long moment, the nurse turned off the flat line sound on the monitor and put her hand on Abe's shoulder. Abe watched Peter's spirit fade out of his tortured little body.

"Safe journey, Peter," Abe said. "Hiawatha."

*    *

Out in the hall, a half hour later, Dr. Hoff walked Abe toward the car park.

"That boy, Kevin," he said. "I checked him in. He was in pretty bad shape, but the emergency doctors deal with that kind of situation a lot, an unfortunate number of times a week. They were pretty sure he would be fine, but he needs a program to help him get away from his gang and their influence. I'll call you when he's about to be discharged."

"Thank you," Abe said.

"I'm sorry we couldn't do more for Peter. Genetic stuff is on the horizon, but that doesn't help now, and I know he leaves a big hole in your heart."

Abe nodded. He unlocked his car door. "I shouldn't have left him."

"You wouldn't have saved Kevin. And now Peter is where he knows you saved Kevin."

Abe looked at the good doctor. "You believe in the afterlife?"

Dr. Hoff nodded. "Don't have any proof that it isn't out there for my patients. And a lot of anecdotal evidence that it does exist, so why would I not choose to believe?"

Abe nodded. "Peter believed. Good enough for me, but I've got to say I'm angry that Peter suffered."

"Me too," Dr. Hoff said. "I loved that little guy."

For the first time, Abe saw tears in his doctor's eyes. He reached out with his hand. Hoff took it.

"Get home," he said. "Sarah needs to hear it from you."

As soon as Abe got in the car, his phone rang on his Bluetooth. "Reese," he said.

"I can't find either Sarah or Ernst. No one at your place, Jackson's house, and Sarah's office is shut up tight. She's not answering her phone."

"The motel Kevin mentioned?"

"The motel is wall to wall trash, and we arrested the fellows in it on charges of making meth."

"Arrested the motel owner?"

"The manager at any rate. He was Templeton – that guy driving the Chevy, would you believe? Clearly implicated. And the gang is not talking about Kevin or Aaron."

Abe sped out of the parking lot. Fear gutted his thought processes. Grief gutted his stomach. He drove to his house and found no one. Lights on, but no one there.

Trying to call Sarah, he drove to nearby Jacksons and drew the same blank. At Sarah's office, he found Ernst's car on a side street with Sarah's right behind it. The hood over the engine of Sarah's was still warm.

He ran to the office door and rang the doorbell insistently.

Sarah answered. "I just got here," she said. "Ernst is asleep on the third floor in his room."

Abe tumbled inside. "Lock that." He ordered as he slammed the door. "Turn off the lights."

She did. "What's going on?"

He pulled her into the inner room where Miguel often worked. "Kevin's at the hospital. Reese is chasing down his dad from a motel on Grand near Columbia. Kevin says his dad wants to kill you."

He handed her his phone. "Call Reese to tell him where we are."

She dialed Reese. As she waited for an answer, Abe put his hands over his face, trying to erase it all. He felt her hand on his back. She asked, "Kevin?"

"Trying to go cold turkey. Found him outside the back door. He's checked in."

Reese came on. Sarah told them where she, Abe and Ernst were.

Abe could hear Reese's voice. "Stay there. I've got plainclothes coming to be outside all your buildings and the church."

"We will stay," Sarah said.

*  *

When Sarah hung up, she looked at Abe. He'd slumped against Miguel's workbench.

She put a hand next to his. "You were outside the backdoor of the hospital when you found him?"

Abe nodded, still gazing at the workbench. "I had to breathe. I shouldn't have been out there but opening the door I saw him."

He lifted a nearby hammer. "I got them to take him in and then I ran up the stairs because the damned elevator wouldn't come and . . ."

Sarah shoved a board beneath his hammer just as he brought it down.

His voice was nothing more than a grunt. "I need to hit. I need to hit. I need . . ."

Sarah went to the other end of the workbench and put a board in a vise, tightened it and hammered a nail into it. As he smacked the board at his end, she pulled out a box of ten-penny nails, took his hammer on the back swing and handed him the heavier one.

"Nails. All over it," she said, gesturing at the other board in the vice.

He glanced up at her, moved to the new board and grabbed a nail from the box. As he gasped out his hurt, every phrase was a nail blow.

"Peter ..."

"Yes," she said, knowing and hurting.

"Peter died ... I got there. He knew I was there. He called for me, his mom and dad, you, Sarah. He said, 'Safe Journey', And died."

*    *

As Abe hammered and sobbed out his grief, Sarah took another piece of wood, already roughly shaped, put it in a second vise and lifted a wood plane from its shelf above the tool cupboard. She covered the pommel of the plane with several thicknesses of quilted fabric.

Abe noticed her trying the plane out with her left hand and right wrist – using it as he would have to. His hammering had slowed, but only a little. But now, he watched her.

She left the wood plane next to the vise and said, "This piece needs some work, if you want to smooth it. Here are several grades of sandpaper. I'll go make you some tea."

As she passed him on the way to the back stairs, she touched his shoulder. "Wear it out," she said. "Peter is worth every inch of anger you feel."

# CHAPTER FORTY-FOUR

Sometime later, he trudged upstairs, exhausted. He found her in her work room sitting in the dark at her drafting table. The only light in the room was a streetlamp reflecting off a long and old cross-cut saw hanging over her desk.

He tried to force his mind away from death and grief. "That your saw?"

"My grandfather's, and his brother's. They bought it soon after they arrived in the Minnesota, and somehow brought it with them to the woods of Oregon. It was how they started. Cutting trees and building homes."

"Miguel says your grandfather was the biggest and the best."

"Yes, a good man who made life for Miguel much better."

Abe looked at her and said, "Peter is at rest."

"No longer afraid for each breath. But his dad is not at rest."

"I cannot sit still. I can't think or write. I can't sleep."

"If you become tired enough, will you sleep?"

"I'm afraid to sleep. I dream. Peter is falling. I cannot catch him. And he is so young and frightened. He opens his mouth but cannot cry because he is too weak. And pieces of the chalice slam into him, cut him, tear him."

Abe sat in her darkened office, staring into the dark hallway and the bedrooms off of it. He closed his eyes on a dream of the wakeful. Pain fought its way from inside him to tighten the muscles in the hollows of his temples and flare his nostrils.

Sarah touched his arm to bring him out of his dream. He turned toward her, his focus blurred. "I warn you every time, Sarah. Get out before it's too late."

"Too late for what?"

Abe jerked. Unsure of the line between reality and dream, he looked down at his arm lying limply in his lap. He watched it with what seemed fear. He looked up at her.

"Sarah, do you dream of me? Do I hurt you?"

"I dream of you. It is never a hurtful dream – always gentle and loving."

"I dream – in my dream, I am a man with two hands. I use both of them when I love you. With you, I am at peace, content. But I begin to want you too much. When I reach out to you, my hand . . . It . . . .. The dream always ends with you running from me, afraid." His voice grew harsh with misery.

Sarah felt his fear for her was as palpable as if the dream had been reality. Somehow, he truly believed he would harm her with his love. The fatigue of his long battle for Peter and the drain of his recurring nightmares showed in the line between his brows and the tension in his throat as he spoke.

Sarah reached out, taking his right arm in her hands. He watched, hypnotized by her long fingers as she untied the leather, unwrapped and folded it. Her voice was soft.

"This arm hides too much. As long as you hide it, you are afraid of it. It is like the wound in your back, ugly in your mind, and kept ugly by your feelings of guilt."

She held his arm, running her fingers over what had been his wrist. Her light caress on the delicate inner flesh made his breast swell. He felt his body yearn for her and he tried to get up, but her voice kept him in thrall. He could not pull away – could not even warn her.

Sarah whispered, "Your arm is just as sensitive as your hand. It feels – It wants touch just as much as the rest of you. You want it to be an inanimate object, but it refuses. That repels you."

Abe bowed his head. He stared at their hands in his lap. His breathing became shallow. Seconds passed in strained silence before his strong left hand grasped both her wrists, lifting her hands away from him.

He swallowed his anguish and forced himself to show her the ugliness of his desires. His right arm reached for her, caressing her cheek and following the contours of her ear, her jaw, her soft lips.

"Yes, it repels me," he said. "I want to do this to you – make love to you with this. I want to touch you with all that is left of me. But with half a body, one hand, one ear, a dragging leg, all I can do is mock myself."

Sarah whispered, "No, Abe. Please don't. . ."

He dropped her wrists and stood abruptly. His hand covered his mouth, stifling a deep moan.

Sarah followed his swift strides toward her office door. Reaching up, she grabbed him by the shoulders. He turned, fear of himself in his dark green eyes. "Sarah, let go. I have to leave before all my restraint is shredded and I hurt you."

"Abe, I want you to love me with both arms. I want all that is you to hold me and show me the love you have tried so hard to keep jailed inside of you."

The gray of disbelief slowly replaced the dark shadow of self-hate. "But you said 'Don't'. . ."

"Yes, don't. Don't talk about yourself that way. You look in the mirror and all you see is the damage that bomb did to your body. But I see the damage it did to your soul and the struggle you have gone through to overcome it.

"There is still one gaping wound in your heart. It doesn't have to be there. You are keeping that wound open – nursing it as you nursed the wound in your back."

". . . my desire for you. . ."

"No. Your distrust of my love."

"Your love?"

"Always. You insist that what we have is a friendship with no physical effects. You refuse to see that I want you to touch me with love. I want it at least as much as you do."

A small, whispered voice came to him. "Dad . . . Love . . . Sarah."

He drew in a sharp breath. All motion between them stopped except for the slow caress of his eyes. She felt him mentally brush over her hair and stroke each feature – brow, eyes, flushed cheeks and lips.

His gaze caressed her throat and hesitated at the top button of her blouse before he looked away and exhaled slowly. When he looked at her again, his hesitation had clearly been replaced by deep passion.

His left arm circled her waist, his hand splayed across her lower back, drawing her toward him.

Sarah knew he tested the truth of her declaration. She wrapped her arms around his body and pushed her hands under his shirt. Her lips found the beating pulse in the hollow of his throat and followed the chords of his neck up to his jaw.

The prickle of whiskers on her lips made her laugh. When Abe looked at her, she tried to suppress the tickle by pressing her lips together. His hand moved lower on her back, lifting her toward him.

"Let me stop that tickle." His mouth took hers with a pressure so subtle that the tickle spread, enveloping her whole body. Sarah shivered against him.

Instead of pulling away as he had whenever she reacted to his touch, Abe groaned softly. His lips left hers and followed the trail of sensation down her throat and back up to her ear.

"Sarah," he whispered, "When this is all over, I want to undress you."

She looked up quickly at his sudden boldness.

"Second thoughts?" His eyes darkened.

"No, Abe – surprised that you believe me."

"I'm not sure I believe you, yet. I expect you to draw away at any moment. But right now, I need you more than ever and you have opened the door."

He continued in a whisper. "This is the wrong night for this, with danger lurking and the police outside our door, but when I love you, I won't hurt you, Sarah, I'm just keeping my foot in the door until you realize you have started something too big for you."

She whispered, "Please believe. I can't be more clear than this. I don't know the ways."

He held her tightly against him, leaning on her desk as he let his left hand move up from her waist to caress her breast.

His right arm betrayed him by moving of its own to caress her other breast. Her dress fabric moved softly under his wrist letting him feel her true reaction.

When his sensitive wrist brushed across her swollen nipple, he stopped, waiting for revulsion to register in her mind.

Instead, she twisted toward his caress. He raised his gaze to see a look of bemused pleasure in her flushed features. He moved his hand and arm over her again, watching her face, unable at first to believe how much pleasure he was able to give her. This was no act put on to massage his ego. This was the real desire of her body for his touch.

As she kissed him, inviting the invasion of his tongue, the tension in her thighs also released.

He invaded her mouth more urgently as he thrust his knee between her legs. His aroused body pressed against her. Her volatile reaction staggered him. She wrapped one long leg around his legs as her arms pulled him tightly to her. Fully clothed, he could still feel the heat of her body. He knew he had more than awakened her. She would be his soon – his completely.

Abe lifted her and strode to her bedroom. Standing next to her small bed, he pulled from her arms and stood with his side to her, breathing deeply, eyes closed.

"Did I hurt you, Abe?"

He brushed his hand over his face. "No, you are wonderful."

"Then what did I do?"

He felt her legs move restlessly.

"You reminded me that you have never been with a man before."

She looked away, embarrassed. "Is it so very evident?"

"Yes, thank God, it is. And because of it, we need to talk."

"You think me wanton."

"Far from it! I think you loving and generous, courageous and the most beautiful of women. I had no idea my unhappy assault on your home was going to include quite this level of intrusion."

Sarah put her hands on his chest. Her voice was soft with confused emotions. "I am not courageous. I want you to love me."

He lowered his mouth to taste the warm honey of her throat. "God knows I want to love you. You have given me such a gift, Sarah. The knowledge that my touch – that all my caresses please you is a gift beyond any I ever expected. I want to fill you with my body. But first, we need to be free of the threat of Aaron and his people."

"I know," she whispered.

He nodded. "And then there is something more."

"More?"

"I want to know that you will marry me when Kevin is safe, and his father is in jail. We can celebrate Peter best by loving each other as he urged us to do."

She hugged him. "After . . . but I can't marry you unless we know . . . unless we know I can . . .we need to make a short affair before we marry."

His own laugh warmed her ear and throat. "I believe the term is `make out' or `Have a short affair'. You are so pure you can't even talk about it straight."

Sarah turned to him with concern. "Am I so pure, that I will not satisfy you, perhaps? Perhaps a short affair will help you learn that I am not able . . ."

"Sarah, I know what you will be. I don't need proof. What has occurred here tonight happened mainly because you were clearly warm and receptive. I could not have made myself even begin to touch you otherwise."

Abe finally understood how deeply her grandfather's influence affected her. For years, Grandfather had unwittingly made her profoundly afraid of being promiscuous. Now she believed she could not make love at all. She'd been suppressing this side of herself for too long.

*"Dad . . . love . . . Sarah."*

"Yes," Abe whispered. His arm touched her throat and slid beneath her chin to lift her toward his kiss. "I will show you, Sarah. When we are safe, I will show you how much pleasure you give me. It will be wonderful – for both of us. I promise."

Sarah, her eyes unable to meet his, took a deep breath and whispered to the wall. "Peter knew I loved you."

He smiled, softly. "He did. I didn't believe, but now I see that he understood."

Abe caressed her throat and said, "When we have this short affair, I will get something to protect you in case, well in case."

She looked up at him, thinking he must be teasing her. She relaxed when she saw that he meant to follow through, and she whispered,

"Um . . . uh . . . Miguel has something you can use when we try this. They are in the bathroom medicine chest."

"What!?"

"I saw him make himself not take them to camp."

Abe sat silent and unmoving for a full minute. At length, his voice broke with humor at the irony.

"I guess Miguel made the right decision for all of us."

# CHAPTER FORTY-FIVE

The two of them lay down on her bed, awaiting dawn and the realization that Peter, lovely Peter, really had died.

For safety, Sarah's phone sat on the table nearby. Abe's remained in his pocket. He held her in his arms, exhausted from hammering out his grief and from the long hours of watching over Peter. She snuggled close to him, holding his head on her breast as he fell asleep.

Hours later, Abe found too much room on the narrow bed for the first time that night. His right arm groped for the soft dress and warmth of Sarah and found empty cotton sheets. He was instantly awake.

His phone rattled in his pants pocket. He pulled it out and answered. "Officer Seneca?"

"Aaron took Kevin from the hospital at gun point. Tied up the nurse and threatened her life."

"Any idea where they went?"

"Aaron pushed Kevin out and said, 'We're getting her.'"

"Her. Sarah."

"We think so. Reese has sent extra police to your place and Arthur's."

"Sarah is at her office, because Ernst came here, and she found him."

"Here. That means you also are there."

"Right. Reese sent me looking for her."

"Got it. I'm sending more police in that direction right now."

"Thanks. I'm not sure where in the building she is right now. I need to find her."

"Go."

Abe took his phone out into the hall. He stiffened.

Rigid, he listened.

A sneering voice rose from the front office, a floor below him. Kevin's father, Aaron.

Abe whispered into the phone. "Aaron is here and threatening Sarah in the workroom."

Seneca said, "We're coming. He has a gun. Be careful."

"Yes," Abe whispered. "Come. I'm going down the back stairs to distract him."

Downstairs, Aaron laughed. "I'm going to ruin you and then I'm going to burn this place down around you. I know they ain't here. And I know they ain't comin' back any time soon."

"Why?" Sarah's voice was shaky.

"You pretend all the time to care about my son – to love my son. Well, let's see a little of that love now, lady. I know you whore with that red-haired man. I seen you with him the other day. Got to be a little of that left for me."

Abe's heart began pumping again. Anger and alarm heated his skin.

Sarah's voice was low and controlled, but Abe knew fear. "Why would you burn down such a big place?" she asked. "Somebody would spot a fire like that and when they find my bones, they'll come after you. Everybody knows you threaten to kill me and Miguel."

"This place'll go up plenty fast and you gonna die of smoke. The way I hurt you, nobody gonna know nothin' from bones. Bones only tell they been cracked. They don't tell that you die from lots of little cuts." The hiss of his dry voice carried venom.

Abe willed Sarah to hear his thoughts. "Reason and keep talking, Sarah. Keep talking."

She said, "Lots of little cuts leave lots of blood and that stain stays there to tell everything. You must need Crack badly not to have planned this a little more."

"Well, so it ain't perfect. That just brings Miguel after me, so I get my chance with him, too."

"Miguel is smarter than I am. He would have felt the air from that broken window."

"He's gonna hate me so much he won't think clearly. Hate makes waste." Kevin's father laughed coldly at his own joke.

"You need money for drugs?"

"Don't play with me, lady. I know you. Don't change the subject. I been waitin' for this a long time. You keep backin' to that wall like that. Pretty quick, I'll be on you."

As Abe crept down the back stairs to Miguel's workshop, he heard the office door open. The next voice he heard was Kevin's. His gasping weak voice seemed as bad as when Abe met him in the alley behind the hospital.

'Dad, ... get out ... policeman you knocked ... come to. any minute."

"I told you to finish him off."

"Not doing it," Kevin said.

"You bastard," Abe heard him say.

"Stop throwing . . .," Kevin said.

Abe wondered what Aaron was throwing.

Abe inched down the back stairs, keeping close to the wall to avoid creaky wood. From Miguel's woodworking room to the right of the stairs, Abe smelled gasoline. He saw the muddy, grease-stained back of Aaron's black and red plaid jacket. In the man's huge right hand was a small gun.

The smell, like strong cleaning fluid and stale body filled Abe's nose.

Abe moved softly into the alcove to the left – the room where he had been working to annihilate grief last night. Even in here the odor of some petroleum product was overwhelming. Abe felt himself become light-headed. He had to get Sarah out of here quickly. He grabbed the long piece of wood filled with nails – a weapon.

In the short hall between the two rooms, he tried not to breathe, but for the little bit of clean air left by the draft from the door Kevin had left open.

Abe saw Kevin in a hospital gown. He stood next to Sarah with his arms spread as if to protect her.

Aaron's back was still hunched over as he closed in on his prey. Seeing Abe, Sarah's eyes widened briefly. Aaron recognized the significance of her look and began to turn.

Kevin lurched in front of Sarah.

Abe lunged, swinging the stick down on Aaron's gun hand. The gun fired as it skittered away. Its echo on the concrete reverberated in both of Abe's ears.

Kevin shouted, "Go, Mom. Go."

And then, Kevin crumpled to the floor.

Sarah started toward Kevin.

Aaron turned on Abe, his broken arm dangling, and his cigarette barely hanging from his mouth.

Abe felt the sting of a deep gash across his right arm and his chest before he realized his mistake. Of course! Aaron had two hands! And a knife.

Abe raised the stick to parry the return slash of the knife. The heavy man grunted. Recovering quickly, Aaron crouched and circled, his knife at attention, his cigarette at ease, limp in his sweaty face.

The glowing end of that white wand held Abe's mind – Something …What? That red glow became more fearsome than the glint of steel.

"Sarah get up the stairs. Get out. Gasoline!"

Out of the corner of his eye, he saw her grab up the skirt of her dress and move toward the gun on the far side of the room. "No, Sarah. Out. Before it's too late. Now! Go."

She hesitated. Aaron smiled and put his bloodied right hand to the cigarette.

"Ernst. Sarah get Ernst. I'll get Kevin."

She leapt toward the stairs just as Aaron threw the cigarette into the stack of wood near her. A wall of flame shot up. Abe could no longer see her. He swung his club at Aaron who was wide-eyed at the fire, just now aware that he too could be trapped by it. Abe's club caught him in the knees, throwing him to the floor in a pool of gasoline and flame. Above Aaron's screams, Abe heard the slam of a door and the complaining groans of a large machine starting up.

The orange light of flame surrounded Abe. The heat seared his eyes and throat. Even his right ear heard the crack of fire.

Blindly, he pulled Kevin from the pool of flame.

The groaning machine grew louder, more painful, filling his mind with awareness of his bloody chest, his burned skin, his throbbing right ear and the screaming youth beneath him.

A white light shot across the room, increasing as the rumble of machinery grew. Abe finally realized the garage door opened. The streetlamp beckoned through the flames. He pulled at Kevin's arm, wild with hope and pain.

Outside, Abe smothered Kevin's hospital gown against his own shirt as he pulled him free of the building. And then he saw the bleeding from Kevin's chest. Aaron's bullet.

A policeman staggered toward him. "That kid . . ."

Abe said, "That kid saved your life. He's been shot. The man who hit you is inside in a fire he created."

"Who are you?"

"Abe Hallowell."

"Oh. Chaplain Hallowell."

"Yes. Help me with this kid."

The patrolman lifted Kevin's legs and they laid him on the grass parking strip.

Behind the patrolman, Abe saw the neighbors coming out in pajamas and robes. "Muhammed," he called to the grocer, "Call an ambulance for the kid."

"I called already das fire department," Booky Kerns yelled. "Ambulance, also."

Muhammed yelled. "Where's Sarah?"

The patrolman clearly was still a little out of it. Abe turned to him. "Stay out of that building. And make sure this boy gets into the ambulance. I have two others to get out of there."

The patrolman stared at the growing flames. "Inferno! How are you going to get to them?"

"Fire escape. Back door. Kerns, tell the police. Kevin's dad shot him. And Kevin's dad tried to kill Sarah. See that they hold him. Somebody get an ambulance and . . . "

Muhammed yelled, "They be here soon. You burned man! and cut bad!" Muhammed reached out to stop Abe, but Abe's bloody arm slithered through his grasp.

"She's still in there. And Ernst. . . I'm going to the fire escape."

"I help you man."

Muhammed followed him around the corner into the delivery drive. They clambered up the fire escape to the third floor. The door was locked and solid.

Abe found the window next to the door. Smashing glass with his fist, he ignored yet another pain. The window lock twisted hard, and the window pushed up slowly. He bent to climb in and was hit in the face with rolling smoke.

"God don't let the fire be in the hall." His thoughts were loud in his mind as he felt the door to the hall. Warm. He flung it open and fell over Sarah's body outside Ernst's door. Ernst's body lay heavy on her arms. Small tongues of flame licked up the wall in Ernst's open room.

Muhammed reached over Abe, grabbing Ernst by the shoulders, roughly bumping his body across both Abe and Sarah.

"Stay awake man. Get her out now. This place goin' be gone any minute." From inside, Muhammed unlocked the fire escape door so they could get out.

Abe scrambled to his feet, lifted Sarah to his bloody chest and pushed himself toward the fire escape door. Sirens screamed down the street and wailed to a halt. More sirens sounded in the far night, coming, coming.

Fireman Frank Richardson appeared on the steps. Frank took Sarah's body. Abe watched numbly as the medics warmed her with blankets. She turned and retched over the side of the gurney. So many people between them and he wanted to be sick for her.

Ernst's still body under the blanket showed no reaction to the respirator. In her sickness, she reached out toward the old man, crying.

Abe saw Frank begin to work on Ernst.

Helpless, Abe looked up at the old building; her life, her home, her hopes for this community, paint peeling in the heat, smoke coming out the roof . . . Suddenly, he charged back up the fire escape.

He heard voices yelling at him. Heedless, he ran to the third floor, crashed through that door to her drafting room. Standing on a chair, he grabbed the crosscut saw from its place of honor over her desk and carried it through the roiling smoke back to the door. It lost a few teeth as he dragged it down the metal stairwell behind him. Twice he had to throw it over the bannister to turn a corner.

Kerns, and the grocer, Muhammed met him as he came down.

"I take dis ting, my house for you, tank you." Kerns relieved him of his crazy burden.

"Kevin?"

Kerns shouted "He inna other ambulance. Gone already. St. Joseph Mercy."

Muhammed's concern made him pushy. "You mad, man? She wild for you. Thinks you burned. Get in that ambulance, man. You sick in a head to leave her and get that thing!"

He shoved Abe, blood and all, into the back of the ambulance.

The attendants hardly seemed to notice him huddled on the floor as they closed the doors and signaled for the driver to beat it out of there.

The siren's wail was not so sweet a sound as Sarah's soft crying or the violent vomiting of Ernst. The old man swore between retches. He was very much alive.

"You Abe?" The ambulance attendant turned him gently onto a blanket and began checking his knife wounds.

Abe nodded. The need to get rid of the smoke was starting to hit him as well.

"It's him," the attendant said. "Tell the lady."

The burns, the pain of the knife wound, his grief for Peter, and sorrow for Kevin and Sarah descended on him. The accumulation of smoke in his system separated Abe's awareness from anything outside his body.

He heard a woman's voice as if in the distance. "Miss Rohann, he's here and he's safe. You must relax now. We'll take care of all of you."

# EPILOGUE

"**W**e're going to need a bigger van," Miguel announced.

Dick laughed, "Do you think we could ever park a van any bigger than this."

"Nope," Miguel said. "Kevin, how about if you and I follow Dick in my truck?"

Kevin looked at Miguel, surprise written all over his face. "Me?"

"Sure," Miguel answered. "You're a better conversationalist. These guys," he pointed to Akesha, Andy and Jeff. "These guys are too invested in winning their game."

In two previous games, Akesha had wiped the magnetic game board of knights and pawns. Andy and Jeff played as a team, and still couldn't beat her.

Kevin said, "How about you, Grandpa?"

Arthur shook his head. "Thanks, Kevin. But I'll ride in the van with Ernst and these kids. I think I want to watch the outcome of this game. You go with Miguel, and we'll meet you at the picnic grounds."

"Well, okay," Kevin said.

Miguel understood that since Kevin had been home only a month from his long-term recovery center, he was feeling a little new to the extended family. He'd suddenly acquired more family than he ever knew about, and he wasn't sure they could love him.

From all his visits to Kevin's center, Miguel knew that most of Kevin's recovery had been psychological. His father was a killer. Did that make him a killer, too? His father was a drug addict. Did that mean he would always be a drug addict himself?

And then, coming home, at sixteen, recovering from a near fatal wound, shot by his own father, a recovering addict, already a formed individual, could anybody see him as a new Kevin?

Miguel intended to help Kevin see himself as the new Kevin.

They were on their way to the cemetery to celebrate Amanda, Peter, and Abe, whose fortieth birthday was today. Abe and Sarah were already at the cemetery.

Abe didn't remember it was his birthday. As usual, he thought about others and forgot to think about Abe. Miguel loved him for it. And in this case, it made it possible for all of them to surprise him with a picnic.

Miguel noticed Kevin looking with pride at the newest building on their block. The shop and home they had all known were being replaced and were nearly finished.

In fact, most of the family already worked there, though most of them lived in Hallowell House. The main floor of the new building had become workshop and office. The second floor hosted a drafting room and a plaster workshop, and the third floor was all Ernst's home, with a fire escape out his bedroom.

This time, the home had fire stops in the walls, which Miguel and Sarah had known were not part of construction in the late eighteen hundreds, when the original building had been constructed. Sarah had always hoped to have enough money to take out the plaster and put in blocks, but the money had never been available. Those blocks between the vertical framing structures would have slowed the fire considerably. Without them, the vertical framing acted as many chimneys directing the fire toward the roof.

'Live and learn,' seemed way too apt in this case.

"So," Kevin said as they climbed into the truck, "who is this Deborah that Dick is picking up at the train station?"

"Oh, I forgot, you never had a chance to meet her. National women's ping-pong champion as of last spring. Abe's foster daughter."

"Where's she been?"

"She's majoring in art at the University of Oregon."

"Art?"

"You remember the graffiti your gang did at the church?"

Kevin ducked his head. "I did it, actually. Dad told me to paint the CX3 because you were working there."

"Do you remember what happened to it?"

"You created that elephant and mouse thing."

"Yup."

"You mean this Deborah person designed it – made the C into the elephant's rump?" Kevin asked.

"This wonderful Deborah artist." Miguel corrected.

Kevin laughed. "Yeah. I thought that mural was funny, but Dad didn't."

Miguel smiled at him. "You were right. It was funny, and a beautiful idea. And by laughing, you already were saying 'no' to all that negative stuff, weren't you?"

"Yes. When Abe found me at the hospital, it was because Dad whopped me around for laughing about the mural."

"Ah. And then Aaron came to the hospital and threatened the nurse and got you out of there."

"I had to leave. He would have stabbed that nurse, and I knew he planned to attack Sarah. I knew I had to stop him."

"That was the best decision, Kevin. It earned you some burn scars, but it also earned you a new life."

Kevin glanced up at Miguel, the right side of his smile a little puckered by the scars that continued down his neck and into his shirt for about six inches, ending just above his bullet scar. "I guess I should think of scars as good things."

"Most of them will heal, but they also are badges of honor, Kev. You saved Abe and Ernst and Sarah that night. Plus, the poor bolloxed patrolman who was guarding the house."

Miguel turned the truck into the train station, following the van. In front of them, Dick pulled up at the turn-around and opened the van's side door. Deborah wheeled out of the train station and over toward the van. Ernst tied the wheelchair onto the ramp, and Dick made Deborah's wheelchair ride the elevator up into the seat."

From inside the truck, Kevin watched all this. "God! She's beautiful."

"Yes, she is. Inside and out," Miguel said.

Kevin looked at him. "You're in love."

"Yes, I am. And hopeful."

Kevin studied Miguel's bemused look. "Think you can wait that long?"

Miguel smiled at him. "For her, I can wait forever. I just hope it's sooner."

Kevin said. "That explains the construction at your building."

"Explains what?"

"Why you bought the porn shop building and turned the main floor into a home instead of a shop and the other floors into apartments. It explains why the construction shop is in that separate building out back and why everywhere in your building is about twice as wide as normal."

Miguel laughed. "You are too observant, Kevin."

"Yeah. I choose that apartment in your building near the fire escape when I go to community college."

"You will be welcomed."

Miguel thought back to the trial that had proven that Kevin had nothing to do with Bruce's death. The gang deaths had all been

Aaron's doing. Nobody, including his own son, had been allowed to question Aaron's perverted judgment.

Aaron's body was only ashes and bone after the fire at Sarah's. But Aaron's handprint had been found on a piece of the gasoline can. Both Sarah and Abe testified that Kevin had never touched the knife, the can or the gun.

At a second trial, the bullies from the blue Chevrolet, Langren and Templeton were sentenced to long terms for money laundering for Aaron and for forcing children, including Kevin, to use and sell drugs. Aaron had held the threat of killing Sarah over Kevin during those weeks.

Today, months later, Miguel and Kevin's truck followed Dick's van from the train station out Interstate 84 and then southeast into the hills. They chugged steeply up into the Willamette National Cemetery.

Peter and Amanda were buried in the Lincoln Memorial Cemetery across the main road from the military cemetery.

Miguel could imagine Peter making up rhymes about being at peace with heroes of war. Miguel also could imagine Peter as Hiawatha, visiting the graves on his hill, greeting the Chinese families and Vietnamese families in his own area, visiting the beautiful mosque nearby, and then running swiftly across the road to salute the heroes of other times.

Miguel had often been up here with Deborah before she left for school, and they had seen gold finch flocks visiting the grasses and berry bushes near Peter's grave.

"What are you thinking about?" Kevin asked. "Sorry . . ."

"No, don't be sorry. I was thinking about Peter. I wish you'd met him."

"I saw him a couple of times. Dad followed Abe when he took Peter to school. He knew Abe had given every motel owner a photo of me and a photo of him."

"So, that threat from Langren about dumping Peter and Andy on the road, that grew out of Aaron's anger?"

"Yes. And I know they also mentioned a girl." Kevin stopped.

Miguel said, "You don't have to elaborate. I can imagine what they said about her."

"Yeah. They were ugly."

"Well, Kevin. That ugliness is in your past. It's in all of our pasts. And now, we're making a new life with a lot more beauty and a lot less ugliness."

Kevin said. "I want to be a part of the beauty."

"And you already are. Here we are. Let's get the picnic baskets and chairs out of the back."

\*    \*

On the hill next to Amanda and Peter's graves, Sarah stood with her arm around Abe's waist. Her own waist was a lot less huggable, but Abe kept his hand on her belly as they faced Peter's headstone.

Sarah said. "Amanda, is little Peter having a good time singing and running about with you?"

Abe chuckled. "Amanda, you and Eleanor Whiting pulled it off. This whole chapel business became a conspiracy between you to make the congregation and Abe Hallowell grow up. We're feeding many, and clothing many, and the new young members are collecting their stories."

Sarah hugged Abe. "Amanda, you saw right through us and knew we needed each other."

"Peter," Abe said. "You were absolutely right about Sarah. Sorry I had trouble believing at the time."

Sarah leaned down toward the grave. "You know your dad. Everybody's lovable but himself. We gotta teach him to believe what he preaches."

Abe had the grace to look sheepish.

"You can see that we're about to have twin boys," Sarah said. "And, if it is all right with you, we'd like to name them Peter Kevin and Andrew Jeffrey Hallowell."

At that moment, a flock of yellow birds landed on the nearby porcelain berry bush.

"There's our answer," Abe said.

Sarah said. "Now, Peter Hiawatha, bring Grandma. Come on down to the picnic area and celebrate your dad's birthday."

Abe stared at her. "My birthday?"

"Yes, Mr. Hallowell. You are about to be forty. And the family wants to celebrate you."

Abe leaned over and pulled his wife into his arms, reaching over her present girth to kiss her.

When he came up for air, Abe said, "It's getting difficult to kiss you adequately around our little boys."

She smiled, "Hard to draw, hard to wash dishes, hard to reach a lot of things."

Abe said, "It's a good thing we have so many helpers at our house."

"It is. And they are waiting down the hill."

She turned back toward the gravestones. "Come on down. Grandpa Arthur is with us."

Abe and Sarah strolled arm in arm down the hill toward the rest of their family.

Behind them, the goldfinch flock swooped from bush to bush.

# THANK YOU!

To the late Dr. David Bell for discussions about caring for a child with Duchenne Muscular dystrophy.

To the children, families and care providers at Albertina Kerr Centers in Portland, Oregon, for your more than one hundred twenty years of service to those with disabilities and those in emotional crises.

To Jane Richardson, Connie Kennedy West, Sister Miriam Kathleen Moran, a triumvirate of hard-working, thoughtful leaders who brought together volunteers from all over the region to turn the Kerr orphanage building into The Old Kerr Nursery and begin three businesses there. For over thirty-five years, the volunteers at The Old Kerr Nursery raised enormous funds to keep the work of the Albertina Kerr Centers financially secure and in the public's eye. Best advertising an agency can have.

These people made it possible for the work of the Albertina Kerr Centers to offer group homes with independent and supported living to adults with disabilities from all over the region.

And my years of volunteering with others at The Old Kerr Nursery gave me and my youngest son a chance to work with adults toward worthy goals. The volunteer opportunities there as head of the garden committee, (when young son was in charge of the wheelbarrow), led to a stint as part of a committee to collect the history of the organization, and finally, to my becoming the author of *To Serve Those Most in Need*, the history of this venerable non-profit as it celebrated its one hundred years. These experiences are what made me realize that I love to write and that I love to write about the best in people when they accomplish seemingly impossible feats together.

Separately, we are each a work of art. But the sum of our parts creates something truly amazing.

# ABOUT THE AUTHOR

Rae Richen is the author of adventures for adults and young adults, of romantic suspense and of the recent Glyn Jones and Grandma Willie mystery series. Join Rae Richen as we explore fear and power, greed and human need in short stories and novels, articles, interviews and essays.

Using family relationships and the backdrop of historical events, Rae Richen writes to bring focus to the themes that drive each of us.

The characters in these stories face a confusing world of hypocrisy with courageous honesty. The humor, friendships, and caring they bring to these situations help them forge new solutions to age-old problems.

Learn more about this author at www.raerichen.com or contact her at rae@raerichen.com .

For a good read of all first chapters, and the history and back story of these novels, sign in as the author's friendly reader at https://www.raerichen.com/guest-area .

# OTHER BOOKS BY RAE RICHEN

*Uncharted Territory* – a father-son adventure in the mountains and in learning to accept and love despite the fragility of life. Learn more: https://www.raerichen.com/books

*Scapegoat: The Price of Freedom* – a teen and his friends struggle with a culture of easy accusation during the McCarthy Anti-Communist era. Learn more: https://www.raerichen.com/books

*Scapegoat: The Hounded* – after September 11, 2001, a grandfather and grandson work to create safety and freedom for friends falsely accused of treason.
Learn more: https://www.raerichen.com/books

*In Concert* – A novel of suspense and romance when a famous musician is stalked by a vicious man who wants to own her and her son. Visit https://www.raerichen.com/in-concert and read the first chapter for free.

*Frozen Trust* – a novel of espionage and romance within the United States during World War II. Visit https://www.raerichen.com/frozen-trust and read the first chapter for free.

*Sentinels of Solitude* – a novel of suspense and love during a murderous land grab in the lush Willamette Valley of Oregon. Visit www.raerichen.com/blog for the stories behind the story.

*A Fool's Gold* , a novel of treachery and romance in the Rocky Mountains of Colorado during the mining fever of the 1880s. Visitwww.raerichen.com/books for more information

*Without Trace: A Glyn Jones and Grandma Willie Mystery*
When Trace Gowan, drummer in Glyn Jones' hip-hop band, goes missing, Glyn and his friends involve Grandma Willie and her connections to prison and police in the search. They find there is a lot more than a kidnapping going on and all of them are in danger. <u>www. raerichen.com/books</u>

Coming Soon: *Calling The Shots, An Anthology of Short Stories:* A confection especially for readers who asked "What happened to Elizabeth in The *Price of Freedom*? To Dick Street of *In Concert* and in *Those Who Curse You*?"

Learn what caused Gryf and his brother Sam to be the targets of a madman even before they came to the United States – the back story of *A Fool's Gold.*

And see what happened to Lewis James's missing brother, Dicken – a follow-up on Lewis's search for Dicken during *In Concert.*

Rae Richen has given us short stories to reveal where these characters lives intersected with the stories in the novels and where they went after we last saw them.

At the same time, in other stories, Rae Richen also has created whole new worlds and characters that you will want to follow and cheer for as they attempt to untangle their complicated lives.